BARK IF IT'S MURDER

"It seems that dog has been at the center of quite a lot of trouble lately, hasn't he?"

"It's not his fault."

"No, I'm sure it's not." He stretched and rubbed at the back of his neck, before stifling a yawn. "But someone finds him interesting."

"You think someone came here to steal Stewie?"

He spread his hands. "I'm not sure what to think. The dog was present when Mr. Fuller was murdered. Now that he's here, your house gets broken into."

"Almost," I said, though the distinction was minor.

"You've had no issues before with break-ins. There's no recent activity in this area. No warning signs. Whoever was here, I'd put money on it that it had something to do with that dog . . ."

Books by Alex Erickson

Bookstore Café Mysteries
DEATH BY COFFEE
DEATH BY TEA
DEATH BY PUMPKIN SPICE
DEATH BY VANILLA LATTE
DEATH BY EGGNOG
DEATH BY ESPRESSO
DEATH BY CAFÉ MOCHA

Furever Pets Mysteries
THE POMERANIAN ALWAYS BARKS TWICE
DIAL 'M' FOR MAINE COON

Published by Kensington Publishing Corporation

The Pomeranian Always Barks Twice

Alex Erickson

KENSINGTON BOOKS
www.kensingtonbooks.com

KENSINGTON BOOKS are published by

Kensington Publishing Corp.
119 West 40th Street
New York, NY 10018

All Kensington titles, imprints, and distributed lines are available at special quantity discounts for bulk purchases for sales
promotion, premiums, fund-raising, and educational or institu-
tional use.

Special book excerpts or customized printings can also be cre-
ated to fit specific needs. For details, write or phone the office of
the Kensington Sales Manager: Kensington Publishing Corp.,
119 West 40th Street, New York, NY 10018. Attn. Sales Department. Phone: 1-800-221-2647.

Kensington and the K logo Reg. U.S. Pat. & TM Off.

First Kensington Books Mass Market Paperback Printing: April
2020
ISBN-13: 978-1-4967-2450-2
ISBN-10: 1-4967-2450-X

ISBN-13: 978-1-4967-1993-5 (ebook)
ISBN-10: 1-4967-1993-X (ebook)

10 9 8 7 6 5 4 3

Printed in the United States of America

1

The hum of two small wheels on hardwood brought a smile to my face as I hefted a bag of dog food from the floor.

"Hey, Wheels," I said, turning and carefully stepping around the calico, who had come up behind me. "I'll get yours in just a minute."

She meowed once, and then sped over to the food dish, where she would wait patiently until I returned.

Wheels was only two years old, but had faced enough hardship for a lifetime. Born with useless, stunted back legs, she was abandoned and left at a shelter by owners who didn't want to have to deal with her condition. She could have given up on life, but that simply wasn't in her nature. A set of snazzy wheels, attached to a comfortable harness, kept her mobile, and boy, did she ever take advantage of it. She'd give any healthy four-legged feline a run for their money if it ever came down to a race.

I shouldered the dog food and carried it to a back room where I was currently housing two aging beagles, Leroy and Toby. The room had once been a laundry room, and it still held the washer and dryer, but now, it was mostly used to house rescues. It meant the clothes often came out smelling like cat or dog, but honestly, in this house, everything did.

Both dogs started barking up a storm as I opened the door and stepped inside, careful not to let them out. I didn't think either would hurt Wheels, but it was always better to be safe when unsure. They'd never been around a cat before, and despite their age, might play a little too rough for her.

Leroy was hard of hearing and had arthritis throughout most of his body, while Toby was blind in one eye. The dogs came to me just recently, and were soon to be on their way to a loving, furever home, where they'd hopefully live out the rest of their days in comfort.

"Quiet," I said, knowing neither would listen. They lived up to their beagle reputation, woofing and baying like they wanted the world to hear. "You don't want to upset the neighbors."

Loud, ear-pounding woofs were my only response.

I filled both dishes, checked the water to make sure it was fresh, and then, with both dogs quieter now that they were eating, I returned to where Wheels waited. I cracked open a can of cat food, gave her half, and then covered the other half for later.

"Ready to go, Mom?" my son, Ben Denton, asked, poking his head into the room. His hair was getting long, but he didn't seem to mind. It was flung fashionably across his forehead, but was thankfully out of his eyes. He used his fingers to brush it back, often with the crooked, mischievous smile he had on his face now.

THE POMERANIAN ALWAYS BARKS TWICE 3

I glanced around the room, and satisfied all the animals were taken care of, I nodded. "Let's go."

We left the house, Ben in the lead, and with the keys to the van in his hand. His name was written across the back of his shirt in large, blocky white letters, as was the name of my rescue, Furever Pets. Beneath that was our slogan: *Purrfectly Defective.*

Like Ben, I was wearing the rescue shirt with my name, Liz, between my shoulder blades. Unlike him, however, mine was coated in hair that would clog even the clearest of drains.

When I'd started rescuing pets that were often considered unadoptable, I was told not to waste my time or money on shirts or on the van with "Furever Pets" painted across both sides and the back.

"Why bother?" some asked. "No one wants a ratty old dog or cat with health issues."

Which was exactly the point. Everyone wants kittens and puppies, yet there are thousands of animals out there that need loving homes. Some have health issues, other physical deformities, but that doesn't mean they are any less cuddly or in need of a family who will take care of them.

Ben hopped into the driver's seat and I got into the passenger's side. I checked the back to make sure we had everything we'd need for the pickup, and then gave him the thumbs-up; it was time to go.

Today's pickup was going to be a tough one. An older man who could no longer take care of himself, or his elderly Pomeranian, was going to be moved into an extended care facility. It was always hard to take animals away from their owners, but in situations like this, it was often necessary.

"I think Amelia has a new boyfriend," Ben said. He checked his speed, and slowed down, likely because I was in the van with him. He glanced at me to make sure I hadn't noticed, which, of course, I had.

"Why do you say that?" I asked. As far as I knew, my daughter was just as single as her older brother.

"She left for class an hour early today. I bet they've found a quiet spot to get to know one another, if you know what I mean." He waggled his eyebrows.

"You're one to talk," I said. Ben was a good-looking guy in his early twenties, and he was smart, but he had a tendency to bounce from one girlfriend to the next. My husband, Emmanuel—Manny to everyone but his mother—thought it was a good thing, said he was getting it out of his system now, and that it would help him later in life. I wasn't so sure I agreed.

But who was I to judge? He was a grown man at this point, even if I still often thought of him as the mischievous teenager he'd once been.

Ben chuckled at my comment, and let the conversation drop.

I sat back and tried not to think about what my daughter may or may not be doing. She was in her second year of college and had yet to settle on a major. She wasn't interested in helping out with the rescue, nor did she want to follow in her father's footsteps and become a veterinarian, like Ben. I hoped she'd figure out what she did want to do with her life soon, because it can quickly pass you by if you aren't careful.

The house came into view a few minutes later. It was an old farmhouse that had been pretty well maintained over the years. The siding was showing its age compared to the addition on the far side, but it was pretty clean. A faded red barn sat out back. The property might have once been big, likely a farm, considering the house, but was now parceled down to only a couple of acres.

The neighborhood itself was quiet, despite being situated in an otherwise busy end of town. Grey Falls was once a small farming village that had turned into a city of about twenty-five thousand. Still, it felt more like a small town than a real city, thanks to how it was spread out, rather than up.

We pulled in behind a pair of cars and a van I recognized immediately.

"Oh, no," I muttered, getting out and eyeing the offending vehicle.

"What are they doing here?" Ben asked.

"Nothing good."

Pets Luv Us was sprayed across the side of the van. Kittens, puppies, rabbits, and hamsters were all drawn in intricate detail throughout the logo. The outside of the van itself was a startling pink, and looking inside, so was the interior. Even the steering wheel was buried beneath a frilly pink cover.

I walked past the van, trepidation growing. I passed by a ceramic Pomeranian holding watch out front, before reaching the front door and knocking. When no one answered, I hammered harder, hoping I wasn't too late.

"Mom, over here." Ben was standing at the corner of the house. He waved me over, and then, before I could say anything, he started for the back.

I followed after him reluctantly. We were expected, but I hated walking around a property without express permission to do so. You never knew how someone might handle the intrusion.

I caught up to Ben just as a small gathering of people came into view, situated around a concrete patio. A worn, dirt path led from that to the red barn.

Timothy Fuller was seated in a wheelchair, his Pomeranian, Stewie, in his lap. The old man looked angry, and quite frankly, annoyed. Behind him, an African American woman dressed in nurse's scrubs looked on with concern. Standing a few feet away was a couple I didn't know, but looking at the man, I assumed he was related to Mr. Fuller. They had the same dour look, the same harsh eyes, it was impossible for them *not* to be related. Next to him was a woman I took to be his wife. She was pretty, but had an arrogance about her that already rubbed me the wrong way.

And then there were the other two people. Duke Billings, a broad-shouldered man with dark brown hair, cut short, was looking on. He stood beside a woman in a pink tank top and white shorts that would look more at home on a beach than while working. Her blond hair was pulled back from her face, which was carefully made up with precision.

Courtney Shaw. My nemesis.

She was saying something to the couple, but before she finished, she caught sight of me. A frown creased her perfect features and her head cocked to the side. "Liz? What are you doing here?"

"I could ask you the same question," I said, before turning to Timothy. "I'm here to pick up Stewie, Mr. Fuller, as we agreed."

Timothy scowled and placed a protective hand over his dog. "This isn't what I expected," he said. His voice came out ragged and harsh. Deep wrinkles lined his face, and were a shade darker than the rest of his skin, as if he'd spent a lifetime smoking and it had somehow seeped into the creases of his flesh.

"I was here first," Courtney said, placing a well-manicured hand on her hip. "I believe that gives me the right to take the dog."

"Mr. Fuller called me," I said, keeping my voice level. I couldn't believe Courtney would try to pull this here, in front of a man who was about to give up what very well might be his only companion.

"He may have, but that doesn't change the fact I'm the better option." Courtney cocked her hip and turned back to the couple. "As I was saying, I promise you, I will find the perfect home for Chewy."

"Stewie," Timothy barked. "Are your ears broken, missy?" He looked her up and down. "Or does stupidity come with the outfit?"

Courtney flushed as the man she was talking to said, "Dad!"

I grinned, but my mirth was short-lived when Timothy turned his beady eyes on me. "What are you laughing at? I swear, I'm surrounded by idiots." He turned in his chair. "Meredith! These people are giving me a migraine. I need to lie down." He scowled at everyone in turn.

"Yes, sir." The nurse gave me a look I could only describe as pitying, before turning the wheelchair and maneuvering it—along with Timothy and Stewie—through the back door, into the house.

"See what you did?" Courtney said, turning on me. "Why must everything you do end up so . . ." She looked me up and down. "Disheveled."

I refused to get into an argument with Courtney; not here. I turned to the couple she'd been talking to. "I'm Liz Denton with Furever Pets. Timothy called me to take possession of Stewie. This is my son, Ben."

"Yo." Ben waved a lazy hand, then shoved it into his pocket.

"Tim Jr.," the man said. "But call me Junior. This is my wife, Alexis." He glanced back toward the back door. "Dad can be difficult. I honestly don't care which one of you takes the mutt, just as long as it's gone." He kicked at a chew toy lying on the patio next to him, knocking it into the yard.

"This is a very trying time for all of us," Alexis added. She was wearing a flowery white dress and sandals. Every time she shifted her feet, she'd check to make sure she wouldn't step in something. Neither of them looked to be dog people, which probably explained why I was here.

"You'll be glad to know, I've already found a good home for Stewie," I said, not that the couple cared what I did with him. All I earned for my comment was a dismissive shrug.

"You mean, you'll dump him off onto one of your friends," Courtney said, butting in. Duke took a step back, and, like Ben, kept out of it. "I will personally vet any and all prospective adopters before I sign off on them and let them take Chewy."

"All for a tidy profit," I muttered, and then louder, "And it's Stewie."

"Whatever."

"I'm more concerned about him finding a home that can take care of his needs," I said, focusing my attention back on Junior. "As I understand it, Stewie is an older dog, likely with a few health issues that will need to be looked after?" I made it a question.

"No clue," Junior said.

"I have a personal connection to a good veterinarian who can look him over," Courtney said.

"My husband *is* a veterinarian," I countered.

"Maybe we should go," Duke said, finally speaking. "Come back later."

"If we leave now, she'll take him!" Courtney made it sound like I'd be doing something illegal.

"It's in my right to do just that," I said, trying to keep from getting angry, but the heat was still in my voice.

"You all need to figure it out on your own time," Junior said, taking his wife's arm. "And do it somewhere else. I have more important things to do."

And with that, he turned and led Alexis into the house.

"Now look at what you did," Courtney said, throwing both hands up into the air.

Before I could retort, the back door clicked open again, and the nurse, Meredith, stepped out.

"I'm sorry about that," she said. "Mr. Fuller gets worked up easily. Parting with his dog is hard on him, as you well know."

"I completely understand," I said. "I don't want to get in the way, or cause him undue stress." I glanced at Courtney when I said the last. "If you'd like to show me to Stewie, I can be on my way."

Courtney made a mewl of protest.

"Mr. Fuller won't part with him just yet," Meredith said. "In fact, he told me to tell the both of you to work it out amongst yourselves. He doesn't want you fighting over his dog."

"I'm not fighting over it," I said, but dropped my eyes to my feet as I did. I supposed I was, but honestly, I had all the right in the world to be there. It was Courtney who was butting in where she didn't belong.

"If you come back later today—*one* of you—I'm sure he'll be more willing to part with Stewie." Meredith flashed us an apologetic smile. "He'll be in a better mood after a nap." Something in the way she said it made me wonder about that.

She turned, returned to the house, and left the four of us alone.

"Well, great," Courtney said, both hands finding her hips. "Now what are we going to do?"

"We do as the man said," I said. "Let's find somewhere and talk about it."

"Really?" Courtney's eyebrows rose. "You expect me to . . ." Duke laid a hand on her shoulder, causing her to trail off. "Okay, fine," she huffed.

I shot Duke a thankful look before asking, "Where do you want to go?"

"My place," Courtney said. "It's closer than yours." Which was true, but not by much. She walked past me, making sure to take a wide berth, and vanished around front.

"We didn't mean to intrude or step on anyone's toes," Duke said. "We'll work it out."

"Thanks," I told him. I wasn't sure why he put up with Courtney's drama. It wasn't like the two of them were dating or anything, so it must be something else. Maybe she had dirt on him and he stayed on to keep her quiet. That made more sense.

We made our way back around front. Courtney was already seated in the van, engine running. "Come on, Duke, let's go." He doubled his pace and got in next to her. "See you soon," she said, before driving off.

"Want me to drive?" I asked, watching her go. When Ben didn't answer, I turned. "Ben?"

"What?" He turned around, face a light shade of red. "What were you saying?"

I looked past him. A woman in a bikini was watching us from the house next door.

"Do you want me to drive?" I asked him. "Or do you have something else to do?"

He grinned. "Well, if you don't mind . . ." He glanced back over toward the bikini-clad babe. She waved him over, biting her lower lip seductively as she did.

I held my hand out. "Keys," I said with a roll of my eyes. He dropped them into my palm without looking away from the woman. She looked to be his age, fit, and exactly his type. "I'll be back in an hour or two. Think you'll be all right?"

"Definitely," he said. He started to walk away, caught himself. "Thanks, Mom." He gave me a quick kiss on the cheek, before jogging over next door.

"Men." I shook my head, but couldn't help but smile. One day he would settle down, but today was definitely not that day.

I got into the van, honked once to Ben, and then, regretfully, I was on my way to Courtney's, where the company wouldn't be so pleasant.

2

Courtney was out of sight by the time I was on the road, but I knew where I was going. I knew her address, thanks to previous interactions with her, but had never actually been inside her house. Admittedly, I was kind of curious to know if her home was as pink and obnoxious as she was.

Careful to keep my eyes on the road, I picked up my phone from the cup holder where I usually kept it. With only a quick glance at the screen, I hit a button and it dialed for me. It rang twice before there was an answer.

"Hey, Liz. How's the pickup coming?" Manny asked, sounding chipper, like always. Even when I'd told him I was pregnant, back before either of us were ready to take such a big step in our lives, he'd taken it in stride, not so much as blinking. His positive stoicism was part of the reason I loved him so much.

"We're running a little late," I said. "I won't be bringing Stewie in for another couple of hours. There's been an unforeseen complication."

"Oh, boy, that doesn't sound good. What happened?"

I answered with a question of my own. "Guess who was already there when we arrived?"

"Oh, no."

"That's what I said." I gave him a quick rundown of what happened in Timothy's backyard. "I'm on the way to have a sit-down with Courtney and Duke now. Hopefully, I'll get this all worked out quickly so we won't have to wait until tomorrow to get Stewie his checkup."

"I can stay late if that helps," he said. "I've got some paperwork I could be doing, so it isn't like I'll be bored."

"I'm hoping it won't take *that* long." But with Courtney, it was hard to tell.

"I do have some shocking news of my own," Manny said. "You weren't the only person who had to deal with someone uncooperative today."

I groaned audibly. I already knew what was coming. "Joanne?"

"In the flesh. I stopped by the house not long after you left to grab my lunch since I forgot it when I walked out the door this morning."

"I'm going to have to staple it to you if you keep forgetting it," I said.

He laughed. "You might need to do that. Anyway, Joanne came storming over the moment I pulled into the driveway. Apparently, Leroy and Toby have been barking all day and night for the last two days and she's had enough."

"That's not true!" Granted, beagles tended to have a loud bark, but to say they'd been barking all day and night was an outright lie.

"I know," Manny said. "She said she was going to

call the cops if it didn't stop, but I managed to talk her down for now. Just beware when you get home. She's in one of *those* moods. I wouldn't put it past her to accost you the moment you get out of the van."

Great. Not only did I have Courtney to deal with, but now my nosy neighbor was making her presence felt. I swear, that woman lived to complain. Just last week, she went on a rant when she caught me coming home from the grocery. While I stood there, arms loaded down, she'd spent nearly twenty minutes complaining that my shutters were the wrong color. She claimed it brought down the value of the neighborhood—whatever that meant.

"I'll deal with her," I said, though I wasn't looking forward to it. "Did you see Amelia this morning?"

"No, but I heard her. She was up and moving before I left."

Which was saying something. While Manny's office didn't open until eight, he was often there by six, checking on any animals they'd kept overnight.

"Okay, well, Ben said she left early this morning. I was curious to know why. She's never up before the sun."

"Can't help you there. Maybe she's got a test today and decided to study for it."

"She left an hour early," I said. "And she could have studied at home, but she didn't."

"You never know, she might have discovered what a library is, and spent her morning studying there."

That was about as likely as Ben ignoring a pretty girl, but I said, "Maybe."

"If I see her, I'll see what I can find out."

"Okay, thanks." Courtney's pink van came into view, parked outside her house, which had lime-green siding and pink trim. It honestly looked like an overlarge dollhouse, and not in a good way. "I've got to go. Courtney calls."

"Good luck."

"Thanks." I was sure I'd be needing it.

I hung up and parked next to her van. Side by side, I did have to admit, hers stood out a lot more. But then again, it wasn't like it was a competition. We could both be doing good work, if only she'd stop acting like I was trying to invade her space every time we were in the same general area.

There was a time when Courtney and I might have been friends, despite the fact she was nearly ten years my junior—and looked closer to twenty. A love of animals often brought people together, and while I might not approve of how she ran her rescue, she was still an animal lover.

But for some reason, she got it in her head that we needed to be rivals. This wasn't the first time she'd tried to steal an animal out from under me, and I had a feeling it wouldn't be the last.

I got out of my van and brushed myself off the best I could manage. When you dealt with animals all the time, it was inevitable that you'd end up wearing their hair like a second coat. Some, like Courtney, took great care to lint roll it away every chance she got. Others, like me, just dealt with it. Why bother when you're just going to get hairy again the moment you sat down?

Noting neither Duke nor Courtney outside, I went to the door and pressed the bell. A sound akin to the first chimes of a princess theme sounded inside. A moment later, the door opened, and a smiling Courtney stepped aside.

"Liz! I'm so glad you came." She sounded bubbly, and awfully friendly, considering we'd just been spitting insults at one another.

"Courtney," I said, nervous now. This wasn't like her, not even remotely.

I entered the house and followed her into the kitchen where a pitcher of iced tea sat on the counter, along with a trio of glasses. The entire room was decorated with strawberries. We're talking strawberry wallpaper, strawberry coasters. Even the oven mitt hanging on the side of the fridge had strawberries on it.

And it was clean. There were no musty animal smells here. Taking a deep breath, I smelled lavender, and maybe vanilla. I didn't see a candle in sight, but did note a few of those plug-in scents around the room.

"Where's your son?" Courtney asked, seeming to notice his absence for the first time. "Ben?"

I was actually surprised she remembered his name. "He's with a friend," I said, though I was pretty sure he'd never met the woman in the bikini before today. It was then I noticed Ben wasn't the only one missing. "Where's Duke?"

"He had a few chores he needed to do today," Courtney said, eyes darting around the room. "He didn't need to be here for this, so I told him to go ahead and take care of them."

I narrowed my eyes at her, wondering. Something in her tone told me she wasn't exactly telling the truth.

Of course, Courtney didn't notice my distrust, or at least, pretended not to.

"Tea?" she asked, reaching for the pitcher.

"Sure."

She filled two of the glasses, sliding one over to

me. "I don't know why we have to fight like this all the time," she said. "We're after the same thing. We only want what's best for the animals."

"We do," I allowed. "And I'm sorry if I snapped at you back there. I just want Stewie to find a good home. This is already going to be hard enough on him being taken away from his daddy."

Courtney took a sip of tea, set her glass aside. "His owner, you mean. I swear, I don't understand why people sometimes act like animals are the same thing as children."

Which was probably one of the main reasons we didn't get along. She might love animals, but she didn't seem to understand the connection people had with their pets.

"Mr. Fuller is going through a really tough time," I said. "He's about to lose his dog and be moved from his home. We shouldn't be making this harder on him than it already is."

"I agree."

"Which is why I think you should let me take care of Stewie's adoption. Timothy called me and asked me to take him in because he didn't want him to end up in the shelter. A dog that age might not find a home. You know how it is."

Courtney's gaze drifted out the window, toward her backyard, as if she'd lost interest in the conversation. I could see a flower garden, perfectly maintained grass, and a small crab apple tree. I wondered if she took care of the maintenance herself, or if she paid someone to do it. I imagined the latter. I couldn't see Courtney on her knees, digging in the dirt.

"I suppose I can't change your mind," she said, returning her attention back to the kitchen. "Though, I could use the extra money."

I couldn't suppress the twitch of my left eye when she mentioned money. Sure, sometimes I charged an adoption fee, especially when the cost to spay or neuter, along with the other required tests and procedures, exceeded what I could justify. But I didn't charge anything more than what I put in for the animal's care, and often, asked for less.

Courtney, on the other hand, earned a tidy profit on her rescues—and I use that term lightly. She tended to pick up kittens and puppies, knowing how quickly they were often adopted.

So, why the great interest in one old Pomeranian?

"I'm sure there are some kittens who still need a home," I said. I was going for diplomatic, but it came out sounding cynical. "People are always dumping them."

"True." She didn't sound convinced. "I guess I'm trying to expand my efforts, you know? There are so many pets left on their own these days. Do you know, I came across a pair of pretty Persians at the side of the road just last week. Someone left them there, completely abandoned!" She shook her head as if she couldn't imagine someone doing such a thing. "Thankfully, I came along."

The jingle of a small bell drew my eye. A gorgeous blue-eyed, white-furred Siamese strode into the room. The bell was attached to a blue collar that matched the hue of her eyes. She glanced at me briefly, and as her owner was wont to do, dismissed me immediately. She strode over to Courtney and waited for her to pick her up.

"Have you ever met Princess?" Courtney asked, picking up and stroking her cat.

"Not until just now." I longed to reach out and pet her, but kept myself in check. I wouldn't put it past

Courtney to be offended, or for the cat to bite my hand off, if she took after her owner.

"She's my perfect little angel." She kissed the top of Princess's head, and then set her back down. "I've had her since she was a kitten."

"She's beautiful."

And as if she understood me, Princess raised her chin, swished her tail, and then sauntered off, looking about as close to a runway model as a cat could.

"I've entered her into a few shows. She's won all of them." She frowned. "Well, except for one, but that wasn't her fault. The judge was prejudiced against her. And I think he was sleeping with one of the other owners."

"I'm sure he was," I said, resisting the urge to roll my eyes.

"Excuse me a moment." Courtney followed her cat out of the room, leaving me alone in the kitchen.

I sipped at my tea and considered what I could say to change Courtney's mind about Stewie. Even if she did take him on, it was unlikely she'd earn much of a profit from him. And with Courtney, profit was all that mattered.

She returned a few minutes later, and I had yet to come up with an argument I thought would work. She didn't explain her absence, just resumed her place at the counter and said, "Well, I suppose you can go. Take Chewy and do whatever you want with him."

I almost corrected her again, but decided it wasn't worth the effort. If she hadn't gotten Stewie's name right by now, she never would.

"Thank you," I said, happy we hadn't spent hours arguing. I did wish she would have given in *before* Timothy had kicked us out, but what's done is done.

Courtney didn't appear inclined to walk me to the door, so I showed myself out. On the way, I noticed the living room was done in light, summery tones. It made me wonder if the bathrooms were likewise matching, perhaps seashells or ocean vistas. How someone could live like that, I'd never know. It made the house feel like a model home, not somewhere where someone actually lived.

I stepped outside and got into my van. Before I started it up, I called Ben to let him know I was coming. Not surprisingly, I only got his voicemail, so I left him a brief message, one I doubted he'd get until later. His entire attention was likely focused on Ms. Bikini. I'd be lucky to convince him to leave her to come home.

Checking the clock, I realized it had been almost an hour since I'd left him, though it sure didn't feel like it. It was going to take another twenty minutes to get back to Timothy's house. Hopefully, Ben would be done with his flirting by then, though I doubted it.

As I drove, I started to get worried about Duke. Why had Courtney waited until after we'd gone to her house before giving in? It wasn't like we talked about Stewie all that much. Had she been buying time? I wouldn't put it past her to have sent Duke to pick up Stewie while she distracted me. I only hoped that if that was the case, Ben noticed and stepped in.

Yeah right. The chances of him noticing Duke were about as good as him answering his phone to talk to his mom while he was entertaining a good-looking woman in a bikini.

I turned onto the street on which Timothy Fuller lived, and nearly slammed on the brakes when I saw what awaited me.

Flashing red-and-blue lights illuminated the house. A police cruiser sat parked just off the road, wheels firmly in Timothy's yard. An ambulance took up the space behind the cars in the driveway.

I'm too late. Poor Junior. I knew Timothy was ill, but hadn't realized it was *that* bad. I hoped he hadn't had a heart attack or stroke because of the fight with Courtney. Stress wasn't good for someone with a bad heart, not that I knew exactly what was wrong with him. And then to think about Stewie, having to see his owner die. It was going to be brutal on the poor thing.

I parked behind the police cruiser, not wanting to get in the way of the ambulance, but wanting to be on hand in case someone needed me to take the Pomeranian. As I got out of the van, I could hear other sirens in the distance, and wondered if they were headed here, or were going elsewhere.

Only a few neighbors stood outside, watching. I didn't see Duke anywhere, which made me feel bad about suspecting him of doing something behind my back. He might work with Courtney, but he wasn't a bad man.

Checking next door, I saw the woman in the bikini watching, but Ben wasn't with her as far as I could tell. He must have gone inside to help when Mr. Fuller had gone down.

I started forward, but was stopped as a policeman approached.

"Excuse me, miss," he said, holding out a hand. "Please step back." He was an older man with dark skin, hair gone to gray, but the command in his voice was strong enough that I stopped in my tracks.

"What happened?" I asked. "I was just here an hour or so ago."

Before the policeman—whose name tag read *Perry*—could answer, someone else called to me.

"Mom?"

"Ben?" I looked around, but didn't see him at first.

And then I noticed the open cruiser doors. Seated inside, hands cuffed behind his back, was my son.

"What's going on here?" I asked, voice pitched to a near wail. "Why's my son sitting in your car?"

Officer Perry looked pained as he took me by the elbow and guided me back a step, away from the cruiser. "I'm sorry," he said. "I didn't know you were related."

Okay, that was great and all, but it didn't answer my question. "Please, Officer. What's going on? Ben? What happened?"

Ben didn't answer. Neither did the policeman.

"Did you know the man who lives here?" he asked instead.

I glanced toward the house. I could see movement inside, through the windows, but couldn't make out exactly what was going on. Another police officer stood outside, wiping his hands on a wad of paper towels. He looked young, and pale, which made me all the more frightened.

A pair of paramedics moved from the ambulance and headed around the side of the house, out back. Voices drifted from back there, sounding farther away than just the patio. *The barn?* I wondered.

"I just met him today," I said. "We were here to pick up his dog, Stewie. He's a Pomeranian." Not that the last was important. "We left a little over an hour ago. I was coming back for the dog. Is Timothy okay?"

"No, he's not." Officer Perry's voice had gone grave.

I felt myself go faint, though I'd suspected as much. "He's dead?"

"Yes, ma'am." Perry's grip on my elbow turned supportive. "Are you all right? Do you need to sit down?"

"No, I'm fine." Though I felt anything but as my gaze locked on Ben. "My son . . . Why's he here?"

"I'm sorry to inform you, but he's currently under suspicion."

"For what?" I asked.

Officer Perry looked grimly from me, to Ben, and then back again before answering.

"For the murder of Timothy Fuller."

3

I soon found myself trailing after a police cruiser on its way to the station downtown. I could just barely make out the back of Ben's head through the rear window. He was keeping it bowed, never once looking up. In prayer, or in shame, I didn't know.

My brain felt numb, each thought slow, confused, as I tried to make sense of what I'd been told. Old man Fuller was dead. And somehow, someway, the police thought Ben was involved in his death, which was insane. He might have broken a heart or two in his time, but never had he physically hurt anyone. He'd never even gotten into a fight at school as far as I was aware.

I considered calling Manny to let him know what was going on, but wasn't sure what I'd say. Maybe after I'd talked to the police, and we got everything sorted out, I could let him know. Hopefully, I'd be taking Ben home, and we could laugh about it over the dinner table.

Not that Timothy Fuller's death was a laughing matter.

Behind me, Junior followed, Alexis in the passenger seat beside him. Apparently, they'd arrived shortly after I did, having left during the hour in which I'd been dealing with Courtney. I never saw them until we were on the way to the police station, and even then, I had yet to speak to either.

The cruiser pulled into the station lot, and around the side, where I wasn't allowed to follow. I parked in one of the spaces out front, as did Junior. He got out and was around the front of his car, to mine, before I could so much as open the door.

"This is on you," he said, leveling a finger my way.

"Excuse me?" I said, pushing my way out of my van, forcing him a step back. "I had nothing to do with your dad's death. Neither did Ben."

"I know what you're after," he said. "And there's no way you, or anyone else, is going to get it. I will die first!"

"I don't know what you're talking about!"

"Yeah, right." He bared his teeth at me in a feral smile before he spun away. "Alexis! Come on." He stormed toward the front doors of the police station.

Alexis narrowed her eyes at me, shook her head, as if disappointed in me for whatever it was they thought I'd done, and then she followed after her husband. They both looked back at me once, and then went inside.

I stared after them, mouth agape. All I wanted was the dog. I didn't care about the family drama, or whatever it was he thought I was interested in. At this point, all that mattered to me was Ben and Stewie.

Everyone else could drive off into the sunset for all I cared.

Still, the accusations bothered me. Junior had no right to accuse me of anything.

But there was nothing I could do about it now. I smoothed down my hair, closed and locked my van door, and then followed after the Fullers.

The front of the police station was dominated by large plate glass windows that looked out over the lot, as well as a good chunk of downtown Grey Falls. The courthouse was across the street, though there was little activity going on there at the moment. When I entered through the front doors, I passed through a metal detector, which was currently turned off, much to my relief. If I had to stand there and wait for someone to pat me down, I'd explode.

Alexis and Junior were already seated in red plastic chairs near the wall. About a dozen cops were milling around, each seemingly busy with their own worries. I'd never been inside a police station before, and had no idea what I was supposed to do now that I was in one. Did I stop someone and ask them where Ben was? He wasn't anywhere in sight. Did that mean they took him straight to a jail cell? Or was he locked up in a room with a muscle-bound detective screaming at him to talk?

Before I could panic, Officer Perry appeared. "Mrs. Denton. Please, this way."

"Can I see him?" I asked, following him past a glowering Junior, and down a short hallway. "Can I see my son?"

"Not yet," Perry said gently. I found I actually liked him, even though he was the man who'd told me the police thought my son capable of murder. None of this was the officer's fault. "I'll see what I can arrange once we get some things settled."

I didn't like it, but what was I going to do? Screaming and crying wouldn't help. Getting in his face would only land me in hot water, if I wasn't already there. If they suspected Ben of murder, what did the cops think of me?

So, I did the only thing I could, and followed meekly behind Officer Perry, hoping that somehow, this turned out to be one big mistake.

The kindly officer led me down the hall, to a closed door. He knocked on it twice, and then, when no one answered, he opened the door. "Please," he said, motioning for me to precede him.

I entered the room, worry eating at my gut. It was small and stark, and no one else was in there. The walls were a faded white, the floor hard tile. There were no big one-way mirrors like you'd see on TV, but there was a camera in the corner, watching my every move. A table with four plastic chairs pushed beneath it awaited me in the center of the room.

"Wait here," Perry said. "I know it isn't exactly welcoming, but it's better than out there." He jerked a thumb toward where Junior still sat. "This will give you a little privacy while you wait for someone to come talk to you."

"Thank you," I said, pulling out a chair. It's metal feet squeaked loudly against the tile.

"Someone will be with you shortly for your statement. I want to make it clear that at this time, you aren't in any trouble."

"That's good to hear."

"Do you need me to get you something? Coffee? Some water?"

"I'm okay." If I tried to drink anything, I'd likely choke on it.

"Sit tight." Officer Perry gave me a warm smile, and then closed the door, leaving me alone.

I sat and placed both hands atop the table. I knew they'd ask me about Ben, about his whereabouts when Timothy Fuller was killed—murdered, did he say? I was in shock, I knew, and fear was growing with every passing second. I couldn't tell them much of anything about Ben, other than to vouch for his character. He'd left me to go talk to a woman I didn't know, whose name I didn't know. After that, I knew nothing.

It didn't look good. Not one bit.

There were no clocks on the wall, so I checked my watch. The second hand seemed to crawl around the face in slow motion. I drummed my fingers on the table, stared into the camera, and did just about everything but pace.

Ten minutes, and three watch checks later, a burly police officer with a crew cut and a bushy mustache entered. He was wearing a faded suit and tie, badge clipped to his belt. He looked like he might have played football back when he was younger, but much of the muscle had gone to fat. His skin was tanned, eyes squinted, as if he spent many hours outside, looking into the sun. Maybe not football, then. A farmer?

"Mrs. Denton, correct?" he asked, checking a sheet of paper he'd brought in with him. His voice was deep, a little raspy, and in no way was it friendly.

"I am. Please, call me Liz."

He settled into one of the chairs before glancing up at me. "Liz, I'm Detective Emmitt Cavanaugh."

My hands tightened into fists. Was it good that a

detective was taking my statement? Or did it mean things were quickly spiraling out of control?

"What can you tell me about what happened?" Cavanaugh asked, sitting back and resting his hands atop his stomach in a relaxed posture that was completely at odds with the gravity of the situation.

"I'm sorry, sir, but I wasn't there."

He flashed me a tight smile. "Humor me."

"Ben didn't do it, I can tell you that," I said. "He would never hurt anyone, and had no reason to."

"Noted. You're his mother, correct?" He made it sound like that would be a strike against him.

"I am." I straightened my back, met his eye. "Which means I know him better than anyone."

"I'm sure that's true." Cavanaugh glanced down at the page in his hand. "Why was he at Mr. Fuller's home today?"

"We were picking up Stewie." At Cavanaugh's pinched brow, I added, "The Pomeranian. Mr. Fuller was a sick man. He was going to be moved to an extended care facility that didn't allow pets. He called us a little over a week ago, asking if we could find his dog a home. We did, and were there to pick him up."

"I see."

"We help people," I said. "Ben and I. And we help animals that many people couldn't care less about. Ben's a good person, and would never hurt anyone, especially a man like Mr. Fuller. Who he barely knew, I might add."

"You were there for the dog, then?" Cavanaugh asked.

"We were."

"And you weren't present with your son at the time of the murder, because . . . ?"

"There were, um, unanticipated complications."

Cavanaugh leaned forward, folding his hands on the table before him. "Such as?"

Trying my best not to sound too bitter, I told him about the brief encounter outside Timothy Fuller's home, making sure to note Courtney and Duke were uninvited guests, and how Junior and his wife were short with us. I told him how we were all kicked out, how Ben went over next door, while I went to speak with Courtney.

Cavanaugh nodded as I spoke, but he didn't seem all that interested in the story. Admittedly, none of what I said sounded like it had anything to do with Timothy's death, but it was all I had.

"Duke was missing too," I said, feeling a little bad about throwing him under the bus like that, but what else was I going to do? "At the time of the murder, he was supposed to be with Courtney and me, but he wasn't."

"And what's Duke's last name?"

"Billings."

Cavanaugh produced a pen from his pocket and scrawled Duke's name across the sheet of paper. "While you were at the house, did you see anything else suspect? Were there any strange people hanging around? An argument that might have escalated?"

"No, there was nothing like that." But boy, did I wish I *had* seen something. "Are you sure Timothy was actually murdered?" I couldn't keep the pleading out of my tone. "He could have been sicker than anyone thought and died of natural causes."

"We're sure." Cavanaugh didn't even hesitate in his answer.

"It could have been a heart attack," I pressed. "Or

a stroke. He was in a wheelchair, so maybe he tried to get up on his own and fell. That sort of thing happens all the time, right?"

"He didn't."

"How do you know that for sure?" I was starting to get frantic.

"Probably because of the knife we found sticking out of his back."

All my words dried up right then and there. How could anyone stab an old man in the back, one who was so sick, he was confined to a wheelchair? It didn't make sense.

Detective Cavanaugh must have sensed my misery, because he leaned forward, eyes and voice softening. "Did you know the deceased well, Mrs. Denton?"

"No. While we talked on the phone twice before today, this was the first time I'd met him in person."

"What did you talk about on the phone?"

"About Stewie," I said. "That's all."

"So, you have no idea why anyone would want to kill him?"

"None."

"Your son, Ben, he met him at the same time you did?"

"He did. Up until this morning, neither of us knew Timothy Fuller, or his family."

"Are you sure about that? There's no chance Ben might have met him elsewhere?"

I met his eye. "Positive."

Cavanaugh scratched at the stubble on his cheeks before heaving a sigh. "Mrs. Denton, I know it's hard for you to understand right now, but we didn't arrest your son on a whim. We have evidence that places him at the scene of the crime."

"What kind of evidence?" I asked. It came out as a mere whisper. *This can't be happening.*

"We have a witness."

I blinked at him, slowly, not quite sure I'd heard him right. "A witness? To the murder?"

"No," he admitted. "But someone did see a young man matching your son's description entering the deceased's home. He was inside for maybe ten minutes, before hurriedly fleeing from the scene. A few minutes after that there was a scream from out back, where the body was found."

"A scream?" A glimmer of hope formed. If Ben had left before Timothy Fuller had died, then there was no way he could have done it.

"Mr. Fuller's nurse found him. She screamed and then called the cops. Apparently, she was folding laundry when the murder took place. She came in to check on Mr. Fuller and found him missing."

"Missing?"

"He wasn't where she left him," Cavanaugh said. "She claims Mr. Fuller often wheels himself out to the barn out back when he's upset, so she went looking for him there. She found him." He didn't make it sound like a good thing.

"But . . ." I swallowed, cutting my own words short. But what? *They have a witness!* "There are lots of young men who look like Ben," I said. "Maybe your witness didn't see him clearly."

"That may be the case," Cavanaugh said. "But how many young men run around town with their names written across the back of their shirt?"

"His shirt?" Just like the one I was currently wearing. *Oh, no, Ben.* "It's not possible."

"I'm afraid it is." Cavanaugh started to reach out,

as if he might take my hand to comfort me, before catching himself. He folded his arms instead. "Mr. Denton was seen going into the house, his name proudly displayed on his back. He was seen not just entering, but running away afterward. I hate to tell you, but it's looking like he's our man."

"It had to be someone else," I said, but I knew I was fooling myself. If someone saw Ben's shirt, then Ben was the one in it.

But that didn't mean he'd *killed* Timothy Fuller. There were all sorts of reasons why he might have run away.

"Maybe he found the body and it scared him," I said. "So, he ran. Maybe he went to get help, or tell someone." Like the woman in the bikini. *But why not Meredith?* "Maybe he saw the murder take place and was running away."

"I'm sorry, Mrs. Denton. There was blood on his shirt, and he's said nothing about witnessing the murder."

"But . . . He couldn't have." Tears welled in my eyes. I refused to let them fall.

"I'm sorry," Cavanaugh said. "I imagine there aren't many people running around with those shirts, are there?" He pointed at my chest where the rescue logo was printed.

"No."

"There's yours, your son's. Husband?"

"Yes. And a daughter." I had a shirt printed for Amelia, but she never wore it.

"No other employees?"

"No," I said. "Just us."

"And no one else named Ben would have a shirt like this, I'm guessing?"

"No." I'd only printed enough shirts for the family, so there was no chance anyone else would have one. *Am I sure about that?*

Cavanaugh stood. "I'm sorry," he said yet again, and he sounded like he meant it. "We'll find out exactly what happened. If it turns out Ben is guilty, all he needs to do is cooperate. The judge might go easy on him then."

I nodded. It all felt so surreal, I wasn't sure what was happening anymore. Could he really be talking about Ben going before a judge? Did that mean prison? My stomach clenched at the thought. "Can I see him?"

Cavanaugh bit down on his lower lip, chewed a moment, and then shook his head. "I think it's best you let us deal with this for now. Let us talk to him, see what he has to say. Come back tomorrow. You should be allowed to meet with him for a few minutes then."

It was like a knife to my own back, but there wasn't a thing I could do about it, but go along with it. Somehow, someway, Ben found himself smack-dab in the middle of a murder investigation. And not only was he a suspect, it was sounding more and more like he was the *only* suspect.

"Go home," Cavanaugh said. "Get some rest." He opened the door to the small room. "And if you think of anything you might have forgotten to tell me, don't hesitate to call." He handed me a card with his name and number on it.

"I will." Heart heavy, I stepped out into the hall. Cavanaugh followed me all the way to the front room, where Alexis and a clearly agitated Junior were still waiting.

"Mr. Fuller," Detective Cavanaugh said. "I'm ready for you now."

Junior rose, but instead of going straight to the detective, he stepped closer to me, putting us practically nose to nose. "You won't get away with this." He very nearly hissed the words.

And then, before I could formulate any sort of response, he spun on his heel and strode down the hall.

Detective Cavanaugh and his pinched eyes watched me for a long couple of seconds. I could almost hear the questions flying around in his head, before he finally turned to follow after Junior.

Completely confused, I met Alexis's eye, hoping she might explain what it was Junior thought I'd done, but all she did was huff and look away.

What in the world is going on here?

Feeling as if the entire world was conspiring against both Ben and me, I left the police station, head down. I got into my van, and with numb fingers I started it up.

And then, with nowhere else I could go, I did as Detective Cavanaugh had told me to do, and headed for home.

4

I glanced out the window for what had to be the twentieth time in the last ten minutes. Manny was on his way home, but had been forced to wait for one of the other veterinarians to show up to replace him before he could leave. If it had been me, I would have been out the door, regardless of whether anyone was there or not, but Manny had always been overly responsible, even when his own flesh and blood was in trouble.

"What am I going to do, Wheels?" I asked, pacing away from the window. "Ben needs me, but I can't do a thing to help him." I felt completely useless, lost.

Wheels trilled and wound between my feet the best she could. Her tires bumped up against my ankles like bumper cars. It didn't exactly hurt, but it wasn't comfortable either. I reached down, petted her for a few minutes, and then resumed my impatient pacing.

Leroy and Toby were quiet, for which I was thankful. When I'd come in, they'd started barking immediately, needing to go out. Once their bladders were empty and they were given fresh water and treats, they settled right down for their naps. Thankfully, Joanne hadn't come over to see what all the fuss was about. I didn't think I could have handled her complaints without completely losing my cool.

"Calm down, Liz," I muttered, forcing myself to stop pacing. It wasn't doing anyone any good, and if I kept it up, I'd pace myself right into a frenzy. I needed to find something to do, something to keep my mind off Timothy Fuller and his murder.

But instead of doing something constructive, like prepping adoption paperwork, or planning dinner, I found myself heading up the stairs, to Ben's room. The door was closed and I very nearly knocked before I remembered that he wasn't there. I closed my eyes and rested my hand on the wood, in the hopes I could *feel* him in it.

No such luck.

Pushing open the door, I entered his domain.

Ben was at an age where he could get a place of his own, but he'd chosen to stay home to make it easier for him to help out with the rescue. I was under no illusions that he wouldn't eventually leave us, but for now, I was happy to let him stay. He didn't cause trouble, didn't eat us out of house and home, and the fact that he was over twenty and still lived with his parents wasn't hurting his ability to date.

His bed was made, nightstand uncluttered. His computer was turned off, and a few scattered papers lay atop the desk beside it. I crossed the room and checked them, not sure what to expect. It wasn't like I truly believed Ben planned to kill Timothy Fuller and left evidence lying around.

Still, my chest was tight as I checked the papers to

find they were printed pages from the internet about canine arthritis in beagles. He'd circled a home remedy that was supposed to help with the pain and wrote, *Tell Mom*, beside it.

"Oh, Ben." I touched the writing, as if I could feel him in the words, before returning the pages to his desk. I couldn't take it anymore, so I left the bedroom, closing the door behind me.

Ben had always wanted to work alongside his dad, and occasionally did when the office was shorthanded, though more often than not, he spent much of his time with me. Maybe, once all of this is over, I'd finally tell Manny to hire Ben on full time. It was about time we let him fly free.

If he ever comes home again.

I stamped down on that line of thought and turned toward Amelia's door. I would not think like that. Ben was coming home, even if I had to find the killer myself.

"Amelia?" I asked, knocking on her door, though I knew she wasn't home. Her car hadn't been in the driveway, and I would have heard her moving around if she was.

Still, I gave it a good twenty seconds before knocking again, this time louder. As expected, no one was there to answer.

Feeling like an intruder in my own home, I pushed open the door and glanced inside. Unlike Ben, who tended to clean up after himself, Amelia let her messes lie. Her bed was unmade. A pair of candy wrappers lay on the nightstand beside the bed. Her laptop was gone, the desk a mess of textbooks and stacked papers. In other words, the room of a college student.

She wasn't on the bed, earbuds in, while she scanned

a textbook. Nor was she sitting at her desk, hammering out a paper the night before it was due. She was gone, living her life, learning to become whatever it was she decided to be.

What I wouldn't give to have her there with me now.

I started to close the door when I noticed an index card poking out between a pair of books on a shelf next to the door. I went to push it in when I noted there were numbers printed on it. I tugged the card free and saw it was a phone number, and a name.

"C. Chudzinski," I said aloud. The mysterious new boyfriend? A professor looking to help his favorite student? It was written in Amelia's handwriting, and there were no other notes telling me who C. Chudzinski might be. The books were old YA novels she no longer read, so they weren't any help either.

I shoved the card back where I found it and left the room, closing the door behind me. Whoever it was, Amelia would tell me in her own time.

A car pulled into the paved driveway. I bolted down the stairs and to the door. Wheels followed after, anxious because she recognized the sound of Manny's Ford. He struggled a bit with the weird automatic transmission that always caused the entire car to shudder when he pulled to a stop or started to go. It gave him away every time he came home.

I threw open the door and hurried outside to meet him. His curly hair was dark, and falling into his eyes. His brown eyes were worried as they found me. He was still wearing what I always called his pet scrubs—blue fabric with kittens and puppies printed on them. Somehow, despite how ridiculous they were, he made them look good.

"Where is he?" Manny asked, stepping past me,

into the house, like he expected Ben to be waiting there for him.

"He's still with the police," I told him. "They're going to hold him overnight! What are we going to do, Manny?"

He ran his fingers through his hair as he turned back to face me. "What can we do?" He sounded far calmer than I did, though he was still worried. I could see it in his eyes. "You said they think he killed that man?"

"The detective told me they have a witness." I still couldn't believe it. The witness had to either be corrupt, or blind. "But I know it's not possible." And then, quieter. "It's not possible, is it?"

"Of course not, Liz." He wrapped me in a hug. He smelled like wet dog and sanitizer, but it comforted me anyway. "Ben will be fine."

"How do you know?" I asked. I could feel my fragile grip on my emotions slipping. Ben was my son. He was in jail. There was no way I could get past that.

Manny stepped back and somehow managed a smile. "Trust in the law," he said. "And if that doesn't work, trust in Ben. He knows how to handle himself. We all know he didn't do it, and the police will eventually realize that. They'll find who killed that man, I promise."

Oh, how I wished I could believe that.

"Now, tell me exactly what happened," Manny said.

Taking a few moments to calm my nerves, I went over it again. It wasn't any easier than when I'd told it to the cops. Actually, it was worse. I kept wondering how things would have gone if I would have done things differently, convinced Timothy to hand over

Stewie right then and there, or if I'd refused to let Ben run off with the woman in the bikini.

"Do you think Duke could be responsible?" I asked about halfway through the tale.

"Duke?" Manny's eyebrows, which were thick and dark, met in the crease between his eyes. "Why would you think that?"

"He wasn't with Courtney when I met with her at her house. He could have gone back to Timothy's to sneak Stewie away while I was there. He might have gotten into a fight with him over the dog, accidentally killed him. Or what if, when he got there, he found Timothy's body after someone else, like Timothy's nurse, killed him? Duke could have told the police he saw Ben to cover his own tracks."

"That doesn't sound like Duke."

No, it didn't, but I didn't have anything else to go on.

"Maybe it was Junior," I said, mind spinning as I searched for someone else who could be responsible for the murder. "He was accusing me of all sorts of things, none of which made any sense. He acted like I had some ulterior motive for showing up. Maybe he decided to blame Ben for a murder *he* committed instead."

"Or, he's simply upset," Manny said, as levelheaded as ever. Unlike his mother, who was as excitable as a Chihuahua on a bad day, Manny rarely got worked up. And even when he did, he still managed to exude calm, which often helped keep me from completely flying off the handle.

"You're probably right," I said. Blaming others wasn't going to help Ben. Not unless I found proof.

An idea started to form, one that I was reluctant to dismiss. Manny wanted me to trust the police, but so far, they'd accused Ben of murder on the word of a single witness. That didn't inspire much confidence in their abilities.

"Come on," Manny said, taking my arm and leading me to the table. "You should eat. I'll whip up some sandwiches for the both of us."

"Sure," I said, though I was far from hungry. I sank down into a chair and turned my idea over in my head, tried to see where it could go wrong.

The easiest thing to do would be to stay put and wait for the police to work things out on their own. It was what they were trained to do.

But I'd seen those made for TV movies where the police arrest the wrong man, and without intervention, would have ended up convicting him of the crime. Could I really take that chance with my son's life?

Manny was humming as he made a pair of tomato sandwiches. I knew what he'd tell me to do, that there was nothing more I could do, that I should let the police handle it and stay right here at home, doing nothing.

But it wasn't like I was thinking of doing anything more than chatting with a person or two to see what they had to say. What harm would there be in that?

I forced a smile as Manny handed me a plate. If I let him see the thoughts working behind my eyes, he would surely try to stop me.

"Did you get a chance to talk to Amelia yet?" I asked, changing the subject away from Ben and his predicament in the hopes Manny wouldn't pry into my thoughts. I took a bite of my sandwich to hide my nervousness.

"No," Manny said, wiping tomato juice from his chin. "Do you really think something is up with her?"

"I'm not sure," I said. "She's never been secretive before." I considered telling him about the name and number I'd found in her room, but decided it was really none of our business. She was a grown adult at this point and was allowed to have her own secrets.

"All kids go through it," Manny said.

"I guess. Ben thinks she might have a new boyfriend."

Manny looked surprised. "Really? It would be news to me. Do you think we should talk to her?"

"I don't know. She's been kind of moody lately." Thanks to Ben's current predicament, my mind was traveling in some pretty unsavory directions. What if it was drugs? Alcohol? What if she was struggling in school and was about to drop out? What if it was a cult?

And then, thinking of the name and number, as well as Ben's guess about her current relationship status: What if she was pregnant?

"It's probably nothing," Manny said. "She might have wanted to get a jump start on the day. Nothing sinister about that."

"I hope so."

We finished our meal in silence. I shouldn't have brought Amelia up because now I was worried about *both* my children, when by all rights, I should be focused on Ben.

"I should be getting back," Manny said as he gathered the plates and put them into the sink. "Theresa came in to cover for me, but said she can't stay long. If you need me to stick around here, I can always call Ray and see if he can make it."

"No, that's okay," I said. "You should go. It's not like there's much else we can do but wait." I went over and kissed him. It was shocking how calmly he was taking it all in. The man was a rock, unfazed by anything. "Thanks for talking me off the ledge."

"Always." He kissed my forehead, and then grabbed his keys. "If you hear something, call me immediately."

"I will."

He started for the door, stopped. "Liz?"

"Hmm?"

"Do you know if Ben's talked to an attorney yet?"

"No, I don't. They wouldn't let me see him."

Manny nodded, seemingly to himself. "All right. I'll call Lester, just in case."

"Do you think he can help?" Lester Ives was an attorney we knew, but I wasn't sure he knew anything about murder cases.

"Can't hurt," Manny said. "And Liz?"

I hugged myself as I said, "Yeah?"

"It'll be okay."

"I'm sure it will." I forced a smile.

He winked, blew me one more kiss, and then he was gone.

As soon as the door closed, I sagged against the wall, exhausted from keeping on a brave face. I went from having what felt like the perfect life, to wondering if I was going to get through the day with either of my children at my side.

"You can do this," I muttered, pushing away from the wall. I was all butterflies and nerves inside, but I refused to let Ben go down without putting up some sort of fight.

I took a few minutes to make sure Toby and Leroy were taken care of, taking them both out back for one more potty break, and then making sure they had enough food and water. Then, once that was settled, I picked up the phone and called my pet sitter, Lenore Cosgrove.

"Hi, Lenore, it's Liz," I said when she answered, keeping the fear for Ben out of my voice. I didn't need to worry her. "Do you think you'll be able to come in and keep an eye on the dogs for me? I know it's short notice, but it's an emergency."

Lenore chuckled a dry, raspy laugh. "Of course, I can," she said. "Give me a moment to grab my shawl and I'll be right over."

"Thank you so much," I said, relieved. "I'm not sure how long this will take. I have to run some errands, but Amelia should be home to relieve you before too long." At least, I hoped she would be.

One crisis at a time, Liz.

"It's no bother at all," Lenore said. She grunted, and I imaged her rising from her rocking chair, where she liked to sit to knit. "I was hoping to get another chance to spend a few hours with those two dogs of yours before they're gone. They're blessings sent straight from Heaven, let me tell you."

"They are," I agreed. "I'll see you when you get here."

We said our goodbyes and I put a can of soup on low heat as I always did for Lenore when she came over. She lived only a few houses down, all by herself. She was eighty-five, and looked every day of it. When her dog, Bobo, had died, many thought she would go with him, she was so depressed.

Thankfully, in a moment of inspiration, I asked her if she might like to spend some time with a pair of puppies I'd recently taken in, thinking she might want to take one home with her. She didn't want to go that far, but she did enjoy spending time with them. One thing led to another, and before long, I was paying her to pet sit whenever I knew I was going to be out for more than a couple of hours. She'd probably do it for free, but I'd never ask her to do such a thing.

"Lenore's coming over," I told Wheels, who'd followed me into the kitchen. "Be good for her, okay?"

Wheels purred, rubbed her head against my leg, and then rolled over to her water dish. It was as close to a "yes" as I was going to get.

Lenore showed up fifteen minutes later, back stooped, but with a broad smile on her wrinkled face. I let her in, showed her the soup, and then left her to the mercy of the elderly dogs who loved her just as much as I did.

With the animals squared away, I got into my van, started it up, and headed back to the scene of the crime.

5

No other cars sat in Timothy Fuller's driveway as I pulled to a stop. The house didn't just look empty; it *felt* empty. There was no police tape strung across the doorway like I'd expected there to be. I supposed that since the murder took place out back, there was no reason to seal up the house. The front door would be locked, but the curtains had been pulled wide, as if someone had decided to let in the sun before leaving. The ceramic Pomeranian out front looked weathered and alone.

I wondered where Stewie was being kept, and prayed someone hadn't called the shelter to come and get him. From what little I knew of Junior, I wouldn't put it past him. I knew for a fact the shelter was already overfull, and with a good many of the dogs being puppies, or young enough to still act like a puppy, Stewie wouldn't stand a chance.

I got out of my van and walked over to the window and peered inside. Old furniture sat amid machines I didn't recognize, but were obviously there for health reasons. A mask sat on the armrest of the couch, attached to a box by tubing. Another machine stood near the wall, next to a small statue of a soldier.

It was heartbreaking, really. How hard had Timothy's life been before his untimely demise? It couldn't be easy getting to sleep with a mask like that covering half your face. And then to be confined to a wheelchair, so he couldn't go out and do things on his own. To go through all that, and then be murdered? I couldn't imagine.

Had he been a soldier once? A businessman? Was his inability to walk due to his illness, or something else?

Looking at the state of his living room, it was no wonder he was cranky earlier this morning. I would be too if I had to live like that.

I checked for some sign that Stewie might be inside, but other than a chew toy resting against the far wall, I saw nothing. No crate, no wag of a tail, no water dish.

I considered knocking on the glass to see if I could cause the dog to bark, but decided against it. No sense agitating the little guy if he was inside, not after what he just went through. I'd have to check with Junior later and see where Stewie had gone so I could get him and take him somewhere safe.

Putting my back to the window, I scanned the street. I had no idea who the witness who fingered Ben as the killer might be. It could have been a passerby, a friend of the family.

Or it could have been someone living in one of the nearby houses.

I was counting on the latter.

The houses in Timothy's neighborhood were spaced apart, so that I could only see three houses clearly from my vantage point near the front door. The house to my right was where Ben had gone when I'd left for my powwow with Courtney. Another across the street appeared empty. There were no curtains in the windows, and a *For Sale* sign sat out front.

That left the battered house beside the empty, which was occupied by an older man who was currently sitting in a rocking chair on his porch, watching me. All the other houses were shielded from view by trees, or were too far away for someone to have been able to read Ben's name on his shirt.

I decided the old man was the best place to start.

He tracked my progress across the yard without giving anything away. He held a mug in one hand, and wore a sagging straw hat over dark eyes and skin. As I approached, he raised a gnarled hand toward me in greeting.

"Hi," I said, stepping up to the front porch, but didn't ascend the stairs. "I'm Liz. Do you have a minute to talk?"

"Sure do," the man said, voice slightly accented, as if he'd lived much of his life in the South. "You can call me Clarence, if you please. Would you like some coffee?" He raised his mug. "There's plenty."

"No, thank you." At his gesture, I joined him on the porch and took a seat in a neighboring rocking chair. From there, I had a clear view of Timothy Fuller's front door. "I hope I'm not intruding."

"Don't worry yourself," Clarence said. "It's been a long time since someone joined me on my watch. Wife's been gone nearly fifteen years now, bless her heart. It's about time a pretty woman sat beside me again. I promise, she won't mind."

"I'm sorry to hear about your wife," I said, and meant it. The old man seemed friendly enough, and

I hoped he could tell me something that would save Ben.

"Me too, darling. Me too."

It felt wrong to go from his dead wife to my son's predicament, so, instead of jumping in right away, I took a moment to gather my thoughts, eyes drifting back to the Fuller house. I tried to remember if I'd seen Clarence outside at any point earlier, but I'd never once looked his way.

"Shame, isn't it?" Clarence said, nodding toward Timothy's house. "These sorts of things happen in all neighborhoods these days, I suppose. Still, hard to wrap your mind around it when it happens right across the street."

"Did you see what happened?"

"I did, I did." He took a drink from his coffee. "Saw the boy that did it too."

"You saw him? And you told the police?"

"I did." He looked me up and down. "Wore a shirt just like you. I might be old, but my eyes are as good as they ever were. Or at least, near as can be." He chuckled. "Saw him go in myself, name splashed across his back as if he was afraid someone might forget who he was. Was only inside for a few minutes before he came running from around back, looking as if the devil himself was after him."

"Did you get a look at his face?" Good eyes or not, there was a decent amount of distance from the porch, to Timothy Fuller's front door. I wasn't sure even *I* could make out a face, and I had pretty good vision.

"No, I didn't."

"Was he wearing a mask?"

"No, ma'am. Just happened so quick. Since people were going in and out all day, I just assumed it was another one. Didn't pay him no real mind until he bolted."

A glimmer of hope formed in my chest. He hadn't actually seen the murder, which meant all he had was Ben going in, which could mean anything. "Are you sure he was the one who killed Mr. Fuller?" I asked. "He might have come across the body and panicked."

"Could be, I suppose," Clarence said. "Can't say I'm all that surprised someone finally did in old man Fuller, either way."

"Why do you say that?"

"Tim wasn't a good man to be around." Clarence clucked his tongue, took a drink before going on. "He treated everyone as if they were beneath him. Was a mean old man, grown from a mean young boy. You should have seen the way he treated that nice nurse of his. Couldn't help but hear it, the way he carried on, yelling at her. Blamed everything on her, even if he done did it himself. Shame to treat a good woman that way."

I wish I could say I was surprised, but I'd seen a hint of his unsavory behavior when I'd met him. And sadly, it appeared Junior was a chip right off the old block.

"Who do you think would have a reason to kill him?" I asked. "If it wasn't the man you saw, I mean."

Clarence laughed as if I'd just told one of the funniest jokes he'd heard in a long time. "Who didn't?" he said. "When you're that mean, just about everyone you come across will want you dead eventually. Now, I ain't saying it's right or nothing. No one should be put down before their time. I reckon Tim pushed somebody a little too hard and they finally snapped."

I wondered if that included his nurse, Meredith.

From the sound of things, she'd put up with a lot of abuse. And with the way Detective Cavanaugh talked, it sounded like she was in the house at the time of the murder. It wasn't hard to imagine her following him out to the barn and killing Timothy in a fit of blind rage. Then, while she's cleaning up, Ben shows up for Stewie, sees the body, and panics.

But why run? And who called the police?

"Did you see where the guy in the shirt ran to?" I asked. "After he left, and before the police picked him up."

Clarence raised the hand with his coffee and pointed. "That way. Came from there as far as I could tell, and ran right back after the deed was done."

I followed his gesture, some of my hope dwindling. It was the house where the bikini-clad woman lived.

"You know, didn't I see you that day?" Clarence asked, turning in his rocking chair to get a better look at me. "I did, didn't I? You came with the boy."

"I was there earlier, yes," I said. "Ben is my son." And he was twenty-two, but I supposed anyone under the age of thirty-five might be considered a boy to a man like Clarence.

"I should have suspected," he said. "Why else come talk to an old man like me if you didn't have cards in the game."

"It's not like that," I said. "Well, I guess it is, but it's hard, you know? I'm sure Ben didn't kill Mr. Fuller. He doesn't have it in him. I just don't know what else to do with myself. I thought if I talked to some people, I'd be able to figure out who might have done it."

Clarence nodded, eyes meeting mine. He seemed to search for something there, expression going grim. "I reckon you'll do just that," he said, nodding as if he'd found whatever he'd been looking for. "You look the determined type."

"I am." I pointed toward Bikini-girl's house. "Who lives there?" I asked.

"That'd be Selena Shriver." A wry smile crossed his lips. "Vixen she is. She sometimes lays out in her yard wearing one of those teeny little bikinis that can't help but draw the eye. Does yard work in it sometimes too. Think she enjoys the attention, and well, with a . . ." He trailed off, chuckled. "Well, now, you don't need to hear what I think about that, do you?"

No, I didn't. "Thank you," I said, rising. "It was nice talking to you, Clarence. You've been a big help."

"You too, Liz. Come see an old man again sometime, would you? It can get awfully lonely out here all by myself."

"I will." And I think I actually meant it. He might have accused Ben of killing Timothy Fuller, but there was no malice in it. He'd simply told the police what he'd seen, and they'd made their deductions from there. I couldn't hold that against him.

I descended the stairs and crossed back over to Timothy's driveway. I stopped by my car and considered what to do next. No one was home, and I didn't know where or how to contact Meredith, Junior, or Alexis about Stewie. I was pretty sure they wouldn't help me prove Ben's innocence, even if they knew who'd actually done the deed.

I couldn't shake the feeling that one of them might be the true killer. Did I really want to associate with a murderer, even for the sake of a dog?

Yes, I realized, I did. Especially if it helped Ben.

But that would all have to come later. For now, I

needed to clear my son's name, and there was one person who could provide him an alibi.

I turned toward Selena's house. It was small, but tidy, with a flower bed running along the side I was facing, looping around to the front. The house was tucked back a little farther from the road than Timothy's house, so I couldn't see the back from where I stood. A single car sat under the carport out front, telling me someone was likely home.

"Might as well," I mumbled. If nothing else, I could get a good look at the girl Ben had been so taken with.

I crossed the short distance to her yard. I glanced back and saw Clarence was still watching me. I waved, and he returned the gesture before rising and heading inside.

Now, in front of Selena's house, I noted how good the flowers looked, each vibrant and lively. A pair of cute garden gnomes were hidden amongst them, seemingly watching me from the cover of petals and leaves. The morning paper was lying halfway down the driveway, and I walked over and picked it up. It would give me a good excuse for knocking.

I approached the front door, mentally prepped myself for what was to come, and then knocked.

It took only a few seconds before the door opened and Selena Shriver peered out at me, a quizzical expression on her face. "Yes?"

Up close, she wasn't just pretty, but drop-dead gorgeous. No wonder Ben had abandoned me for her. She had sparkling blue eyes, and blond hair that held the faintest red hue. It appeared entirely natural. She wasn't wearing a bikini now, but the sundress revealed nearly as much leg.

I handed over the paper, feeling frumpy in my

hair-coated shirt. "Hi, my name's Liz Denton. Ben's mother."

She blinked at me. "Ben?"

"The guy who came over here earlier. To talk."

Selena set the paper on a stand just inside the door. "Oh, that's right. I completely forgot all about it after what happened."

"Was he with you when Mr. Fuller was . . ." I cleared my throat. "Killed?" I finished lamely, hating how the word sounded.

There was a thump inside. I tried to look past her, but Selena moved to block my view. "It's my cat," she said. "Always likes to knock things off the table to see who's at the door."

Which was one of the things my Wheels couldn't do. "Was Ben with you when you found out about Mr. Fuller?" I asked again.

She glanced behind her, then back to me. "He was here when the police arrived, if that's what you're asking," she said.

"And before?"

She refused to meet my eye. "We talked some, that's all."

"Was Ben here the entire time?" I pressed. Why was she being so evasive? "The police think he killed Mr. Fuller. Please, if he was here, you've got to let me know."

Another thump, this one a little louder. It sure didn't sound like something falling over. "I'm sorry, I have to go," she said.

"Wait!"

But it was already too late. The door closed and I heard the definitive sound of the door being locked.

I stood there a long moment, debating on whether

or not to knock again. Selena seemed nervous, but then again, I was the mother of an accused killer. She might think I was trying to implicate her in something, or worse, coming after her.

But hounding her wouldn't make her cooperative. If anything, it might make her turn against Ben, if she hadn't already. She could very well be the only person in the world who could vouch for him that wasn't related to him.

I turned away and returned to my van. Something wasn't right, but I couldn't figure out what it was. Ben had gone over to meet Selena; I'd seen it myself. Clarence saw him go into Timothy's house later, and leave at a run, right back to Selena. She claims he was with her when the police arrived, so it tracked. But why not tell me if he was here the entire time? What was she afraid of?

And had Ben called the cops? Was that why he ran back over, wanting to get to his phone? Meredith had called the murder in, sure, but that didn't mean Ben hadn't as well.

Or had Ben fled for another reason entirely? Maybe Timothy Fuller had been alive and kicking when he'd arrived, and he'd taken out his anger on Ben, which caused him to leave in a rush. Then, someone else killed the old man, meaning Ben would have had no idea that he'd been murdered, not until the police had arrived.

But there was blood on his shirt.

Or so Detective Cavanaugh had said. Perhaps there was another reason for why it was there. Nothing said the blood belonged to Timothy Fuller. As far as I knew, Ben had tried to pet Selena's cat, earning him a sharp slash across the hand. Or perhaps he *had* found the body, checked for a pulse, and gotten blood on him in the process. It didn't mean he killed anyone.

I started up the engine and backed out of the driveway. I might have been told to come back tomorrow, but I couldn't wait any longer; I needed to talk to Ben.

6

It was much to my relief that when I pulled into the Grey Falls Police Station lot, Junior's car was gone. I didn't have it in me to deal with his groundless accusations, not after the day I'd had. I found an empty space, parked, and then headed inside.

I went straight to the front desk, where the young cop I'd seen outside Timothy's house was currently sitting, furiously scribbling away at a piece of paper. He glanced up when I came in, looking as if he didn't know which way was up.

It wasn't a good sign.

"I'm here to speak with my son, Ben Denton," I said, approaching the desk and putting as much command in my voice as I could manage.

"Um." The officer glanced around, seemingly unsure how to handle me. His name tag read *Mohr*.

"He was arrested earlier," I said. "Wrongfully accused of murdering Timothy Fuller."

"Oh. Yeah." Officer Mohr cleared his throat, red

climbing up his neck. "That was pretty rough." He gave me a sheepish smile. "Let me see if I can find someone who can help you."

"I dealt with Officer Perry earlier," I said. I figured he'd be more likely to let me in to see Ben, rather than Detective Cavanaugh. I'm sure there was someone else higher up who I could talk to, but it was likely the higher up the chain I climbed, the more resistance I would meet.

"Perry . . . Perry . . ." Officer Mohr tapped his chin with his pen. He appeared genuinely flummoxed by the name.

"Older man. Gray hair. Dark skin. He was at the house too."

"Oh! Reg!" The lightbulb must have finally clicked on. "He's been pretty good to me so far. Nice guy. I hear he might retire in a year or two. It'll be a shame if he does."

"It will be," I said, growing impatient. "Can I speak to him?"

"Sorry, he's gone for the day. I'm not sure when he'll be back. I'm guessing tomorrow."

Well, crap. "What about Detective Cavanaugh?" I asked, my stomach churning at the thought of dealing with the burly detective again. He hadn't been all that hostile, yet he hadn't come off as very friendly either. Right then, however, he was the closest thing I had to an ally.

Officer Mohr paled. Apparently, Detective Cavanaugh's name meant something to him, unlike everyone else's.

"Detective Cavanaugh?" he asked. "I . . ."

Thankfully, the man in question entered the room before Mohr could say something he might regret. It was obvious the young cop wasn't a big fan of the detective. At this point, I wasn't so sure I disagreed.

"Mrs. Denton," Cavanaugh said, making a beeline over to me. "What are you doing here?"

"I'm here to see Ben," I said, raising my chin. I refused to show weakness now, especially if that weakness sent me home.

He sighed. "I thought I told you to come back tomorrow."

"I know, you did, but I need to see him." My voice trembled slightly. "Please," I said. "Just for a few minutes. I want to make sure he's okay."

Cavanaugh stared at me for a long couple of seconds without blinking. His face gave nothing away, no hint of compassion or anger. I wasn't sure what to make of this man, whether he was on my side or thought I'd given birth to a cold-blooded killer.

His unreadable face was probably why he'd become a detective. I hoped that it also made him a good one.

Cavanaugh's face finally broke into a frown before he turned away from me. He took two steps, and then glanced back, eyebrows raised. "You coming?"

"Oh! Yeah, of course." I hurried after him.

Cavanaugh's stride was long, practically forcing me to run to keep up with him. "He tried to call you," he said as he led me down the hall. "Tried at least three times, but never got an answer."

"I don't have my cell on me." It was still sitting in the cup holder of the van. I mentally kicked myself for not remembering it. "He could have called his dad." Manny would have answered a call from Ben, even if he was in the middle of an exam.

"He never tried as far as I'm aware. I think he wanted you." He glanced at me out of the corner of his eye. Was that respect I saw there? "The kid's tough."

"He is." But for how much longer? Sitting behind bars couldn't be easy on him. Ben had never been in trouble like this before in his life. He'd never even gotten a detention, or even so much as a warning when he was in school. I wasn't going to say he was a complete angel, but if anyone was a near thing, it was Ben.

We came to a stop outside a closed door. "All right. Here's the rules."

I opened my mouth to say something, but closed it quickly when Cavanaugh's eyes narrowed.

"You get five minutes," he said. "If that's a problem, then you can turn around and walk away now."

"Five minutes is fine." Though, honestly, it sounded like no time at all.

"Understand, I don't have to let you see him. He's being held because he's a suspect in a serious crime. He's cooperated so far, but I feel he might know something more. Talking can only help him in the long run."

"I see."

"I will be in the room when you talk to him. He has yet to request counsel, otherwise we'd be waiting for the attorney to arrive."

"My husband is contacting someone for him," I said.

Cavanaugh nodded. "It will be made clear to Ben, as I'm making it clear to you now, that anything he says can be used against him. Do you understand?"

"I do. And thank you," I said. Maybe my first impression of Detective Cavanaugh had been wrong. He might be tough, might be investigating my son for murder, but he seemed like a fair man.

"Go in and take a seat. I'll go get him and bring him to you in a few minutes."

I nodded, unsure I could speak. I was starting to shake, and my throat felt tight. I was going to see Ben. What if this was the last time I'd get a chance to sit down with him outside a prison?

Cavanaugh strode away, and I shook off the unpleasant thought and entered the room.

It was the same room in which Cavanaugh spoke to me before, yet somehow, it felt darker, colder. I took a seat, nervously glancing at the camera in the corner. No one else was in the room with me. I could hear voices from down the hall, and a clunking sound, like someone was repeatedly kicking the wall.

"Everything's going to be all right," I muttered, needing to hear the sound of my own voice, lest I drive myself crazy. The room was too quiet, despite the sounds from elsewhere in the station. I felt horribly alone, and could only imagine how Ben must feel.

It took Cavanaugh a good ten minutes to return. Ben was cuffed, and was wearing a set of blue clothing with *Grey Falls Police Department* written across the left breast, and *GFPD* on the back. It broke my heart seeing him like that. It made him look guilty, even though I knew deep in my heart he wasn't.

"Hey, Mom," Ben said, a nervous smile on his face. He was trying to play it cool, but I could tell he was scared. I wouldn't even have to have seen him to know that. There was a faint tremor to his voice, a strain that wasn't there before.

"Ben." I forced myself to return his smile. I was pretty sure it looked just as shaky as his own.

"I'll be right here," Cavanaugh said, closing the door. He took up position next to it.

"Thank you," I said, and then motioned for Ben to take a seat across from me.

He sat down awkwardly, thanks to the cuffs. I considered asking Cavanaugh to remove them, but figured I might be pressing my luck if I did. He'd already conceded more than he probably should have by letting me speak to Ben.

"How are you holding up?" I asked.

"Okay, I guess. I'm still trying to process exactly what happened."

"Me too." I glanced at Cavanaugh, and then scooted my chair around to the side of the table so I could take one of Ben's cuffed hands. "Are you sure you're okay?"

He shrugged one shoulder, looked down, past our hands, to the floor. "It's not like I'm doing backflips of joy," he said. "But no one has mistreated me. And while they think I killed Mr. Fuller, they haven't yelled at me or threatened me in any way."

"Good. Have you talked to anyone yet? An attorney?" While Manny was going to call Lester, it didn't mean Ben hadn't already talked to someone.

"No, just the cops." Ben shifted uncomfortably in his seat. "Detective Cavanaugh already gave me the whole spiel about implicating myself and whatnot. He told me I could have an attorney present if I wanted, but, right now, I'm okay. I mean, it's just you."

"Yeah, it's just me." And I prayed I didn't do or say something to make his situation worse. I scooted closer to Ben, lowered my voice. "What happened at that house?" I asked. I wasn't sure if Cavanaugh was listening in, but if he was, I wanted to keep whatever was said between my son and me private, at least until I knew whether or not it would help.

"I don't know," Ben said, keeping his own voice lowered. "I didn't know he was dead until the police showed up."

"You didn't discover his body?"

"No." He shuddered. "If I had, I probably would have freaked out. Knowing he was dead was bad enough."

I started to ask another question about Mr. Fuller and his family, but caught myself. I needed to start from the beginning.

"The girl, Selena, do you know her?"

"Yeah." He paused. "Well, I don't really *know* her. I've seen her around town once or twice, but we'd never talked. Today was the first time I'd actually spent any time with her."

"How long were you with her? Before the murder, I mean."

"Right up until the police showed up." Ben released my hands, folded them in his lap as best he could. "I went over because, well, you saw her."

"I did."

"I couldn't resist." Some of the old Ben came back when he smiled. "We talked for a few minutes and I guess we hit it off pretty good because she invited me inside."

"Really?" I asked in my mom voice.

He rolled his eyes. "We were just hanging out," he said. "Besides, I'm twenty-two. It's not like we were doing anything stupid or illegal."

"I know that." Though it was easy to forget sometimes. As any mother knows, you never truly look at your children as anything but, no matter how old they get.

"So, we were together, hitting it off pretty good, when I heard the sirens. We went to see what was happening, and I saw the police go into Mr. Fuller's house, and then around back, to that red barn of his. There were ambulances coming too. I went over to make sure he was okay, and the cops wouldn't let me in. It didn't take long before I realized the guy was dead. I was about to call you when one of them cuffed me and read me my rights. I couldn't believe what was happening."

My heart went out to him. "You didn't see anything or anyone strange hanging around?" I asked, knowing it was unlikely. Once Ben was in a woman's orbit, he paid everything else little mind.

"No. Mr. Fuller—Junior, not the older one—and his wife showed up shortly before they cuffed me. He completely lost his mind when he heard his dad was dead. I guess I don't blame him."

"Lost his mind, how?"

Ben shrugged. "Started yelling. One of the cops had to restrain him at one point because he was trying to get into the barn. I think they took him inside the house after, but by then, I wasn't paying much attention to him. I had problems of my own to deal with."

"What about Timothy's nurse?" I asked, imagining the scene. It had to have been chaos.

Ben shook his head. "I never saw her. I assume she was still there because someone said she found the body."

"You're sure no one else was hanging around," I asked, not really sure who I expected there to be.

"Pretty sure," Ben said. "But I wasn't really aware of much. Once you left, I only had eyes for Selena. If I hadn't heard the sirens, I doubt I would have even known anything was going on next door."

"Ben, a witness saw you enter Mr. Fuller's house *before* the police arrived," I said. "And he said you ran off after only a few minutes."

Even as I spoke, he was shaking his head. "No way. I didn't even make it that far. The police stopped me. And I definitely wasn't over there before the police got there. You can ask Selena."

I might have to do that, I thought. "He said he saw you specifically," I prodded, hoping he could tell me something that would explain how Clarence could be so wrong.

"It's not possible," Ben said. "I was with Selena the whole time. I swear!"

I studied him, tried to determine if he was lying to me for some reason. I wasn't sure why he would, not unless something really had happened between him and Timothy Fuller that he didn't want me to know about.

"Think carefully, Ben," I said. "The man I talked to was pretty sure he saw you. He had no reason to lie."

"Well, he's not telling the truth either," Ben said. "Because I never left Selena's house; not until the police showed up."

I didn't think Clarence was lying outright, but he must have been mistaken.

Of course, there was one other explanation as to how Clarence could have seen someone wearing a shirt with Ben's name on it. Everyone knew Ben and I wore those shirts. It wouldn't be hard to get one made. In fact, the shirts were made at a local graphic design place downtown. If someone was planning on killing Timothy Fuller, they could very well have had shirts made ahead of time.

But that would require prior knowledge of our visit. Who all knew Ben and I were going to pick up Stewie?

Timothy did, of course, but I doubted he planned on murdering himself. His son and daughter-in-law were new in town, but I found it unlikely they knew Ben's name before we got there. Nurse Meredith would have known about our visit, but it would be kind of hard to mistake her for Ben, even from as far away as Clarence was.

Duke knew you were coming.

And I didn't know where he was when the murder took place.

I couldn't believe I was entertaining the thought that Duke Billings would frame Ben for murder, but I couldn't help it. Nothing else made sense.

"I'm going to figure this thing out," I promised Ben.

"I hope so," he said. "I didn't do anything wrong."

Which reminded me of something . . .

"The police say there was blood on your shirt. If you never went over to Timothy's house, how did it get there?"

"I don't know," Ben said. "I wish I did."

I did too. "Your dad's calling Lester Ives for you in case you need him. He'll want to talk to you soon, probably today."

Ben paled, as if mentioning the attorney by name had suddenly made everything real.

Cavanaugh stepped forward. "I'm sorry, but I have to take him back now."

I rose, and then gave Ben a hug when he did the same. "Stay strong," I whispered into his ear. Ben merely nodded.

Detective Cavanaugh took Ben's arm and led him away as soon as we parted. I waited in the interview room for Cavanaugh's return.

"He's innocent," I said as soon as he stopped outside the door.

"I'm sure you believe so," he said. "And if it's true, neither of you have anything to worry about."

"He couldn't have done it," I said, unsatisfied by his confident tone. "He was with a woman at the time, one who can verify his story."

"Selena Shriver," Cavanaugh said, gently taking me by the elbow and leading me out of the room and back down the hall. "I know."

"Did you talk to her?" When he didn't answer, I pressed. "She should be able to confirm his alibi. Talk to her if you haven't. And find Duke Billings. He might have something to do with Timothy's murder."

Detective Cavanaugh's jaw tightened the more I spoke. He guided me all the way past the front desk, and then right out the door. He didn't release me until the sun was shining on both our faces.

"Mrs. Denton, please let us do our jobs. We know what we're doing."

"But Ben . . ."

"If he's innocent, then he'll be fine. I can't have you pressuring me or anyone else involved in the case. We'll talk to everyone and get their statements. I'll figure out what happened."

"What about bail?" I asked, mind searching for any way I could take Ben home with me.

"It hasn't been set. At this time, we're just holding your son, not charging him. Because of the nature of the crime, I'm keeping him for thirty-six hours. I might apply for more time if no new evidence appears."

"But . . ."

"Mrs. Denton." The tone of his voice said he was done humoring me. He was likely regretting ever letting me talk to Ben, which didn't bode well for any return visits I might make. "It's better I hold him without charging him, even if it's longer than you'd like."

I lowered my head and nodded. I didn't like it, but he *was* right.

"Go home," Cavanaugh said once he was sure I wasn't going to argue any longer. "Get some rest. If I need to talk to you again, I'll call on you. Otherwise, you have no reason to be here."

Another "But" formed on my lips, but I bit it back. "I'm sorry," I said. "I'll go."

He patted me on the shoulder, nodded once, and then stepped back to watch me go.

I *did* leave as I said I would, but home was not my destination. Ben's life hung in the balance. I couldn't just sit by and do nothing.

7

Duke Billings lived just outside of town, in a large ranch house that sat on about three acres dominated by trees. The house felt warm and inviting from the outside, and I knew from experience, it was the same on the inside. There was a sort of rustic charm to the place, everything being done in shades of brown and green. It was about as close to living in a log cabin in the woods as anyone could come without actually doing so.

A black cat lay atop the front stoop, washing its paws. As soon as I pulled into the gravel driveway, it leapt up and bolted around back.

I'd only been to Duke's house once before, and that was when his wife had broken her ankle three years ago. Even though he worked with Courtney, we got along well enough, so I decided to bring them a cake decorated with get well puppies. Both Duke and his wife seemed to have appreciated the gesture, though I never was invited back.

I approached the front door with trepidation. What

if Duke *had* framed Ben? He wouldn't be happy about seeing me now. If he'd killed one man, what would stop him from doing the same to me? I doubted our history, limited as it may be, would save me.

The door opened as I stepped up onto the stoop where the cat had been. Sasha Billings filled the space, a curious look on her face. She was a big woman, and I didn't mean fat. She stood nearly six feet tall, had midnight-black skin, and was built like a linebacker. When she'd broken her ankle a few years ago, it hadn't been doing dainty work, but rather, in one of those competitions where contestants flip gigantic tires and uproot trees with their bare hands.

Needless to say, she scared me.

"Liz," she said, crossing her massive arms across her chest. She made broad-shouldered Duke look small. "For what do I have the pleasure?"

"Hey, Sasha. Is Duke home? I'd like to talk to him for a few minutes."

"Sorry, he's not. I think he's on a run with Courtney, but he could be out with a few of his friends by now. Said he needs to blow off some steam."

"Do you happen to know where he's going?" I asked, thinking that if he and Courtney thought they could swoop in and steal Stewie now, they'd have a serious fight on their hands.

She shrugged. "I never asked. I don't expect him back until later tonight. Do you need him now? I could call him if it's important."

"No, that's okay." While I wanted to talk to Duke, I didn't want to drag Sasha into it. She might not know anything about the murder, or Ben's involvement.

Sasha and I faced each other wordlessly as I debated on what to tell her. Her dark eyes bore into mine, making me feel smaller and smaller by the moment. There was no malice there, just intensity. She'd give Detective Cavanaugh a run for his money if it ever came down to a staring contest between the two of them.

"I ran into Duke earlier," I said, finally breaking the silence. "There was some miscommunication between us and we ended up on the same job. It was mostly Courtney's fault, but we've got it all worked out now." I hoped.

"That's good."

"Unfortunately, the man whose dog we were picking up died. The cops are saying he was murdered."

Sasha's eyes widened. "Really? That's terrible."

"The police think Ben did it."

"Well, now, that's just stupid. He'd never do such a thing. You raised that boy right."

I felt all warm and fuzzy from the compliment, but didn't let it sway me from what I had to say. "It's why I was hoping to talk to Duke," I said. "I was with Courtney when the murder happened. Duke was supposedly running errands at the time, and I was hoping he might have stopped by the Fuller house while doing them. He might have seen something that could help Ben."

"Supposedly?" Sasha's eyes narrowed dangerously. "What are you implying?"

"I'm sorry," I said, taking a quick step backward. I didn't think she would actually hurt me, but just the thought that she *could* if she wanted to, was enough to make me nervous. "I didn't mean it that way. Courtney could have told him to go back to the house in the hopes Timothy would give up his dog while I wasn't there," I said. "If that was the case, it would make sense that she would lie about where he really was.

I'm trying to piece together what happened for Ben, not start anything with Duke."

Sasha seemed to accept my explanation because the muscles in her arms stopped bulging. "I'm sorry, but I can't help you. Duke left this morning to pick up an animal and has yet to return home. As far as I know, he's still with Courtney, and if he's not, he planned on getting together with a few friends later. There's no telling when he'll be home."

"Okay," I said. "I guess I can call Courtney and see if they're still together. I'm sorry to have bothered you." I turned and started to head back to my van.

"Liz, wait."

I turned to find Sasha coming toward me. My natural instinct was to tense and prepare to make a run for it, but when she reached me, she wrapped her big arms around me and squeezed.

All the air was immediately pressed from my lungs like I'd been caught in a vise. Thankfully, the hug was brief and she released me before I suffered any internal injuries. I staggered back and sucked in a deep breath.

"I'll have Duke call you when I hear from him," Sasha said. "This has to be hard on you and I know if it were my kid in trouble, I'd want to get answers too."

"Thank you," I said, managing to not gasp the words.

She nodded once, and then abruptly turned and walked back into the house. She waved once before closing the door.

Rubbing at my chest, I returned to my van and climbed inside. Sasha meant well, but boy, she was a lot stronger than she realized.

A trio of small black heads peered at me from the window as I backed out of the driveway, gravel popping under my wheels. The kittens couldn't have been more than six months old. I wondered if the cat I'd seen outside was the momma or the poppa. Either way, I knew they were in good hands. For all our differences, Duke was a good man. It made me feel worse about suspecting him of being involved in Timothy's murder, but I wouldn't just drop it, not until Ben was safely back home.

I drove back to Courtney's house, wondering how I was going to question Duke without outright accusing him of anything. Ben was in trouble, but that didn't mean I needed to make enemies of people who were already my business rivals. If I pushed too hard, there'd be no way we could ever work in the same town again.

I kept wondering what would make Duke, or anyone else in Grey Falls, want to frame Ben. It seemed like a pretty convoluted way to go about murdering someone. I mean, why not kill him and blame it on Junior? Or even Timothy's nurse, who was in the house at the time? There were far better people to implicate than Ben, who'd only met the old man for the first time today.

I pulled up in front of Courtney's house and frowned at her empty driveway. Her pink van was gone, and no other cars occupied the space. Neither Duke nor Courtney were there and I had no idea where they might have gone, or even if they were together.

"Well, now what?" I asked the empty van. I couldn't drive around town looking for them. Not only would it take all day, but Grey Falls was a pretty big town sizewise. The chances of me running into them was as likely as me randomly stumbling onto evidence that would set Ben free.

I picked up my phone and checked the screen. Three missed calls. I checked voicemail to find it was Ben's calls from the jail. The first two were pretty basic.

"Hi, Mom. It's me." And then he'd hung up without saying anything more.

The third call made my heart ache.

"Hey, Mom. I've been trying to call, but I guess you don't have your phone with you." He laughed. "I guess I'll talk to you some other time. I miss you."

I pressed the phone to my chest and fought down the urge to cry. If the real killer wasn't caught, these voice messages could very well be the last recordings of Ben's voice I'd ever receive.

I made sure to save the voicemails, and then instead of returning the phone to the cup holder, I shoved it into my pocket. It felt strange there, but I wasn't going to miss another call from him, not if I could help it.

Pulling away from Courtney's, I decided to make one more quick stop to lay to rest some of my doubts. If someone *had* planned on killing Timothy and had a shirt made to frame Ben, then there would be a record of it. I could call and ask, but felt it better if I asked my questions face-to-face.

I made the short drive downtown to Graphics to a Tee, the graphic design T-shirt place where I ordered all my shirts. I knew the owner, Bethany Calhoon, well enough that I thought she'd tell me what I wanted to know without taking it the wrong way. She liked Ben, and would do anything she could to help.

I just hoped she had something to offer.

Downtown Grey Falls was rundown, and kind of depressing. Many of the buildings were older, and could use some TLC. The sidewalks were cracked, gravel pounded into the holes, rather than actual repairs. Law offices sat beside more offices, with little in the way of businesses to draw attention to the main drag. An artists' community took up the southern end of downtown, near defunct railroad tracks that held the skeletons of a dozen train cars.

It was sad to think that things could have been different. Grey Falls had gone from a farming town, to a bustling, growing city, only to have it all collapse as businesses moved on to bigger, seemingly better cities. There was still growth, but it had moved to the northern and southern ends of town, leaving the downtown to decay.

I parked in the parking lot across the street that served as a general lot for the five artistic businesses attached to it. There was nothing in the way of foot traffic here, but I did note there were quite a few people shopping in some of the stores. All five shops were crammed into a single, long building that bordered the railroad tracks.

I passed by Axiom Pottery, and entered Graphics to a Tee. Bethany was working at her laptop behind the counter. She gnawed away at a pen cap as she hunched over the keyboard and mouse, her red ringlets pulled back in a loose ponytail. She held up one hand without looking my way, moving the mouse slowly, eyes squinted, but unblinking, as she stared at the screen. She bit down hard on the cap, moved the mouse slightly to the left, and then clicked.

"There!" she said, sitting back with a weary sigh. She admired her work a long couple of seconds before turning to me. "I swear, people get pickier and pickier every day."

"Rough day?" I asked, coming to the counter.

"Some lady wanted me to make her a shirt, but didn't like the *B*s after I printed them off. She claimed they sat too far apart, if you can imagine." She popped the cap from her mouth and set it aside. "It was her design, yet it was *my* fault." She rolled her eyes skyward. "What can you do?"

"Not much, but keep at it, I imagine."

"You've got that right." She stood, placed one hand on her lower back and pressed. It cracked audibly. "What can I do for you, Liz? Need more shirts made up? I'm a little behind right now, but I'm pretty sure I can squeeze you in rather quickly if you don't have many changes."

"No, I don't need any more. But I do have a question about them."

Her face darkened for a heartbeat before clearing. "Is there something wrong with the last batch?" she asked.

"No, nothing like that."

"Good. You've had those ones for what? A year or two now? I can't believe you've waited so long to get a refresh." Bethany was a big believer in changing styles every year to keep people interested. It not only kept her busy, but when you came right down to it, it worked. If your designs were outdated, then people thought *you* were outdated. Not good for a business.

I glanced around the small space as I tried to come up with some way to ask what I had to ask without sounding accusatory. Bethany was a friend, and I didn't want to make her think I believed she would do something to hurt Ben.

Shirts hung on nearly every available wall space, all designs by Bethany. These weren't the custom designs requested by her customers, but ones that popped straight out of her own head. Many were fantasy or sci-fi based, with dragons or spaceships or other fantastic images. Others were mere swirls of colors. All of them were fantastic.

"Are you all right, Liz?" Bethany asked, leaning on the counter. "You look stressed."

"I am," I said, but instead of going into the why, I decided to dive right in and ask my question. "Has anyone come in recently looking for a shirt design like mine?"

She looked confused when she answered. "Like yours? Like one similar?"

"No, as in, they asked for an exact copy. Maybe they said they were getting it made for Ben?"

She shook her head. "I don't recall anything like that. I get a few requests here and there that infringe on trademarks, but nothing involving Furever Pets."

"What about spares coming up missing?" I asked. "Did you print off a few more than we ordered, like a test run maybe?"

Bethany straightened, her expression showing concern. "What is this about, Liz?" she asked. "Did something happen with one of my shirts?"

"Well, sort of." I told her briefly about the murder, leaving out most of the details. She didn't need to know how Timothy died, or that Ben was flirting with a bikini-clad woman when it happened.

I did tell her my theory about it being a frame job, that someone might have killed Mr. Fuller and then blamed Ben for it, using his shirt to throw off the police.

Needless to say, she looked skeptical.

"No one came in looking for a Furever Pets shirt," she said. "And no, I don't print off spares or test runs. If I do print one, and it turns out wrong, I scrap it. I don't believe I had any issues with yours, so there was never a spare floating around."

"Are you sure?" I asked, heart sinking.

"Sure as I can be. It's been over a year, so there's always a chance my memory is a little fuzzy, but I'm almost positive you have the only copies of that shirt in existence."

There *were* the old shirts lying around, the ones from previous years, but as far as I was aware, they were all stuffed to the back of Ben's and my closets. I supposed it was possible Ben had given his old shirts away once we retired the designs, but it was unlikely they'd end up in the hands of anyone involved with Mr. Fuller. I seriously doubted Courtney would ever lay hands on a filthy old Furever Pets T-shirt, even if she thought it would help her in some way.

"All right, Bethany, thanks."

"Anytime."

I left, torn. On one hand, I was disappointed I didn't have an easy answer for Ben. On the other, I was kind of glad Bethany didn't have anything to do with the murder, even indirectly. If she'd made a shirt for someone else, one just like mine, with "Ben" across the back, it would make me lose trust in her, even if it really wasn't her fault.

Of course, there was probably more than one Ben in town. Just because the shirt looked like a Furever Pets shirt, didn't mean it was actually one. Sure, it would be a massive coincidence for the person who killed Timothy Fuller to be wearing one at the time of the murder, but it wasn't impossible. Unlikely, yeah, but not impossible.

I pulled away from Graphics to a Tee, but once more, chose not to go home. I was desperate and hoped that a talk with Selena Shriver, however brief, would help ease my mind.

8

A somber tone hung over the neighborhood as I pulled into Selena's driveway. Clarence wasn't outside with his coffee, and I found I kind of missed having him there, watching my back. Next door, a pair of cars sat in Timothy's driveway.

Junior and his wife, I assumed. If the police had already finished with their search, it was likely the house had been turned over to the family. Junior had a lot to do now that his dad was dead, but I guess he'd been planning on doing much the same anyway. It wasn't like Timothy would have been able to take most of his things to the extended care facility—if he'd lived that long.

I made a mental note to head next door after I finished talking to Selena. If nothing else, I hoped they'd allow me to take Stewie so I could get him his preadoption checkup. A dog his age could have all kinds of conditions. Manny could treat many of them with the right medicines, and I always preferred to know everything there was to know about an animal before sending it out.

I knocked on Selena's door, hoping she'd be more willing to talk to me now than she was earlier. I needed to know what happened at the time of the murder, and other than the killer, she might be the only one who knew.

No one answered at first, so I knocked again, this time harder. I was pretty sure she was home; her car was under the carport. I was about to try for a third time when the door opened and a harried-looking Selena peered out at me. Her hair was a mess, her clothing rumpled as if she'd been lying down when I'd knocked. She smoothed down her dress and hair, looking guilty for what I assumed was her midafternoon nap.

"You're back," she said, sounding about as excited by my presence as she might a door-to-door salesman.

"I am," I said. "Would it be all right if I came in? I'd like to talk to you a little about Ben."

She looked behind her, gnawed on her lower lip, before nodding. "I suppose you might as well." She turned and walked away.

Taking a deep, relieved breath, I followed her in.

For as nice as the house was outside, the inside of Selena's home looked sparse and downtrodden. The furniture was old, ratty in places. The wallpaper on one wall was peeling at the seams, and the floor had old worn-in stains that would likely never come out.

It was like walking into college housing where the rent was exorbitant and the living conditions were barely, well, livable. It made me wonder if Selena was renting the place since she was kind of young to own a house of her own, on her own.

We passed by the living room, and went into the dining room, which consisted of a small, circular table, and a trio of empty chairs.

The fourth was occupied.

"This is my friend Jason," Selena said, moving to stand behind one of the chairs, rather than sit down. A cat-shaped clock hung on the wall by her head, tail swishing the seconds.

"Hi. Jason Maxwell." He stood and held out a hand. He was wearing a flannel with the sleeves pushed up, over a plain white shirt and jeans. His hair was shaggy, and in serious need of a trim. Even as we shook, he was forced to blow it from his eyes.

"I'm sorry to intrude," I said, wondering if Jason was part of the reason Selena could afford the house. Friends sharing rent wasn't all that surprising, even though it was coed habitation. It did make me wonder, however. It would be just like Ben to get himself involved with a woman who was already seeing someone. "I just have a few questions about what happened earlier."

"I wish I could help," Jason said, sitting back down. He stretched his legs out and crossed his ankles. "I just got here a little while ago and missed all the action."

And he didn't seem too broken up about it either. "Did you know Mr. Fuller well?" I asked him.

"Not really," he said. "I've never really talked to anyone in the neighborhood, other than Selena." He glanced at her, smiled. "We've been together since middle school."

"Best friends," Selena amended. "We're practically attached at the hip."

Jason laughed. "That's true. I do wish I was here when the guy was murdered. If the killer had come

over and tried that here, I would have dropped him."
He balled up his fists and punched the air.

"It's horrible what happened," Selena said, seemingly embarrassed by Jason's flippant tone. "I've
known Mr. Fuller for years. A lot of people didn't like
him, but he was never mean to me. I've helped him
carry his groceries in a few times when his nurse was
preoccupied."

"Do you have any idea why anyone would want to
hurt him?" I asked.

"None. He wasn't the best neighbor in the world,
but like I said, I had no problem with him. He used
to yell at people a lot." She ran her hand along the
back of the chair in front of her. "I already told the
police everything I know."

"I'm not here to accuse you of anything," I said,
making sure she looked at me when I said it. "I just
want to understand what happened, and how Ben
got himself involved."

"Wrong place, wrong time, maybe," Jason said. "It
happens to the best of us."

"There's really nothing I can tell you," Selena said.
"I do wish I could help, but I'm just not sure how I
can."

"Tell me what happened," I said. "From the beginning. What did you and Ben do while he was here?
Where did you go? Did you hear or see anything?"

"Honestly, there isn't much to say," Selena said,
looking to Jason, as if for help. He shrugged. "He
came over, and at first, I figured he just wanted to
ogle me like so many guys want to do."

"Can't really blame them," Jason said, waggling his
eyebrows at her.

Selena ignored him. "At first, I was happy just to
talk since I was kind of bored at the time. He was

nice, didn't stare. He didn't even ask me out on a date or anything. We just talked. It's rare to see a single man with manners these days." Another look Jason's way.

He merely snorted.

"What happened then?" I asked, glad Ben had left such a good impression on her. It was nice to know I'd raised him right.

"We came inside and had some lemonade." She paused. "Do you want some? The pitcher is in the fridge. It'll take only a minute to grab it and pour us all a glass."

"No thank you."

She seemed torn, as if she wanted to flee the room and grab the lemonade anyway, before finally going on. "After a little while, we went out back to enjoy the sun. I'd already spent half the day swimming, and thought it would be nice to lounge around the pool. Ben agreed. There was nothing sinister in it, or even romantic."

My gaze traveled toward the kitchen, and the back door. I could just make out the in-ground pool out back, and the lawn chairs on the patio around it. The furniture outside was a far cry better than what was inside.

"Mind if we go outside for a minute?" I asked, nodding toward the door.

Selena looked to Jason, who shrugged, seemingly disinterested in the entire conversation. In fact, he appeared almost angry, though he was hiding it well behind his smile and bangs.

"Sure."

Jason remained behind as Selena led me into the small kitchen, and out the back door to the pool. More flower beds lined the house back here, and a small rose garden bordered the property. The water was clear, not a leaf floating inside it. A pair of towels lay beside the chairs.

It was strange how different the outside of Selena's house appeared compared to the inside. Was it all for appearances sake? Did she simply spend more time out here, which in turn, caused her to take better care of it?

I walked over to the edge of the pool, and then turned toward Timothy's property. Because of how her house sat back, I couldn't see much of anything in the front, though I could see the back door and patio clearly over the short hedges that served as a natural fence separating the properties. Police tape was strung across the front of the red barn where I assumed the body was found. No one was currently outside but the two of us.

"Were you out here when the police arrived?" I asked. "By the pool, I mean?"

"We were." Selena crossed her arms over her middle and was standing near the back door. She looked nervous, and a little sick. "I was dozing there when it happened." She nodded toward one of the chairs.

"With Ben here?" I asked, surprised. Normally, when you had a guest, especially one you'd just met a few minutes prior, you didn't up and take a nap with them sitting beside you.

"Ben excused himself and went inside to use the restroom," she said. "It took him longer than it should have, but I figured he might not be feeling too good. He'd seemed nervous, like he was afraid of something. I didn't think anything of it until later." She met my eye, looked frightened. "I think he went straight through the house, and over next door. I was sitting here the entire time and never suspected—or saw—a thing." She shuddered.

I fought back an urge to leap to Ben's defense. She didn't know he could never have done such a thing. She didn't know him, not like I did. And with the murder happening so close to her home, it had to be hard to make sense of everything that had happened. Ben's arrival probably seemed like he was trying to cover for something sinister.

"Did you hear him leave the house?" I asked.

"I didn't," she admitted. "But he must have. The police say he had blood on his shirt and Mr. Ellison across the street said he saw him, so it had to be him, right?"

"Did you see the blood?" I asked. "I'm assuming you saw him when he came back over." If indeed, he'd left.

"No. It wasn't like I was looking for it. And since I was sleeping right up until I heard the sirens, it wasn't like I had time to notice it. After that, I was focused on what was happening next door." She hugged herself. "Can we go back in now?"

I glanced at Timothy's house once more, and then nodded. "Yeah."

We returned to the dining room, a cloud seemingly hanging over the both of us. Jason was still sitting in his chair, fiddling with his phone. Selena resumed her place behind the table, as if wanting to keep it between us.

No one spoke right away. I was at a loss. I knew Ben couldn't have killed Timothy, yet everything kept pointing at him as the murderer. Why would he leave Selena to go next door? It made no sense; not unless he heard something and was concerned for Timothy's health.

Had Ben heard the murder taking place? If so, why hadn't he simply called the police and let them deal with it? And if he had, did Detective Cavanaugh know? Did he even believe him?

Jason shoved his phone into his pocket and broke the silence. "Is everything all worked out between you two?" he asked, sounding impatient for me to leave.

Selena looked at me for an answer, one I didn't have. I felt like she should know more, that she should be able to tell me something that would save Ben, but all she'd done is make things worse. If she told the police he'd left for a little while, right before Timothy was discovered, then that was one more witness against him.

But what else could I do? It wasn't like I could force her to tell me something that wasn't true, just because I wanted to believe it. Maybe everything she said was the truth, at least the parts she knew for a fact. Ben might have gone to the bathroom, not because he wanted to use it, but because he was prepping himself to ask Selena out. It would be just like him to primp before making his move.

But instead of a date, his absence caused him to end up in jail.

A new thought came to me as I stood there, unsure what to say. I glanced around the room, noticed the absence of anything resembling a feline.

"Where's your cat?" I asked.

"Her what?" Jason asked, seemingly amused by the question.

"Outside." Selena offered me a smile that was two parts nervous, one part embarrassed. "Jason doesn't like cats, so I let her out when he's here. He doesn't even realize I still have her."

"Oh," I said, noting Jason's bewildered expression. The guy really was that clueless. "I was just wondering where she was. I'm a sucker for animals and was hoping to say hi."

Selena's smile turned wooden. "Sorry," she said, before Jason popped to his feet.

"Well, if that's all, we really need to get going. We're meeting some friends in town and are already going to be late."

"I'm sorry to have kept you," I said. "Thank you for your time. And I assure you, Ben had nothing to do with Timothy's death. It's all a big misunderstanding."

"I hope not," Selena said. I couldn't tell if she was just being nice, or if she sincerely hoped Ben was innocent. She seemed friendly enough. I don't know if she was girlfriend material, at least, by my standards, but she was the type of woman I could see Ben going for.

Selena and Jason followed me to the front door, but didn't join me outside. They watched me as I got into my van, and even waved when I looked back at them.

If they were hoping I'd drive away and they'd never see me again, they were mistaken. I wasn't going away, not until Ben was free.

But for now, it was time to leave them in peace. I started up the van, and backed out of Selena's driveway. Instead of heading for home, I drove the short distance to Timothy Fuller's driveway, and pulled in behind one of the cars there. Selena and Jason had stepped outside to watch where I was going, and continued to stare as I got out of the van.

I waved at them once, earning myself another return wave. They looked perplexed, like they couldn't figure out why I was still hanging around. A part of me was wondering the same thing. All I seemed to be doing was digging a deeper hole for Ben, one I was afraid he'd never be able to climb out of.

Yet giving up wasn't in my nature. And there was still a dog I could be helping.

Putting Selena and her friend out of mind, I approached the front door. Steeling myself for the verbal abuse that was likely to come, I raised my fist to knock.

Something crashed inside the house. It was followed by a woman's scream and the frantic bark of a dog.

Eschewing politeness, I pushed open the door, and forced my way inside.

9

Expecting another murder to be taking place, I was prepared for a fight.

Instead, I found Junior standing, his back to me, arms out wide, as if trying to encircle a large ball. He was cursing under his breath as Stewie, who was backed into the corner Junior was facing, yapped at him. In the doorway leading to the kitchen, Alexis was using one hand to hold Meredith back, another was pressed to her mouth, as they both looked on.

"What's going on in here?" I asked, my immediate concern going to the dog. One of Timothy's medical machines was lying on its side near Junior. It was likely the source of the crash I'd heard.

"It's none of your business," Junior growled, not looking my way. He eased slowly forward. "Stop barking you mutt!"

Stewie continued his yapping. Junior muttered under his breath, and then reached out to touch the agitated dog. Stewie growled and snapped at him, causing Junior to jerk back.

"I'd leave him be if I were you," I said.

"You have no say in this," Alexis said from across the room.

"They're trying to take Stewie when by all rights, he should stay with me," Meredith said. She probably could have pushed Alexis away to help the dog, but she didn't. Chances were, she was afraid of what Junior might do if she tried.

I, on the other hand, had no qualms about stepping in when an animal was in danger. "Step away from the Pomeranian," I said, voice hard. "Now."

"Leave us alone," Junior said. He made another grab for Stewie, and nearly lost a finger for his trouble.

"Is everyone okay?" Jason's voice startled me as he and Selena appeared in the doorway behind me. "We heard shouting."

"We're fine!" Junior practically roared it. "Alexis, get these people out of here."

Alexis took a step toward us, but stopped when I gave her my best glare. Meredith moved toward Junior, but Alexis held out a hand, choosing to resume her duties guarding the nurse, rather than risk my wrath.

Stewie barked twice, seemed to notice the influx of new people at the door, and then, ears pinned back, he bolted.

For an old dog, he moved pretty fast. He ducked under Junior's lunge, and made straight for the stairs next to where Alexis and Meredith stood.

"Grab him!" Junior shouted.

Instead, Alexis squealed and leapt aside. Meredith tried to make a grab for the dog, but missed, nearly falling over as she did. Stewie whined as he vanished up the stairs, and out of sight.

"Damn it!" Junior righted himself and then kicked the downed machine. He glared at it a moment before spinning on me. "No one told you to butt in."

"I wasn't butting in," I said. "I heard a crash and thought something might be wrong."

"What's wrong is that everyone is trying to stop me from taking my property," Junior said, before turning to his wife. "Go find the mutt." He pointed at Meredith when she started to move. "You. Stay."

Meredith sucked in an angry breath. I didn't blame her. Junior was treating her about as well as he was Stewie. If he pointed that finger at me, he was liable to lose it.

Alexis hesitated, as if unsure she should leave Junior to the rest of us, before finally chasing after Stewie. She made clicking noises with her tongue as she went.

"Does anyone care to explain what I just saw?" I asked. "Because if I even suspect you were going to harm that dog, I'm calling the cops."

Junior snorted. "Like they'd do anything."

"He's trying to take Mr. Fuller's dog," Meredith said before I could tell him exactly what kind of trouble he'd be in if he was found to be abusing an animal. Most people didn't realize how harsh the penalty could be. "I told him it wasn't his place to decide what happens to him, but he won't listen to me."

"You aren't anyone," Junior said. "And this *is* my place. Dad's dead. Someone has to take care of the beast."

I took a step toward him, but refrained from slapping some sense into him. "You didn't want the dog," I said. "You said as much earlier today."

"I've had a change of heart." The smile he gave me was condescending. "That dog is about the only thing in the place that meant anything to Dad. I'd like the memento."

"Stewie isn't an object," I said.

"We'll, uh, get out of the way," Jason said from behind me, taking a step back with Selena. I'd completely forgotten they'd come over.

"Sorry to intrude," Selena said.

And then the two of them scurried away, leaving me and Meredith to face off against Junior alone.

"Mr. Fuller told me that you weren't to have him," Meredith said to Junior. "And I don't think you should either. He didn't believe you would be a fit pet owner."

I had to agree with that assessment.

"He told you that, did he?" Junior said. "Is it in his will? Or did you record him when he said it? If so, I'd love to hear it. Well? Do you?"

Meredith's eyes narrowed and she took a threatening step forward. "Are you calling me a liar?" she asked in a low tone. "Because, if you are, I'm going to slap that smirk right off your face."

Junior paled. "No," he said, taking a step away from the woman who was indeed bigger than him. "But I think it would be best if the dog stayed with me until we can sort everything out. No harm in that is there?" He looked to me, expression suddenly contrite and friendly.

I wasn't buying it.

"I don't think he wants to go with you," I said.

Junior's teeth clenched, though he continued to

smile. "If it turns out the best thing for the beast is for it to go with you, then I'll turn him over, but not until we're sure."

I didn't like it, but there really wasn't much I could do. I wasn't sure if I still had any right to take Stewie, or if Timothy's wishes were void the moment he died.

"Stewie has an appointment with the vet today," I said. "I could always take him to get checked out and we can go from there." I hoped by the time Manny finished the exam, I'd find a way to keep the Pomeranian out of Junior's hands legally.

"Cancel it," Junior said as Alexis returned, a squirming Stewie tucked under one arm. "He's coming with me." His fake friendliness was gone now that his wife had control of the dog. "Alexis, let's go."

"I don't think you should," Meredith said.

But there was no stopping him. Junior took Stewie from Alexis's grasp—earning him a nip on his hand, I noticed with some satisfaction—and they bullied their way past me, and out the door.

"Should we call the police?" Meredith asked, joining me as we watched Junior shove Stewie into a carrier he had in the back of his car. He shook his hand as if he'd gotten bitten again. Good. The man deserved it.

"I'm not sure they'd help." At least not yet. Once I could produce proof that Stewie was supposed to be in my control, then maybe I'd involve the cops.

Junior paused getting into the driver's seat so he could glare at us where we stood. I had a feeling he was considering whether or not to kick us out of the house, but must have decided it wouldn't benefit him in any way. He climbed all the way into the car, started the engine, and a moment later, they were gone.

"I don't know what to do," Meredith said, walking over to Timothy's fallen machine and righting it. "Ever since Timothy died, I've been out of sorts."

"The police said you were here when it happened," I said. "It had to have been hard on you finding him like that."

"It was." She started for the kitchen, paused. "I need a drink. Care for some iced tea? I made it earlier today."

"Sure."

We went into the kitchen and gathered around a small floating island counter. The kitchen appeared dated. I don't think any of the appliances were made after 1980, and the wallpaper hadn't been popular for at least fifty years.

Meredith opened the fridge, pulled out a container, and set it on the counter before grabbing two plastic cups from the cabinet. "Timothy always broke the glass ones," she said, filling each with tea. "It got so bad, I bought him a plastic set, and that included bowls and plates. I think he broke them on purpose, just to watch me clean up the mess."

I took one of the cups and took a sip. "It sounds like it was hard working for him," I said.

"It was." She leaned against the counter and held her cup in both hands. "Every morning, when I woke up, I dreaded coming here. I only live five minutes away, yet I always made it take thirty."

"Why'd you keep doing it?"

She shrugged, took a drink. "Timothy might have been hard to work with, and he treated me like I was here for his entertainment most of the time, but I was still doing a good thing. He couldn't take care of himself, and if I didn't do it, I doubted anyone else would."

"I heard Mr. Fuller was pretty difficult," I said, thinking back to what Clarence had told me. "It seems like you weren't the only one he treated badly."

"That's the truth." She chuckled. "But it's over now." She seemed to realize how callous that sounded, so she added, "Not that it's good that he died the way he did. I still can hardly believe it."

"Did you see anything that day? Something that might make you suspect something like that might happen?"

"No," she said, looking into her tea and swirling it around as she thought. "There was the argument out back, but you were there for that. Afterward, Mr. Fuller got into a fight with his son, just a petty spat, and he and his wife left. I got Timothy settled then, and then went to deal with the laundry. Honestly, I went just so I wouldn't have to listen to him. The man could complain when he really wanted to. I didn't see or hear anything, other than Stewie barking, until I came out and found them both missing."

"Stewie was barking?" I asked, my mind immediately latching on to that. *Barking like he had been to Junior just a few minutes ago?*

"He does that a lot," she said with a fond smile. "The little rascal rarely stays quiet." The smile faded. "But now, I'm beginning to wonder if I should have paid more attention to him. If I would have come out to check on him, then . . ."

"Then you might have been killed too," I said, not meaning to make it sound like a threat, or even a warning, but Meredith's eyes widened and she placed a hand on the counter behind her as if to steady herself.

"I never even thought of that before now," she said.

"Do you have any idea who might have wanted to harm Mr. Fuller?" I asked.

"Anyone and everyone, I'm sure," Meredith said, regaining some of her composure. "As I said, he didn't treat anyone very nicely, and that included his own flesh and blood. Why, I wouldn't put it past Junior to have come back and finished the old man off himself."

"Do you really think he'd kill his own father?" I asked. While I didn't like Junior—or his wife for that matter—I found it difficult to believe he might murder his dad.

"If he thought he'd get something out of it, sure," Meredith said. She set her tea aside and leaned toward me. "There's a rumor that Timothy had been secreting money away for years. He didn't have a lot in the bank, and the property isn't worth all that much, but the hidden bundle was supposed to be rather large."

"Really?" I asked. "Is there any truth to those rumors?"

She shrugged as she picked up the container of tea and returned it to the fridge. "I honestly couldn't say. If Timothy was hiding money, I've never seen it. It wouldn't surprise me if he was. He didn't trust banks, or anyone else for that matter. But if he did have a stash hidden around here, I wouldn't put it past Junior to come sniffing around for it."

I wondered if that was why he was here, and I didn't just mean today.

I took a long drink of my tea as I thought it over.

Junior didn't appear to get along with his dad, yet he was here in Grey Falls anyway. Maybe he was here to see Timothy off to the home, but what if he was after the old man's money? He heard the rumor, decided he deserved the payout, but knew that if the house was sold, whoever purchased it would be in control of the cash—if they ever found it.

So, he pretends to leave after their fight, follows Timothy out to the barn, and then kills him.

But would he really kill his own father just to get at some money? Seeing how he treated everyone else, I wouldn't be surprised if he had.

"I really should get going," Meredith said. "I came here to pick up Stewie when Junior showed up. The poor dear was crated in Mr. Fuller's room after the murder. The police told me it would be okay if I took him to watch over him while they sorted this mess out."

"I guess Junior figured it was his right to do the same." Though why he would, I didn't know. I didn't believe for one second he cared about the dog, or thought of him as a memento of his dad's memory.

Meredith gave me a look that echoed my own thoughts. There had to be ulterior motives in play here.

I followed Meredith to the front door and outside. She locked the door, checked it twice, and then turned to me. "You need to fight for that dog," she said. "I keep saying Mr. Fuller didn't care for anyone, yet he loved his dog more than life itself. Don't let Junior keep him."

"I'll do my best." And I meant it. I had no intention of letting Junior walk off with an animal he clearly despised.

But it did make me wonder; why did he take him at all? It didn't make sense, especially after this morning, when he'd told me he wanted nothing to do with the Pomeranian.

"And I'm sorry about your son," Meredith said, fishing in her purse for her keys. "He seemed like a nice enough guy."

"He didn't kill Timothy," I said, needing to say it, if not for her, then for me.

"I'm sure that's true," Meredith said. "When I saw him afterward, he didn't look like someone who'd just killed a man. He looked worried, and was looking to help."

"He would do that," I said. Could that have been how he got blood on his shirt? If he tried to resuscitate Timothy, he would have had to touch him. It's easy enough to imagine him getting blood on his hands while performing CPR and then wiping them on his shirt afterward.

Of course, Ben said he didn't go into the house; the police stopped him. Perhaps he was scared to admit he'd gone in earlier and tried to help? Or maybe he blacked out and forgot all about trying to save Timothy Fuller.

I was grasping, but knew there had to be a reason for the blood on his shirt, other than Ben killing Timothy.

Meredith reached out and squeezed my arm, before heading to her car. She got inside, waved, and then drove off, leaving me the last person at the house. Even the car next door was gone, telling me Jason and Selena had finally left to meet with their friends.

My motherly instincts were screaming at me to do something more, to go back into the house and look around for anything that might help Ben, but I realized if something had once been there, the police would have already taken it.

With nothing left to do, I went to my van. It wasn't my place to snoop around. I'd done what I could, and it wasn't enough. I had to hope the police found enough evidence to set Ben free.

I got behind the wheel, and finally headed for home.

10

Dinner was on, and nearly ready, by the time I returned home. Manny was standing at the stove, stirring a pot of vegetable soup, a faraway look on his face. I kissed him on the cheek and it seemed to break him out of his reflections.

"Hi, hon," he said, sounding almost dreamy. "Ready to eat?"

I wasn't the slightest bit hungry, but nodded. "Where's Amelia?"

"Her room." Manny moved to the cupboard and retrieved the bowls. "She wanted to get some homework done. Hey, Wheels."

The cat in question rubbed her head against Manny's ankle, and then rolled over to her dish, giving him a sad look, despite the fact there was food there—it was just pushed to the edges so there was a hole in the center. As far as Wheels was concerned, that meant it was empty.

Cat logic.

As Manny poured her some dry, I headed to our

bedroom, where I swapped out my hairy shirt with a clean one. I took a few minutes to steel myself against the idea of eating dinner without Ben, and then I crossed the hall and knocked on Amelia's door. When she didn't answer, I opened it a crack and peered in.

"Dinner's ready," I said.

Amelia was sitting on the bed, her cell phone pressed to her chest. She looked guilty of something—eyes wide, breathing hard—when she nodded. "I'll be right down."

I hesitated only an instant before closing the door. Something was up with her, but I had a feeling it was far less life altering than what Ben was going through. Or, at least, I hoped it was. *Maybe Ben was right, and it's a new boyfriend.* It wouldn't be the first time she'd tried to hide one from us.

I headed back downstairs, memories flooding in. Amelia's last boyfriend had been five years older than her, prone to forgetting what he was doing—in the middle of doing it—and had the IQ of a rock. I'm not sure where she'd found him because he was definitely not college material. He hadn't lasted long, for which I was grateful. I hoped Amelia had learned a lesson from that brief fling and was making better decisions now.

The food was on the table when I returned, with Manny sitting in his usual place, staring at the empty chair where Ben normally sat. I'd just taken my own seat when Amelia came bounding down the stairs.

"How was your day?" I asked her, wondering if she even knew about Ben. I hadn't talked to her, and if Manny hadn't filled her in, she might not yet realize why her brother wasn't sitting at the table with us.

"Fine, I guess," she said, and then, easing my worries about having to tell her what happened, she added, "Better than Ben's." She scowled at her bowl.

"Ben will be okay," Manny said. "We all will."

Amelia's scowl didn't ease. She brushed her blue-tipped hair out of her face and started eating. Each bite was taken with force, as if she were angry at the stew for Ben's predicament.

I watched her nervously a moment before asking, "Did your father tell you about him?" I glanced at Manny, who nodded.

"He did, but I'd heard about it earlier. Some detective came to see me at school. Guy had them take me right out of class, in front of everyone. I'm not in high school anymore, and it was an aide that got me, but people talk, you know? They all probably think I'm into something illegal by now."

"Was it Detective Cavanaugh?" I asked, temper flaring. He shouldn't have gone to see my daughter in school. Granted, she was an adult. And it was a college, not high school. But still, I felt I should have been informed.

"I think so. He asked me some questions and then left. Was no big deal." She stirred her vegetables around, but didn't take another bite. She dropped her spoon and sat back. "How did this happen?"

"We don't know, honey," Manny said.

"He was with someone at the time of the murder," I said. "Don't worry yourself too much about him. I'm sure she'll vouch for him when the time comes." Though after my conversation with Selena Shriver, I wasn't so sure about that.

Amelia snorted. "He was with a girl, huh? I'm not surprised."

I chose not to speak my mind on the matter. Ben was a grown man. He could do what he pleased when it came to women, though as his mother, I didn't have to like it.

Instead of talking about Ben's questionable dating habits, I changed the subject to something I could deal with. "Ben said you left for school early today. Did you have a big test?"

Amelia's eyes flickered to me, and then to Manny. "No, I just wanted to get an early start."

"He thinks you might have a new boyfriend," Manny said, leaning forward and smiling. "Any truth to the rumor? Or can we lay that one to rest?"

"No boyfriends," Amelia said, blushing. "I was just anxious to get moving this morning, okay? It's no big deal."

Noting her tone, I nodded. There was no reason to press when we were all already stressed enough. "Okay. I was just wondering. We don't have to talk about it."

"Good." Amelia picked up her spoon, but didn't eat, just pushed her veggies absently around the bowl.

It seemed none of us knew how to deal with the day's developments. I was worried about Ben, about Amelia, but didn't know how to voice my concerns without sounding like a patronizing parent. Manny looked listless. I guess the reality had finally sunk in, and even he couldn't keep a positive attitude.

"I'm done," Amelia said, pushing her half-full bowl away. "I'm going to go upstairs and study."

"Have fun," Manny said. I think he tried to make it a joke, but it came out sounding flat.

Amelia rolled her eyes and rose. She was halfway to the stairs before I stopped her.

"Hey, Amelia."

She turned and gave me a stubborn look, as if she

expected me to continue to grill her about her whereabouts earlier.

"I love you."

She opened her mouth, blinked, and then said,
"Love you too," before she bounded up the stairs and
vanished into her room.

"That was nice," Manny said. "I think she needed
to hear that."

"Yeah," I said, staring after her. I turned back to
Manny. "Does she seem off to you?" Amelia had
never been the easiest child to deal with, but she'd
never been so, I don't know, sullen.

"It's been a rough day for all of us."

"It has," I said with a weary sigh. "I talked to some
more people today. I'm getting the impression that
Timothy Fuller was a pretty nasty man. His son's not
much better. I'm starting to wonder if maybe he
killed his own father for his money."

"Now, Liz," Manny said, pushing his half-eaten
meal away. "Be careful. You shouldn't be talking to
these people. Lester said he'd do what he could for
Ben, and I think we should let him do his job."

"I can't help it, Manny," I said. "It's Ben. And even
if he wasn't currently sitting in a jail cell for a murder
he didn't commit, there's Stewie to think about. Junior took him today. I don't think he's going to provide a very good home for the dog."

"It'll work out."

Oh, how I wished I could be as positive as Manny.
With the way my day had gone, it was hard to see the
bright side of anything.

We finished up our meal, neither of us able to finish our bowls. Manny started in on the dishes, as I
went about cleaning up. I kept wondering what exactly Detective Cavanaugh had talked to Amelia

about. Did he know more than I did? Could he actually think she had something to do with the murder, even though she wasn't there?

Or was he just following up whatever lead he could, talking to the families of both the victim and the accused? I had no idea how any of this worked, which only made me feel that much worse. How was I supposed to relax when I didn't even know if the detective on the case was focusing on the right people?

I'd just finished putting the leftovers in the fridge when there was a knock at the door. Thinking it might be the detective in question, I hurried to answer, ready to give him a piece of my mind—and maybe, to see if he could give me some actual good news.

I opened the door, but before I could so much as say, "Hello," Evelyn Passwater pushed past me.

"What a crazy day!" she said. "I heard about what happened. I can't believe it."

"How are you holding up?" Deidra Kissinger added, as she stepped in behind Evelyn. She gave me a brief hug.

"She's fine." Holly Trudeau brought up the rear. She closed the door behind her as she entered. "Liz is strong. Hi, Manny."

"Hi, ladies," Manny said, an amused lilt to his voice. "I'm all done here. I'll get out of your way."

"Good man," Deidra said. "Leave the ladies to their fun and games."

Manny bowed, and then gave me a quick kiss on the cheek before leaving the room. He never liked to stick around when my friends showed up, claiming he was afraid of what we might say about him while he was there. I'd think he'd be more worried about

what we'd say when he *wasn't* around, but that's men
for you.

"I'm sorry," I said, hurrying over to the table and
wiping it down. "I completely forgot you were coming tonight. I don't know where my head's at."

"It's no wonder," Evelyn said. She was the oldest of
the group, coming in at a healthy sixty-five. I'd met
her when she wanted to adopt a dog, and had come
to me because she wanted one who needed her as
much as she needed him. "I half expected you to call
and cancel."

"Which we wouldn't have allowed," Deidra said.
She was my age, fit and thin. Her hair was dark, cut
short so it curled around her chin. She was another
previous adopter who I'd kept in contact with.

"Let me do that," Holly said, taking the rag from
me. She was the youngest of the group, just recently
hitting her thirties. She was married to Ray Trudeau,
one of the vets who worked at the office with Manny.
He was almost ten years older than her, but it never
seemed odd that they'd gotten together.

I left the women to get settled and found the Scrabble board. We met on the first Wednesday of every
month and played. It wasn't like me to forget something like that, but with everything that had happened, I could be forgiven.

I carried the board to the table and went about
setting it up. Holly had already broken into the wine
she always brought with her. She'd poured everyone
a glass, including me. I noted she'd filled my glass
nearly to the top. She probably thought I needed it.

"I don't believe for one minute Benjamin had anything to do with that man's death," Deidra said, taking her tile rack when I offered it to her. "You should

go to the police and demand they release him this instant!"

"I already talked to them," I said. "They have a witness placing him at the scene, which is probably why they're holding him."

"Baloney," Evelyn said. She drew her tiles and beamed at what she got. "I'm surprised it took someone this long to knock off Timothy Fuller. If anyone deserved to end up with a knife in his back, it was him."

I drew my own tiles as I mulled it over. I groaned inwardly when I noted a multitude of *U*s. "It's been rough," I said, watching as play moved my way. There wasn't much I could do on my turn, so I placed an *X* to form "ax" and "ox."

"Hate moves like that," Evelyn said. "Can't expand the board that way."

"Quit complaining," Deidra said. "You'll win anyway."

"Darn tooting, I will," Evelyn said, emptying her rack and cackling as she began tallying her points.

Groans went around the table.

"How is Manny doing?" Holly asked. "Ray didn't get to talk to him today, other than in passing."

"He's okay, I guess. We're just sort of waiting to see what happens."

"Why?" Deidra asked.

"Why what?"

"Why wait around? Go make some noise. Don't let them make Ben out to be a killer."

Just hearing it, caused me to shudder. "I don't know what else I can do," I said. "We've contacted our attorney and I went and talked to some people, but their stories are all pretty consistent." And then, remembering what Meredith had said, I asked, "Have any of you heard anything about Timothy Fuller having a stash of money hidden away?"

Both Holly and Deidra shook their heads. Evelyn, on the other hand, looked contemplative as she rearranged her fresh set of tiles.

"Evelyn?" I asked when she didn't respond right away. "Do you know something?"

Play had stopped while we watched her. She continued to fiddle with her tiles a moment, before finally answering.

"I used to know Timothy better than most, I guess," she said, eyes darting around the table, not meeting any of our own.

"Better how?" Holly asked.

"We had . . . relations." Evelyn scowled at us, dared us to laugh. When we didn't, she went on. "It was years ago. Hell, a lifetime ago, really. I was eighteen, he was in his twenties. We went out for a few months, and then I broke it off. End of story."

"What was he like back then?" I asked, intrigued.

"A righteous jerk," Evelyn said. "Even back then, he only cared about himself. Never bought me a thing. If we went out for ice cream, I paid for my own. It wasn't like he couldn't afford it either. He had a good job, family had money."

"Thought he was better than everyone else," Deidra said.

"That he did," Evelyn agreed.

"Did he hide money back then?" I asked, thinking back to Timothy's house. Everything had looked old, rundown. If he had money, he must have either lost it, or it had all been eaten up in medical bills. I wouldn't have been surprised either way.

"That's the thing," Evelyn said. "I knew he did, saw him do it once."

"Really?" Holly asked. "How did he handle that?"

"How do you think?" Evelyn smacked the table with the flat of her hand. "He screamed and hollered at me for a near hour about respecting his privacy. He was hiding the money in a loose board in his living room, right out in the open where anyone could walk in on him. I asked him why he bothered, and he just told me it was none of my dang business. When I came over the next day, the board was nailed down tight. I assumed he moved the money after my intrusion."

"Does he still live in the same house as he did back then?" I asked.

Evelyn shook her head. "Was forced to move after a bad storm about fifteen years back. Tree took out the roof and everything inside was lost. He could have fixed it back up, but decided to move on instead. This was years after we parted, so I wasn't privy to his decision making."

So, it sounded like Meredith had been right. Or, at least, she had been at one time. Could the rumors of his hidden stash be remnants of Evelyn's story? He might have spent it all by now. Or was he still saving up, year after year? We're talking nearly fifty years of savings if that was the case. It could very well be a nice and tidy sum.

But was it one big enough to kill over?

"Well, that's all I've got to say about Timothy Fuller," Evelyn said. "And I think it might be a good idea if we forget the entire mess for a night."

"I agree," Deidra said. "You could use a relaxing night, Liz."

"Here, here," Holly added, topping off my glass, even though I'd only had a sip.

I thanked her absently, mind still turning over what

I'd learned. Whether or not Timothy was really still hiding money was immaterial. The fact that people *thought* he was, could be enough motive for murder.

"Now, if it's all the same to everyone else," Evelyn said, a confident grin on her face. "I'd like to start playing again. I've got me a game to win!"

11

Manny was already gone by the time I woke up the next morning. My head was pounding slightly after I'd had a little too much wine. As expected, Evelyn handily won every game of Scrabble we played, but I was okay with that. I hadn't been at my best, though I was starting to wonder if it was time we switched it up and found something she wasn't so good at to play.

I took a shower, and then got dressed in another of my Furever Pets shirts. As much as I would prefer to find a way to help Ben, I had other things I needed to be doing. It wasn't like I was helping anything by constantly asking questions. That was a job for Detective Cavanaugh, not me.

Amelia was leaning into the fridge, rooting around when I entered the kitchen. Wheels was at her feet, making short trills as she begged for scraps.

"I'm surprised you're up this early," I said, checking the coffee pot to find it still hot. I poured myself a mug and leaned against the counter.

"I was thinking of getting out for a bit," she said, closing the fridge, arms laden. She'd put together an egg sandwich and took a big bite. Manny didn't always fry up an egg for everyone before he left in the morning, but I was glad he did today.

I went to the fridge to make my own sandwich. "No class today, right?" I asked.

"Right."

"Meeting anyone?"

Amelia eyed me warily. "Why do you ask?"

"Just curious," I said. I found the cooked egg, slapped it on a piece of bread, added cheese, and a slice of tomato. I considered mayonnaise, but decided against it.

"This doesn't have anything to do with last night, does it?" Amelia asked.

"Nope." I took a bite, chewed. "But with what happened to Ben, I'm allowed to be worried about you."

"There's no need to be worried about me, Mom. I can take care of myself."

"I never said you couldn't."

But it was already too late. I'd lost her.

Amelia picked up her backpack and tossed it over one shoulder. "I'm out of here," she said. "I'm not sure when I'll be home." With her egg sandwich in one hand, she walked out the front door, slamming it closed with a little more force than was necessary.

"Good one, Liz." I heaved a sigh and finished off my breakfast, though by now, it didn't taste quite so good. No one told me parenting would only get harder as the kids got older. I thought it was supposed to be the other way around.

"Where did I go wrong?" I asked Wheels, who was

watching me with interest. When I showed her my empty hands, she wheeled over for a petting, which she took with much purring.

"Sorry," I said, after a few comforting strokes. "I've got some things to do today."

Wheels followed me down the hall, to the door where Toby and Leroy were locked away. They must have heard our approach, because as soon as my hand touched the doorknob, they started barking up a storm.

"Quiet," I said, opening the door and stepping inside. Leroy caught sight of Wheels, who was still sitting outside, and made an awkward leap her way. I closed the door before he could get out, though I did note, Wheels didn't so much as flinch at his lunge.

"No kitty snacks for you," I told the dog, who began howling at the door. I rubbed him behind the ears, which in turn, caused Toby to come over for a rub of his own. At least then, both dogs quieted down.

Today was the day I was supposed to drop both Leroy and Toby off at their new homes. Sometimes, the new pet parents came to my house to pick up their animals, sometimes it happened at the locally owned pet store I frequented. But today, I was delivering them myself. Mr. and Mrs. Keane were older, and both of them suffered from arthritis, much like Leroy. The dogs would work as a sort of therapy for the couple, and I'm sure the humans would be the same for the beagles.

Still, I was sad to see them go. It was never easy caring for an animal, only to give it up after a week or two.

I was in the process of laying soft towels in the bottom of the dog carriers when a pounding echoed throughout the house. Both Leroy and Toby started baying at the top of their lungs in response.

I hurried out of the room, making sure the dogs didn't follow, as the pounding came again. Wheels was gone, likely hiding under a table somewhere, considering the cacophony. The third round of pounding came just as I reached the door, which rattled in its frame by the force of the knocking.

"I'm coming," I said, even as I jerked open the door.

"You've got to do something about those dogs!" Joanne Bandon was shouting even before I had the door open all the way. "No one can sleep in this neighborhood with them making such a racket all of the time."

"Joanne," I said, suppressing an urge to groan her name. "I'm sorry if they're too loud. I'm prepping them to leave now. They'll be gone within the hour."

"Oh." Joanne's short, curly hair was dyed an odd shade of brown that didn't quite go with her features. She was wearing a tracksuit, though I knew for a fact she hadn't run anywhere in the last fifteen years. She had a fondness for donuts, and an aversion to exercise, which, to be honest, I could empathize with.

She'd been my neighbor since the day Manny and I had moved in. At first, she was friendly enough, but soon after the first year, the complaints started. I'd thought that maybe it was something I'd done, but after talking with the other neighbors, I learned it was just the way she was.

"I promise it'll be quieter soon," I said. "I really should get back to them." I started to close the door.

Her foot darted forward, just barely making it into the crack before the door shut all the way. "Then when are you going to do something about that eyesore out front?" she asked, jerking a thumb toward my van. "Just having it there gives me an ulcer. No one else leaves their work vehicles parked out front."

No one else complains either, I thought, but decided to keep that to myself.

"I'm sorry if you don't like it," I said, gritting my teeth. "But I need it to transport the animals. If we are able to afford it, we'll be adding a garage in the next year or two, and then you won't have to look at it anymore." Manny and I had talked about it, but honestly, it wasn't bothering anyone but Joanne.

"In the next year or two?" She made a horrified face. "You could always park down the street a ways."

By "a ways," I was pretty sure she meant the next street over. "I'll think about it," I said, not wanting to argue with her. If I started an argument with Joanne Bandon, it was likely I'd never get out of it—in this lifetime nor the next.

"You do that."

I stared at her expectantly. Her foot was still blocking the door, and I did have some dogs to take care of. "Do you need something else?" I asked, not bothering to hide my impatience.

"Well . . ." She looked past me, into the house, as if looking for something. She bit her lower lip and patted at her curls.

"I'm very busy today, Joanne," I said. "It's been a rough couple of days, so if there's nothing else, I'd really like to finish up here." The dogs had stopped barking, but I knew it was only a matter of time before they started up again.

"It's just that . . ." She frowned, produced a handkerchief from the pocket of her tracksuit. She patted at her forehead with it. It came away with a healthy smear of foundation. What did she do, bathe in the stuff?

"Just that . . . ?" I prodded.

"Ben," she said, withdrawing her foot. "I heard about what happened."

The urge to slam the door and walk away was strong, but I decided to play nice for now. Anger her now, and I wouldn't put it past her to start calling the police every time she heard me sneeze.

Joanne shifted from foot to foot, clearly uncomfortable by the topic, even though she was the one who'd brought it up. "I'm sorry to hear about it, is all. I don't think he is capable of such a thing, not like your—"

"Joanne," I warned. If she so much as insinuated Amelia was the type who was capable of killing someone, Detective Cavanaugh would be investigating another murder, one that would be taking place right here on my doorstep.

She fluttered her handkerchief, seemingly flustered. "No, what I mean to say is, I think he's innocent." Her eyes met mine briefly before she looked away. "I'm not surprised someone offed that man, to be honest."

"You're not the first person who's said something similar." Which didn't help matters much. If Timothy Fuller rubbed everyone the wrong way, who was to say he hadn't done or said something to Ben that caused him to snap.

I, of course, knew it wasn't possible. Ben wasn't someone who angered easily. But Detective Cavanaugh didn't know that. Not yet, anyway.

"I bet it was his nurse," Joanne said with a sharp nod. "I'm almost positive it had to be."

Interested despite myself, I opened the door farther. "Why do you say that?"

Joanne stepped closer, taking my interest for invitation. I remained in the doorway, keeping her from entering the house. "I saw them at the market just last week," she said, easing back, resigned to stand outside. "They were shopping for oranges, I believe. Timothy kept grabbing them and dropping them on the floor. And I think it was on purpose."

Somehow, I wasn't surprised. "I'm not sure how that leads to Meredith killing him, Joanne."

"Meredith?" Joanne asked. "Who in blazes are you talking about?"

"Meredith? His nurse?"

She fluttered her handkerchief again. "I never knew her name," she said. "Not sure it really matters, does it?"

"I guess not," I said, suppressing a sigh.

"Anyway, the nurse tried to stop him from dropping the oranges all over the store, and he started wailing like she was beating him. I swear he acted like she was trying to murder him right in the store. She stopped grabbing at his hands, and instead, started cleaning up. When she bent over to pick up what he'd dropped, he hauled off and shoved her right over. Pushed her right on the keister, he did."

"He abused her?" I asked, eyes wide. "In public like that?"

"That was the only time I saw them together like

that, but I've heard that sort of thing was a regular occurrence with them. I don't understand how that woman ever put up with him, to be honest. He must have been paying her real good for her to have stayed for as long as she did."

My mind immediately went to what Meredith had told me about hidden money. Had she been hoping that he would leave it to her once he died? It would explain why she would have put up with him and his abuse.

But why tell me about the money if she wanted it? And if she didn't know where it was, why kill him? Had she found the stash and decided it was high time to rid herself of the old man? Why not just quit?

It made me wonder why Meredith really had been at Timothy's place yesterday. Was it really for Stewie? Or had she been searching for the money? Junior showing up might have stopped her then, but what about now?

"Thanks, Joanne," I said, stepping back. "You've given me a lot to think about."

A smug smile crossed her features, making me regret the compliment. "Well, I hope you do consider what I said about that *thing* out front. The whole neighborhood would be a much nicer place if it wasn't sitting there."

"I'll think about it," I said, though I had no intention of parking my van anywhere else.

"And tell Manny about the shingles on the left side of your house. I think you need to replace them. I can't understand why you don't make him fix things up a bit more. If he were *my* husband, he'd never get a moment's rest."

And that, I could believe.

I closed the door with a distracted, "Okay, thanks.

I'll let him know." I was sure she'd complain about that at some point, but right then, I didn't care.

Could Timothy's nurse, Meredith, have killed him for his money? Did Detective Cavanaugh know about the public abuse? What happened behind closed doors in that house? He might have treated her better when no one was looking. Or he could have been worse.

And what all did it mean for Ben? If Timothy abused Meredith, wouldn't that give her a greater motive for murder than whatever Detective Cavanaugh thought Ben's might be?

Those thoughts followed me as I returned to the beagles and readied their transport. I poured them each a small bowl of dry food in the hopes it would keep them from bothering Joanne further. While her information had given me hope that Ben might get out of this okay, I didn't want her coming back over to complain about the noise again. Knowing her, she'd call the cops this time, and I really didn't want to have to explain things to them today.

As I gathered dog toys, I wondered if Clarence knew about Timothy's money. His fingering of Ben was the one thing I couldn't figure out. I could come up with all kinds of motives and suspects, but if Ben *had* fled the scene, it still put him at the top of the detective's list.

Maybe Clarence and Meredith knew one another and were working together. She decides to kill the old man, while Clarence uses Ben to redirect the investigation.

It wasn't much of a theory, but it made far more sense to me than believing my son killed a decrepit old man for no reason.

What I needed to do was tell Detective Cavanaugh

what I'd learned and make sure he followed up on those leads. I'm sure he'd learned much of it on his own, but I doubted he'd talked to either Evelyn or Joanne. They both had firsthand accounts about what Timothy Fuller was like. That had to mean something, didn't it?

But for as much as I'd like to march right down to the station and tell him everything, it would have to wait.

I urged both beagles into separate carriers. They went reluctantly, but they went. Once I had them locked inside, I realized it wasn't going to be easy to get them into the van. Normally, Ben was here to lift the heavier loads, and while I wasn't a complete weakling, the beagles weren't exactly lightweight. It might just be better to leash the dogs and take them to the van that way, rather than try to carry them.

My heart ached as I realized that this might end up being a problem for a very long time. If Ben didn't get released, I'd have no one to help me. I'd be on my own, forced to do everything myself.

"Come on," I said, opening both cages. I snagged the leashes from the wall, which caused both dogs to start barking excitedly, thinking we were going for a walk. I leashed them, and then took them out back so they could relieve themselves and run around a little before the car ride. Then, while they played, I carried both carriers to the van, placed them inside, and then opened them. Next, I dropped the ramp built into the van we used for animals that couldn't jump very well.

Satisfied, I went out back, retrieved the dogs, and then led them around front, up the ramp, and into their carriers. Once they were secured in place, I closed everything up, and started up the engine.

"Ready?" I asked them. I was answered with a chorus of woofs. "Then, let's get you home."

Feeling better now that I was focused on work, I backed out of the driveway, and pulled away, happy I was about to brighten someone else's day.

12

I stood, smiling, as I watched Toby and Leroy leap around Mr. Keane. The two old beagles looked like puppies again, their energy was so high. Even Mr. Keane looked twenty years younger as he grinned and tossed a ball across the backyard for the dogs to fetch.

"This is going to be good for Teddy," Phyllis Keane said, watching her husband.

"It'll be good for all of you. A loving pet can shave years off a person."

"I hope we can do the same for those two darlings."

I was sure they would.

I watched the old man and his new dogs play for a few minutes more before leaving. All I'd done was deliver the dogs to them, yet I felt like a hero. Even as I got into my van, I could hear Teddy's hearty laugh, and the bays of the beagles. It was going to be a good match.

Of course, I'd miss them now that they were gone.

Over the years, I've learned not to get too attached to the animals I rescued, but sometimes, it's hard not to. Toby and Leroy, despite their ailments, were good dogs, and deserved to be happy.

Checking the clock, I decided I had time to stop by and see how Manny was doing before getting involved in anything else. I was thinking of making another run at Junior in the hopes he'd finally relent and let me take Stewie off his hands. Now, there was a man who didn't deserve a pet. The sooner I could save the Pomeranian from his grasp, the better.

I was glad to see the veterinary lot was practically empty, which meant there weren't a lot of sick animals at the moment. Manny's car sat beside a beat-up Toyota. A few spaces down was Ray Trudeau's Kia. Beside that was Trinity's—the veterinary assistant—car. There was only one other car in the lot. This one, I didn't recognize.

I parked beside Manny's Ford, and then entered the office.

"Hi, Liz," Trinity said, snapping her gum. She was in her mid-twenties, and I had a feeling she'd been hired more for her looks than any skills she might have. Not that I held it against Manny. She was blond, blue-eyed, and had a figure that made most men drool.

Ben had tried to get her attention more than once, but so far, his attempts have been in vain. I'm not sure if she rebuffed him because she truly wasn't interested, or if it was because she worked for his dad. Either way, I was kind of glad they hadn't gotten together. I sometimes wondered if she forgot her brain at home because, occasionally, she acted as airheaded as she looked.

"Hey, Trinity. Is Manny busy?"

"He's with a husky now," she said. "Just took him in a few minutes ago, so it could be a little while before he's free."

"I can wait."

Trinity flashed me a smile, and then went back to toying with her phone.

The veterinary office was split into two sections. Dogs entered on the right, cats on the left. Any other animals brought in were left up to the owner's discretion. More often than not, birds and rodents ended up on the dogs' side, because not all cat owners kept their animals caged or leashed. While the dogs might bark, they normally didn't cause any trouble with the other animals.

I'd entered on the cat side out of habit. I'd been here with Wheels more times than I could count, so it was second nature to me. Cat magazines rested in a rack by the door. Pamphlets on some of the more common cat ailments lay on a table next to that. On the wall above the benches, a portrait of the world's fattest cat hung, with a warning about all the health issues that could arise for letting your feline grow so large next to it.

I walked past the counter and peered in through the small window atop the first exam room door, hoping to catch a glimpse of not only Manny at work, but at the husky he was checking out. I loved huskies, even if they could be stubborn, but room one was empty. I moved on, past a chart of healthy dog weights—which seemed to be one of the biggest issues people had with their pets—toward exam room two.

I'd just reached the door when it opened and Ray Trudeau appeared, wearing scrubs decorated with jovial puppies.

"Oh!" he said, taking a sudden step back. "I didn't see you there, Liz."

"Hey, Ray," I said. "Been busy today?"

"Thankfully, no," he said. He rubbed at his thick mustache and regarded me with deep-set hazel eyes. "I heard about this whole mess with Ben. How are you doing?"

"I'm surviving. This thing with Ben is throwing me for a major loop."

Ray leaned on the wraparound counter. Trinity glanced up from her phone long enough to shoot him a disapproving glare, before going back to whatever it was she was doing.

"It's gotten to us all," Ray said. "Manny's doing what he can to keep busy, but I can tell his mind isn't completely on his work. He's not going to risk an animal's health, mind you, but I do believe he wishes there was more he could do."

"Don't we all."

Ray reached out, squeezed my shoulder. "I'm sure everyone keeps telling you this, but I'm going to say it too: it'll all work out. These sorts of things always find a way to come out right in the end. It might not seem like it sometimes, but have faith."

"I hope you're right."

A bark came from exam room three then. It sounded more surprised than angry. I was guessing the husky either got her temperature taken, or was given a shot.

"Holly told me a little about what happened," Ray said. "I don't pay much mind to the news, not with it always being so damn depressing all the time. I'm still having a hard time wrapping my mind around the fact Timothy Fuller was killed."

Trinity perked up, eyes drifting away from her

phone. Apparently, murder was a topic she could get into.

"Did you know him?" I asked, not sure I wanted to talk about Timothy's death, but was curious nonetheless.

"A little," Ray said. "I knew his Pomeranian, Stewie, more than I knew the man himself. The old dog had a few minor ailments, but nothing that was life-threatening or would affect his quality of life. Tim would bring him in like clockwork, once a month, just to make sure everything was okay. He wasn't a nice man, but he sure cared about his dog."

"That's what everyone keeps telling me."

"I don't know what the two of them saw in one another, but I will say, Stewie cared about Tim just as much as the old man did the dog."

"Really?" I asked. "What makes you say that?"

"He was always so protective of his owner." Ray chuckled. "Can you imagine such a little dog playing at guard dog? It was entertaining to watch, let me tell you."

"Sometimes, the smaller dogs are the feistier ones."

"That's true." Ray nodded, smiling fondly as he remembered. "About two months ago, Tim came in for his monthly checkup for Stewie, that nurse of his in tow."

"Meredith."

"He was messing around with the pamphlets— Tim, not the dog—and giving her a hard time whenever she tried to tell him to stop. It was kind of like watching a mother with a misbehaving child, to tell you the truth. The nurse eventually grabbed him by the wrist after he'd knocked over half the magazines, and Stewie completely lost it. He started snarling and barking, so much so, I think it started to worry everyone in the room. It surprised the nurse to no end, while Tim cackled like he'd planned the whole thing. Man, he sure got a kick out of it." He shook his head, an amused smile on his face.

I immediately thought back to the last time I'd seen Stewie. He'd been trapped in a corner, barking and snarling at Junior. I'd assumed then it was because Junior was chasing after him, but what if there was more to it than that? What if he was barking at Junior because little Stewie knew who killed his owner and was trying to warn him off?

"How was Stewie with other people?" I asked, mulling it over. Could the Pomeranian serve as a witness to murder? I'm not sure there was any judge in the world that would accept it, but maybe it would give the police a better suspect.

That was, if they didn't laugh me out of the room for suggesting it.

"Skittish sometimes, especially around me. I think he realized I was going to be poking and prodding him, so he ended up trying to run from me most of the time. I often had to have someone hold the dog down so I could check his ears, lest he snap at me. Those teeth of his might have been old and small, but they were still pretty sharp."

The door opened and a couple came in with a morbidly obese tabby. They went to the desk to sign in with Trinity, who looked annoyed to have to stop listening in on our conversation.

"Ah, Mr. and Mrs. Williamson," Ray said. "I'll be right with you." He turned to me. "I guess I'd better get back to work." He put a hand on my shoulder, looked into my eye, face growing serious. "Be good, Liz. Remember, we're all thinking about you."

"Thanks."

Ray took the Williamsons and the fat cat into exam room one. I looked to Trinity, who'd lost interest the moment we stopped talking about the murdered man, and was back to poking at her phone and snapping her gum. I might as well not have been there.

I considered just leaving, but I really wanted to see Manny before I went and did something stupid. I headed for exam room three and peeked in through the window. The husky was standing on the table, coat practically gleaming in the light. The dog had bright blue eyes, and looked to only be about a year old. Her owner was a thirty-something man I'd seen around town, but never had the occasion to meet.

Manny was checking the dog's teeth, and I was surprised how stoically she took the examination. After only a brief look, he stepped back, said something to her owner, and then shook the man's hand. A moment later, dog and owner were on their way, and Manny stepped out to see me.

"Liz," he said, seemingly surprised to see me. "Is there news?"

"No news," I said, giving him a brief hug. He smelled like dog. "I dropped off Toby and Leroy today. It looks like they'll be in good hands."

"Great," he said, eyes following the husky.

"Anything wrong?" I asked.

"Hmm?" He glanced at me.

"With the dog?"

"Oh, no." He smiled fondly. "Apparently, she tried to chew through a rusty metal pipe. Teeth are fine, but I gave her a shot, just in case."

"That's good." The husky was going to be a really good-looking dog when she grew up.

"How about you?" he asked. "Are you doing okay?"

"I wish everyone would stop asking me that," I said, crossing my arms over my chest. "How do you think I'm doing? It's not like I can stop worrying about Ben or what happened."

"I know what you mean," Manny said. "I can't stop thinking about it either."

"I keep playing over the entire thing in my head," I admitted. "But sometimes, I wish I could forget, just long enough to pretend that the world isn't falling down around my ears."

Manny immediately pulled me into another hug. "The world isn't falling apart," he said. "It might feel like it, but it's not. Ben will be fine."

"I wish I could believe that."

"Lester will take care of everything. He called to let me know he was going to see Ben this morning."

"Maybe I should go with him," I said. "I'm sure he'll want to talk to me too."

Manny released me, held me at arm's length. "Go home, Liz," he said. "Let Lester do his job. Try to get some rest if you can. If that doesn't work, then try to find something else to occupy your mind."

"I could get the room ready for Stewie's arrival, I suppose," I said, grudgingly. It needed to be done, but honestly, I had no interest in cleaning the room. I wanted to see Ben.

"Perfect." He smiled, though I could still see the worry behind his eyes. "Do that. Get your mind off Ben for a little while. It'll do you some good."

I wondered if he was doing the same, but decided not to ask him. Manny dealt with things in his own way. Hopefully, he'd understand when I dealt with them in mine.

We said our goodbyes, which included a chaste kiss on my cheek. I did feel a little better after talking to him, but I still didn't think I could focus on much other than Ben's welfare. How did people go on when something like this happened? I was struggling to make it minute to minute without having a panic attack. What if it took weeks before the police found the real killer?

What if they never did?

A flare of panic almost made me rush to my van and drive straight to the police station to find out what progress the detective had made. I resisted the urge and resolved to go home and do exactly what Manny told me to do, even if I'd hate every second of it.

Fate, however, had other plans for me.

As soon as I was behind the wheel of my van, my phone rang. Since I was thinking of Ben and Detective Cavanaugh, my mind immediately latched on to the idea that it was one of them, calling to tell me they'd caught the real killer and that everything would be okay.

I snatched up the phone, and without looking at the screen, I answered. "Hello?" I asked, breathless. "Detective Cavanaugh?"

"No, sorry, Liz. It's Duke."

"Duke?" At first, I was confused as to why he was calling me, and then I remembered my visit to his house yesterday. "Did Sasha tell you I stopped by?"

"She did," he said. "I was going to call last night, but got busy. Before I knew it, it was too late. Figured I'd wait until today to get hold of you. Hope that's all right."

"It's fine." Though, I wondered if the time was really the reason he hadn't called last night, or if he'd needed to come up with some sort of excuse for his actions—whatever they may be. "What can I do for you, Duke?" I asked.

"Sasha said you wanted to talk. I'm thinking that it might be a good idea."

"Okay, when?"

"How about now?" he asked. "I'm free for the next hour, hour and a half. We could meet downtown. Let's say, Sophie's Coffeehouse?"

"Sounds good. I can be there in ten minutes."

"Make it fifteen."

I clicked off, mind whirling. As much as I wanted to forget about Ben's predicament, I couldn't let this opportunity pass. Something was up with Duke and Courtney, and I had a feeling it could very well have to do with Stewie and old man Fuller.

And if that was the case, it might also have something to do with Timothy's murder, and that was something I couldn't ignore.

13

Sophie's Coffeehouse was once an old Victorian house, but had been converted into a business. It was situated downtown, down the street from where the statue of Grey Falls' founder, Sebastian Grey, stood. The house had been converted years ago when the area was rezoned after a long debate on what to do with the area. While the houses used to once be nice, neglect had turned them into an eyesore; hence the re-zoning. The whole street is now filled with old houses, many of them which were once considered mansions, repurposed as businesses.

Sophie's was one of the smaller houses, scrunched between an oddly shaped tanning salon—which looked like someone took a bunch of square boxes and placed them haphazardly on top of one another—and an op-tometrist's office.

I pulled around to the small lot out back and parked. Sophie's was always busy, and today was no different. The lot was nearly full, and when I en-tered, I noted many of the tables were taken. Most people kept their voices down, though there was one boisterous man in the corner who shouted at his companions across the table like they were hard of hearing. His laugh was twice as loud.

"Liz," Duke called, waving his hand to grab my attention. He was sitting in the opposite corner, as far away from the big man as he could get. I had a feeling it was intentional.

"Duke," I said, joining him. "I'm actually surprised you called."

"I'm surprised myself," he said. "If Courtney knew I was here with you, she'd probably explode. She isn't too happy with you right now."

"What a shock," I said, deadpan.

Duke chuckled and waved over the waitress. "Black coffee, please," he said. "And a water."

"Same for me," I said, when she turned to me.

My gaze traveled over Duke's shoulder, and out the window. I could see the top of Sebastian's head, as well as his hand, which was raised in salute.

"I remember telling Ben the story about him," I said, nodding toward the statue.

Duke looked over his shoulder, and then turned back to me. "Sebastian Grey?"

"Yeah. He couldn't believe the town was named after a man whose greatest feat was falling down."

"He did land on his feet."

"True."

As the story went, Sebastian Grey fell out of his wagon, flipped in the air, and somehow, landed on his feet. There were no waterfalls in town, no cliffs. Just a short fall from a wagon. It was said he decided to settle in what would become Grey Falls because he thought the land was good luck since he hadn't broken his fool neck in the fall.

I wasn't sure how much truth there was to the story, but it did make for an interesting tale. Ben had been fascinated by it.

Duke and I fiddled with our napkins and readied our condiments in silence, neither of us quite sure where to go from there. A few minutes later, the waitress returned. She was a perky teenager who looked to be on her first job. She didn't seem to note our somber expressions.

"Here you go!" she said happily, setting down two mugs, and filling each. "Need me to grab any cream or flavored syrup? We just got some bourbon caramel in, if you're interested."

"No thank you," I said. Sugar was more than enough for me.

"I'm good." Duke flashed her a smile.

"Okie! Let me know if you need anything." With a decided spring in her step, she moved on to another table.

"So," I said, scooping cane sugar into my coffee. There were no prepackaged paper packets at Sophie's. Instead, small containers of different sugars and sweeteners sat in a circle. Duke opted for the standard white. "What do you want to discuss?"

He stirred his coffee, took a sip. "You tell me," he said. "You're the one who wanted to talk."

He had me there. "It's mostly about the other day, when Mr. Fuller died." Okay, it wasn't just mostly, but it felt strange sitting there, talking to him, when he might have been involved in the murder. I was having trouble forcing myself to get to the point out of fear of how he'd react.

"I figured as much," he said, eyes never leaving mine.

"When I went to Courtney's house, after Mr. Fuller kicked us out, I expected you to be there."

"And Courtney expected Ben." He held my gaze as he took another drink.

"True. But I know where Ben was. You, on the other hand, I don't. Courtney wasn't exactly forthcoming."

"No disrespect, but what business is it of yours where I was?" Duke set down his mug, and waited me out while I swirled my coffee.

I felt like I was treading on some pretty thin ice. I liked Duke, despite who he worked for. I didn't want to accuse him of anything, but if he had something to do with Timothy's death, I needed to know. For Ben, if nothing else.

"It's not, really," I said when I couldn't take the silence any longer. "But I'm worried. Ben is in a lot of trouble and if I can figure out who was where and when, then maybe I can find a way to help him."

"That's the job of the detective in charge of the case, don't you think?"

"It is," I admitted. "But I'm his mother. I can't just sit back and do *nothing.*"

"Why not?"

It was spoken with such an air of innocence, I almost laughed. It was obvious Duke wasn't a father. No parent could ever look at another parent in distress and ask that.

"I'm not accusing you of killing Mr. Fuller," I said. *At least not yet.* If it turned out he had, I wouldn't hesitate to tell Detective Cavanaugh. "All I want to know is where you were. If Courtney sent you back after Stewie, then maybe you heard or saw something that could help Ben."

Duke paled and hurriedly looked down into his mug.

"You *did* see something, didn't you?"

"I . . ."

"Can I get you two some sandwiches?" our waitress asked, startling me. I'd been so intent on Duke, I'd forgotten where we were.

"No, we're good," Duke said.

I simply shook my head. I refused to take my eyes off Duke, lest he try to sneak away while I was distracted.

"All righty! Let me know if I can get you anything." The waitress scurried away.

"Out with it," I said, the moment she was gone.

Duke's entire body sagged. "Okay, look," he said. "Courtney *did* send me back to the house. Since you didn't follow us right away, she let me out down the road. She told me to make sure that you weren't going to try to steal the dog from us, and then, if you weren't, to do it myself. I didn't want to do it, thinking it was too underhanded, even for her, so I dragged my feet on the way back. I think I was kind of hoping you'd catch me in the act."

I knew it! Courtney *had* been stalling. She'd probably calculated how long she expected Duke to take, which was why she was so abrupt in dismissing me. She'd figured he'd already have Stewie and was anxious to pick him up.

"What happened when you got to Timothy's house?" I asked, keeping my voice level.

"When I got back, I saw Ben right away and thought Courtney was right to be worried. He was next door with a pretty girl in a bikini, and they seemed to be hitting it off. I hung back and watched him, mostly to make sure he didn't see me, and to make sure he didn't head over to the Fuller place. It wasn't long before I realized I was wasting my time."

"He went inside the house?"

Duke nodded. "He did. I waited for a few more minutes after he went inside, just to make sure he wouldn't reappear. When he didn't, I walked up to Fuller's front door and was about to knock when I heard shouting."

I leaned forward, heart skipping a beat. "Who was shouting?" I asked.

"Mr. Fuller and that son of his."

"Junior."

"Yeah, him. Junior was shouting something about being owed, and his father wasn't having any of it. He kept saying that Junior didn't deserve anything of his, and that he wished he'd never showed up. It sounded pretty heated, and I for one, wasn't about to intrude."

"You didn't go in?" I asked, shocked. If it had been me, I'd probably have knocked, just to break up the fight.

Still, if Duke had seen, or at least, *heard* Timothy's murder, that made him a witness. He could tell Detective Cavanaugh everything he knew, and the detective would have no choice but to release Ben.

"No, it wasn't any of my business."

When he didn't say anything more, I prodded. "And then what happened?"

"Then, nothing," Duke said, with a dismissive shrug. "They shouted at one another for a few more minutes, and since I wanted nothing to do with it, I backed away."

"So, you didn't see anything?" I asked. It came out sounding like a whine.

"Not really. Though, while I was walking away, the

door banged open and Junior and his wife stormed out of there. I could hear Mr. Fuller screaming at them, and his nurse was shouting at him to calm down, but they didn't come outside. She sounded just as angry as he did." Duke took a drink, grimaced as if his coffee had turned suddenly bitter. "Junior and his wife sped off, and that was the end of it."

That didn't help me—or Ben—one bit. "Did you see an old man across the street?" I asked. I couldn't remember if Clarence had said whether or not he'd seen Junior leave. If he had, why not say anything about Duke?

"No, sorry. I kept my head down and just walked away. I wasn't interested in being there, though now, I wish I would have paid more attention."

"Did you go back for Stewie?" I asked. "Or see Mr. Fuller when he went out back to the barn?"

"No, I didn't. At that point, I'd lost all interest in the dog," Duke said. "I want to see it find a good home, don't get me wrong, but I wasn't about to stick my nose in the middle of that mess. And then, after what happened . . ." He shook his head.

"Where did you go?" I asked, still hoping he could tell me something that might help Ben, though those hopes were fading. While the fight between Junior and his dad was interesting, it didn't prove anything I didn't already know. The two men didn't get along. That didn't mean Junior had murdered his own father, especially since he'd left before the old man had died.

"I went for a walk. I wanted a clear head while I tried to figure out what I was going to tell Courtney. As you know, she doesn't like it when things don't go her way."

"Tell me about it," I muttered.

Duke smiled, but it quickly faded. "When I heard the sirens, and realized where they were headed, I called her, not wanting to be caught hanging around where I didn't rightly belong. She came and got me, and then proceeded to rip into me for not doing what she asked. She didn't care why, didn't care that an ambulance was there. She just wanted the dog."

"Sounds like Courtney." I could only imagine how high-pitched her shouts were.

"I like her well enough," Duke said. "But sometimes, she goes overboard." He leaned forward, met my eye. "I didn't know you were supposed to be there that day. I swear to you, that was all on Courtney. If I would have known, I would have tried to talk her out of it. We had no right to be there, not if Mr. Fuller called you first."

"You could have told her that when Ben and I showed up," I pointed out.

"I could have," he said. "But then I would have landed squarely on Courtney's bad side. We were already there, so it wasn't like she'd just drop it, even if I asked her to. You only have to see her every once in awhile. I, on the other hand, have to work with her. I opted to stay out of it and let it work itself out. It's safer that way."

"True," I allowed, and then fell silent.

This was far from the outcome I'd been hoping for. I was glad to know I'd been right about Courtney's underhanded tactics, but something still didn't sit right with me about the whole business.

"Why did Courtney want Stewie so badly?" I asked Duke, who drained his coffee and was looking around like he was ready to leave.

"Honestly, I can't say," he said, producing his wallet and dropping a few bills onto the table. "When she called me, she said it was important we got there early, but never said why. Once you arrived, I figured it was because she was trying to beat you to the punch."

There was something to his tone that caught my interest. "But now?"

"Now, I'm not so sure." Duke rose. "I'm sorry if our interference has caused you and Ben trouble. I never intended for any of this to happen, and I'm sure Courtney feels the same way."

Though she'd never say so.

"Thanks, Duke," I said, my mind turning over what he'd said. If her early arrival at Mr. Fuller's wasn't because of me, then why was she there? Something was going on, and I had a feeling Courtney was the only one who knew what it was.

Duke smiled, patted me on the shoulder, and then walked away. Even though I still had questions, I let him go. I had a feeling he wouldn't have the answers.

I remained seated for a few minutes more, toying with my cooling coffee. I wasn't completely satisfied with Duke's explanation of Courtney's motives. Why was she so interested in Stewie? What had Duke meant when he said he wasn't so sure about her interest in the dog? There was something she wasn't saying, and I had no idea how I'd ever get it out of her.

But Detective Cavanaugh might.

I considered calling him and pointing him Courtney's way. It would serve her right for trying to snake the Pomeranian out from under me. And then to lie to my face about Duke's whereabouts . . .

It might serve her right, but it would also make her an enemy for life. I wasn't convinced she knew anything about the murder, but if she did, I intended to find out.

I paid for my coffee, and then left Sophie's, debating on how to handle things without stirring the pot. If nothing else, I could call Cavanaugh and let him know what Duke had told me about Junior's fight with his father. If the detective hadn't heard about it by now, maybe it would give him a lead that would lead him to someone other than Ben.

I was about to turn the corner to head to my van when I saw someone across the street; someone who, as far as I knew, wasn't supposed to be there.

Amelia was leaving one of the businesses, talking animatedly as she descended the stairs. There was no sign on the building, at least none I could see from where I stood. It was a small, brick structure, at least, small compared to the much larger mansion-sized buildings surrounding it.

An older man in a ratty tan suit—I'd put his age at around sixty—was walking with her. They both stopped at the foot of the stairs and faced one another. The older man put a hand on her shoulder and spoke to her, leaning toward her intently.

I moved so I could still keep an eye on them, but wouldn't be immediately evident if they were to look my way. I knew I should just walk away and let Amelia tell me about it in her own time, yet I remained.

It's not like she'd just up and tell me about anything going on in her life.

Amelia and the man spoke, heads very nearly touching, like they didn't want anyone else to overhear what they were saying. Every so often, she would nod. His hand moved from her shoulder, down to her wrist. When she started to walk away, his grip tightened, causing her to stop.

"Who are you?" I muttered, thinking back to the name I'd seen written on the card in her room: C. Chudzinski. Could this be Amelia's new boyfriend?

My gut clenched at the thought. She was still young, just barely in her college years, and this guy was at least three times her age! I had half a mind to stomp over there and demand to know what was going on, but knew if I did, she would never forgive me.

They spoke a few minutes more before the man retreated back into the building. Amelia stood there, alone, a contemplative look on her face, before she nodded once to herself, and then strode meaning-fully toward her car.

Snap decision. I could march across the street and demand to know who the man was, and what he wanted with my daughter.

Or, I could get into my car, follow after Amelia, and see what she was doing. By her determined stride, I was positive she wasn't going to simply drive home and take a nap.

I found myself moving toward my own car without a second thought. Confronting the older man might get me my answers, but it would also infuriate Amelia. If I asked her myself, then perhaps she would tell me on her own. She'd still be mad I followed her, but I had a feeling she'd be far less volatile if the explana-tion came from her own lips.

I hit my car at a run, fumbled with the door han-dle, nearly dropping my keys in the process. Amelia was likely in her car by now. If I didn't move fast, she would get away, and any chance to see where she was headed would be gone.

I jumped into the driver's seat, slammed the key home, and then backed out, nearly clipping the back of a pickup truck parked behind me.

I hit the street just as Amelia pulled away from the curb. I kept well back, just in case she checked her mirrors.

And then, hating myself even as I did it, I settled in behind my daughter to see where she would take me.

14

Amelia pulled to a stop in front of a house not far from Timothy Fuller's home. I, not wanting to be seen, pulled off the road a short distance away and watched to see what she would do. Amelia didn't get out of her car right away, and I wondered if she was reconsidering whatever it was she was doing.

Of course, it also gave me time to reconsider my decision to follow her. As far as I knew, one of her friends lived here. Or she was running an errand, though what kind, I had no idea.

Her car door opened and she popped out, looking almost jittery as she scanned the front of the house. She smoothed down her hair, brushed herself off, and then went to the door.

I chewed on my lower lip as I waited to see what would happen. Something about Amelia's manner didn't feel right to me. She kept looking around nervously as she pressed the doorbell and stepped back to wait for someone to answer.

She smoothed down her hair again, clearly a nervous gesture. It made me wonder if perhaps I'd been wrong when I thought the older man might be the new boyfriend Ben believed she was seeing. Could she be at her real boyfriend's house now?

I almost drove away then. As much as I wanted to protect her and make sure she was safe, Amelia was a grown adult. If she was seeing someone, it was none of my business. It didn't matter who the older man she'd been talking to was. It didn't matter who she was meeting now. It was her life, and I had to let her live it.

Yet, I remained right where I was. After what happened to Ben, I was feeling overly protective, and I wanted to make sure she wasn't making a huge mistake.

The door opened and I audibly gasped when Timothy's nurse, Meredith, poked her head outside. She wasn't wearing her uniform, but rather a light sweater with the sleeves pushed up past her elbows, and a pair of capris. She looked just as startled as I was to find Amelia standing on her doorstep.

The two women spoke briefly. Meredith shook her head once, then a second time, before heaving a sigh and nodding. She stepped aside and Amelia entered the house. Meredith checked to make sure no one else was lurking, and then closed the door.

"What is going on here?" I wondered aloud. Amelia had no business being here, especially after what had happened to Ben. Did she know Meredith somehow? I found it unlikely, which meant she was likely involving herself in the case.

But why?

One thing was for sure, there was no way I was leaving now.

I put the van in gear and pulled in behind Amelia's car in the driveway. I shut off the engine and after making sure I didn't look as harried as I felt, I got out and approached the door. The good news was, there was no yelling going on inside. The bad news was, I couldn't see inside to make sure they weren't strangling one another.

I pressed the doorbell and stepped back, stomach churning. This had to be about Ben, but it made no sense to me why Amelia of all people would be here, even if it was. How would she know who Meredith was? I supposed she could have asked around, but why would she? Did she know something I didn't?

The door opened to reveal Timothy Fuller's former nurse. She took one look at me and her shoulders slumped. She spoke before I could utter a word.

"I guess you'd better come on in too."

Meredith turned and led me down a short hall, into the living room. Amelia was flipping through a notebook when we entered. She was sitting on the couch, that contemplative look still on her face. She wrote something in the notebook, and then looked up, mouth open to speak, when she saw me. Whatever she was originally going to say vanished, and was replaced by a single word.

"Mom?"

"Amelia." I stepped the rest of the way into the room and looked around, hoping to spot some indication as to why my daughter was here. There were a few pictures on the wall of an older couple I took for Meredith's parents. There were no kids, no husband, as far as I could tell. A pair of candles burned on the coffee table, making the room smell of caramel. It was rather cozy, if not somewhat sparse.

Meredith walked past me and took a seat in a rocking chair by the window. A closed wicker basket sat beside the chair, a pair of knitting needles atop it.

"What are you doing here?" Amelia asked, voice rising an octave. She looked to Meredith as if she might have the answer, but I was the one who spoke.

"I could ask you the same thing," I said, crossing my arms and putting on my mom face.

She blinked at me twice, slowly, a realization dawning. "Were you following me?"

"Not at first," I said. "But after I saw you with that man, I was curious." My face started to warm. "I wanted to make sure you weren't getting into anything I should know about."

"You followed me!" This time, it was a statement. "I can't believe you!" She threw herself back into the couch, looking for all the world like the petulant teenager I'd argued with a hundred times before. If she was trying to act the part of a responsible adult, she was losing whatever credibility she might have had.

"I didn't mean to do it," I said. "It just sort of happened."

Amelia snorted and rolled her eyes.

I glanced at Meredith, who was watching us with a resigned look on her face, before turning my attention back to my daughter. "Why are you here?" I asked. "Do you know Meredith?"

"That's none of your business." Amelia's stubbornness came into her voice full force.

"Amelia, what happens to you *is* my business." I could be just as stubborn. In fact, Manny would say she got it from me. "After what happened to Ben, I want to make sure you're okay, and not putting yourself at unnecessary risk."

"I'm fine, Mom," Amelia said. "I came here to talk to Ms. Hopewell."

"Why?" I asked, glancing at Meredith—Ms. Hopewell, apparently. She remained seated, seemingly resigned to let whatever happened, happen.

Amelia's mouth pressed into a fine line, before she answered. "Because I want to help Ben." She crossed her arms over her chest, mimicking my own stance. "Because I heard Ms. Hopewell had more of a problem with Mr. Fuller than she let on." She turned to Meredith. "Isn't that right?"

She didn't answer right away, choosing instead to stare at the floor between us. Her silence gave me time to work through the multitude of questions zipping through my brain.

How did Amelia know any of this? Why did she feel it necessary to confront Meredith herself? I couldn't fathom how she'd gotten involved.

"Is this true?" I asked Meredith when the silence began to stretch on for too long.

She glanced up at me briefly, and then went back to staring at the floor between us. Her dark eyes were unreadable, though by the way she was sitting, I could tell she was nervous; scared even.

"Meredith?" I said, taking a step toward her. "Did you have a problem with Timothy Fuller?"

A sad smile spread across her face then. "You know how it is," she said. "I worked hard for that man, and what did it ever get me? He treated me worse than that dog of his. You saw it. I was someone he used for his own pleasure. He would have discarded me if he'd gotten the chance."

"He hit you," I said, wondering if I was about to hear a confession. "Pushed you to the edge."

"He did," she said. "He didn't care who saw him do it either. Every time I turned around, he was knocking something over, or breaking something, just so he could force me to clean up after him. It made me so mad that sometimes I . . ." Her gaze rose, eyes meeting mine. "I'd never actually do it," she said, voice pleading. "I'd never kill him, even if every fiber of my being begged me to."

"It's not the abuse I'm here about," Amelia said, sitting forward. She flipped open her notebook and scanned the page before continuing. "Everyone knew about his abuse toward you and his family. Mr. Fuller had a history of hurting anyone he could. By all accounts, he was something of a sadist."

Meredith's eyes flickered from Amelia, to me, and then down to her hands. "I should have quit long ago, but couldn't bring myself to do it."

"If it's not about the abuse," I asked Amelia. "Then what? Stewie?"

Amelia shook her head, eyes never leaving Meredith. "It wasn't for love, that's for sure," she said. "That really only leaves one reason why you'd want to do Mr. Fuller harm." She paused for dramatic effect, and then said, "Money."

The hidden stash. Meredith had admitted to hearing about it. Others have mentioned it. And while money was an awfully good motive for murder, I'd never gotten the impression that Meredith was all that concerned about it.

Then again, she *was* at the house the last time I was there. Just because she told me she was there for Stewie, didn't necessarily make it true. The dog could have been secondary, a convenient excuse.

But if she was after the stash, why tell me about it?

Amelia pressed on. "You're about to lose the house, aren't you, Ms. Hopewell?"

Meredith ran a hand over her mouth, and then nodded. "I am."

I was flabbergasted as I stared at Amelia like I'd never seen her before. "How did you know that?"

She ignored me. "You heard Mr. Fuller had money stowed away, and wanted some for yourself, isn't that right?"

Meredith visibly flinched at the question. "It wasn't fair," she said, meeting my eye, instead of Amelia's, like she thought I might be more sympathetic. "He had money, but refused to think about anyone but himself and his dog. I asked him for a little, just to help pay the bills, but he laughed in my face."

"I have it on good authority that he planned on leaving all his assets to Stewie, which in turn, would mean everything would go to his dog's new owner." Amelia tapped her pen on her pad of paper. "That meant, no one else was going to get a thing. Not you. Not his family. Not unless one of you took legitimate possession of the dog, isn't that correct?"

"It is," Meredith said. She sounded sick by the idea. "I was there when he wrote the provisions into his will. Whatever was left after funeral costs was supposed to go to the dog. Can you believe it? A dog!" Her eyes went hard, and for the first time, I saw a woman capable of murder. "I thought I deserved a share of it, after everything he put me through, but there was no way I was going to get it through the legal system. He'd never allow me to adopt Stewie, even though I was the one who fed him, cleaned up after him, for the last couple of years."

"So, since he wouldn't allow it himself, and since you knew the dog would soon be adopted out, you had to do something," Amelia said.

"There wasn't much I could do," Meredith said. "I tried to find the money. Whenever he'd go to sleep, I'd look around. I had to have checked every corner of that house, but I never found it. And then, when Junior arrived with that wife of his, I knew he was after the same thing. Junior is more like his dad than he'll ever admit. He only cared about what he could get out of the old man before he passed. Trust me, there was no love between those two."

I stood just inside the room, seemingly forgotten, mouth hanging open like I was hoping to catch flies. Where had Amelia gotten all of this information? I wasn't even sure the police knew all of this.

"Junior demanded Timothy tell him where the money was," Meredith went on. "We all knew he had it, but Tim steadfastly denied it. He said he'd spent it all years ago, and when Junior tried to force him to tell him, he only laughed."

"They fought?" Amelia asked.

"All the time. I don't think there was a moment where the two of them weren't at one another's throats. The day Timothy died was the worst. I thought Junior was going to strangle him right then and there, but instead, he stormed out of the house and drove off. When he was gone, Timothy took out his frustrations on me."

Which corroborated a big part of Duke's story. I was relieved he seemed to have told the truth, though there were still questions about why Courtney wanted the dog so badly.

"I never killed him," Meredith said, looking from face to face. "You have to believe me. A part of me wishes I had because of all the misery he'd put me through. I never got an extra dime from that man, and now, it looks like I never will." Her head dropped, tears forming in her eyes. I couldn't tell if they were sad tears, or angry ones. "I don't know what I'm going to do."

"Who else knew about the money?" I asked.

Meredith shook her head. "I don't know. It doesn't really matter, does it?" She stood. "Please, I'd like you to go now." She walked to the door without waiting for a response.

Amelia and I shared a look before following after her. As soon as we were outside, Meredith closed the door and locked it. I had a feeling she wouldn't answer if we were to knock.

Amelia stormed over to her car. I followed her, trying to figure out how it all pieced together. I knew in my heart Ben was innocent, but I also believed Meredith when she said she didn't kill Timothy. So, who did that leave?

Junior and Alexis were the most likely of suspects. They had motive, and opportunity. Just because they made a show of leaving, didn't mean they'd gone far. They could have pulled off the road a short distance away, and walked back to the house. Junior could have followed Timothy to the barn, killed him, and then fled.

It still didn't fully explain Ben's role, and why he was seen going into the house and then fleeing a few minutes later. That was something I hoped to work out soon.

"Satisfied?" Amelia asked. She was standing with her car door open, glaring at me.

"About?" I asked.

"That I'm not making some huge mistake? That maybe, just maybe, I know what I'm doing?"

"No, I'm not," I said, matching her defiance with my own. "I saw you with an older man and I think I deserve to know who he is."

"Mom!" She made a frustrated sound. "I have a life, you know? I don't need you poking around in it."

"I wasn't poking around," I said. "I was talking with Duke when I happened to see you with a stranger."

"And you just so happened to follow me here afterward?"

"I was concerned."

"Right." She snorted, looked away.

After all I'd been through, I was in no mood for her attitude, as justified as it might be.

"Go home," I told her. "Don't make any stops, don't make any calls."

"Mom!"

"No, Amelia, go. We need to have a little talk tonight. I can't have you getting involved in this murder investigation, not when Ben's life is at stake."

"Even if it helps?"

"Even then," I said, though after hearing what Meredith had to say, I was kind glad she had. And in all honesty, I was a little proud of her.

"I can't believe this," Amelia huffed and tossed her notebook into the passenger seat.

"Go home," I repeated, just in case she was thinking of defying me. "I'll be there soon. We'll talk, okay?" I touched her on the hand to show her I wasn't truly mad at her, just worried.

She didn't get the message.

Amelia jerked her hand away and then threw herself into her car. She didn't even look at me as she backed out and turned toward home. I hoped she was actually heading that way, and not toward another murder suspect.

Honestly, I didn't blame her for being mad at me. A part of me hated myself for snooping, even if I felt it was justified. Ben was in trouble, and I didn't want anything to happen to Amelia. I couldn't lose both of them.

Still, I felt like a horrible parent, and a bad person, as I trudged my way to my van. She might hate me now, but I was sure I could get through to her once we talked. Maybe if I brought home some ice cream, we'd get through it without a fight.

But first things first . . .

I climbed into the van and pulled out my cell phone. I didn't know what all Detective Cavanaugh knew about Meredith's financial situation, or the money Timothy was rumored to have socked away, but I was going to fill him in. He might not like it that I'd been talking to people, but I had a feeling he'd appreciate the information.

"Grey Falls Police Department, Officer Mohr speaking."

"Hi, Officer, I'd like to speak to Detective Cavanaugh. Is he in?"

"Sorry, ma'am, he's not here. I can pass on your message and have him get back to you." He paused, seemed to realize this might not be a courtesy call. "Unless it's an emergency. I can help you if that's the case."

"Can I get his number?" I asked, frowning. He'd given me his card after we'd talked at the station, but I had no idea what I'd done with it. "It's Liz Denton." I didn't know if Officer Mohr remembered me, but figured having my name couldn't hurt. "I might have some information on the Timothy Fuller murder."

"Oh!" Officer Mohr said. "I remember you now. Like I said, Detective Cavanaugh isn't in. In fact, he's currently out on a call regarding the case. If you're calling about what happened at Mr. Fuller's home, then we already know."

"Something happened at Timothy's house?" I asked. "Other than his murder?"

"I can't say," he said. "I'll let Detective Cavanaugh know—"

I clicked off and started the van.

Something had happened at Timothy's house, something that could very well have to do with the murder. Detective Cavanaugh was currently there, dealing with it. Since I was only five minutes away, there really was no harm in stopping by.

Or, at least, that's what I told myself as I put the van into gear and headed that way.

15

Detective Cavanaugh's car sat behind Junior's own in Timothy Fuller's driveway. Clarence was back, rocking on his front porch, watching on with his coffee mug in hand. He waved as I got out of my car. I returned the gesture, but my attention was mostly focused on the house.

From the front, it didn't appear as if anything was wrong. I took it as a good sign that an ambulance wasn't here, and I was pretty sure if it had been earlier, I would have heard it speed away at some point since Meredith lived so close.

Unless someone was dead. An ambulance wouldn't need to run hot in that case.

I glanced over at Selena's house as I approached Timothy's front door. If she was home, she wasn't outside. I didn't see a car beneath the carport either.

I knocked on the door, mentally preparing for the worst. Someone had already died on the property once. I wouldn't be surprised if it had happened again, especially since it was looking more and more like money was involved. *Please don't let it be someone I know.*

At my feet, the ceramic Pomeranian still stood watch. I was afraid this was as close as I was ever going to get to Stewie again. The thought didn't help my mood.

The door opened, and a perplexed Detective Cavanaugh peered out at me. "Mrs. Denton? What are you doing here?"

"I was looking for you," I said, trying to see past him, into the house. He shifted so his massive frame blocked off my view entirely.

He looked skeptical when he asked, "Why?"

On the way over, I was certain what I had to say would be of dire importance to the case. Now that I was standing there in front of the detective, I wasn't so sure. What if he arrested me for interfering? What if he went after Amelia? And the more I thought about it, the more certain I became that he likely knew everything already.

Before I could come up with something to say, Junior pushed past the burly detective and shoved a finger in my face. "You!" he shouted. "You did this, didn't you?"

"Did what?" I asked.

Junior barked a laugh, looked to the sky. "How convenient for you. You just show up here, acting innocent, when we all know the real reason you're here."

I looked past the clearly irate Junior, to Detective Cavanaugh. "I honestly don't know what he's talking about."

"You'd better come inside," Cavanaugh said. "Mr.

Fuller, please." He placed a hand on Junior's shoulder, and steered him back into the house. Junior complained the entire way, but at least he went.

I followed them inside, but only made it a few steps before I came to a shocked halt just inside the door.

The house was a disaster.

The couch cushions were shredded, as if by a wild animal, as was the couch itself. Anything and everything that could be moved, had been. Even the expensive medical equipment, which I imagined would be going back to a hospital somewhere once the investigation was over, had been opened, electronic parts scattered about the room.

I took another step inside. Peering past Cavanaugh and Junior, I could see the kitchen was in much the same condition as the living room. Alexis stood, bent over, in front of the oven, looking inside. The racks had been pulled free and lay on the floor next to her. Cupboards were open, contents spilled out onto the counter and floor.

"What happened?" I asked, stepping carefully over a broken vase.

"As if you don't know," Junior spat.

"Someone broke into the residence," Detective Cavanaugh said. I noted his hand was still on Junior's arm, keeping him from leaping at me again. "The back door was jimmied open. They went through the kitchen and living room, but it doesn't appear as if they made it any farther."

Did that mean they'd found what they were looking for? Or had Junior surprised them?

"Who would do something like this?" I asked.

"We don't know yet," Cavanaugh said, cutting off Junior's protests before he could get started. "There doesn't seem to be much in the way of evidence. And with the mess, it's hard to tell if something is missing."

"She did it," Junior said. "Why else would she be here? She's covering her tracks!"

"I'm doing no such thing," I said, as much for Cavanaugh's benefit as Junior's. "I wouldn't have known anything was wrong if I hadn't called the police station looking for you." I looked to the detective, hoping he believed me.

"She's a liar!" Junior shouted, jerking his arm free. He paced toward the kitchen, where Alexis joined him, before he spun back around. "It wasn't enough that your brat *murdered* Dad, but you had to go and do *this!*"

"Ben didn't do anything," I said through clenched teeth. "Neither did I."

"So says you," Junior said. "You only care about ruining my life."

"I didn't even know you until yesterday!"

"Right. You conveniently show up whenever I'm around, causing problems for me and my family. What did I ever do to you?"

"Other than accuse me of crimes I didn't commit? I don't know, what could it be?"

"That's enough!" Detective Cavanaugh shouted, face going red. "The both of you need to calm down and keep your mouths shut. Throwing accusations around will get us nowhere."

Junior crossed his arms as Alexis put an arm around him and pressed her head against his temple. I clenched my teeth closed, lest I say something and get myself into more trouble. Junior was hitting every last nerve I had.

"You two, wait for me in the kitchen," Cavanaugh said, pointing at Junior and his wife.

"But . . ."

The detective narrowed his eyes. Smartly, Junior cut his protest short and stormed into the kitchen, Alexis in his wake.

Cavanaugh turned to me. "Care to explain to me exactly why you're here? And don't give me no bull about just showing up, clueless. You have no reason to be out this way."

"I didn't know anyone broke in," I said, feeling the need to defend myself first. "I was with Duke Billings earlier, and then was with my daughter afterward." I thought it wise not to bring up Meredith just yet lest Cavanaugh blow up at me. "They can vouch for my whereabouts over the last few hours."

"Good. I'll talk to them. It still doesn't explain why you're here now."

"I told you; I needed to talk to you."

"Okay then, talk."

Suddenly, I wasn't so keen on spilling my guts to the detective. Maybe it had something to do with Junior in the other room. Maybe it had to do with the way the detective was glaring at me like I'd personally hired someone to sabotage his investigation. Either way, it took me a moment of hemming and hawing before I got to the point.

I kept my voice low as I filled him in on what I'd learned from Duke, about his return to the scene, just before Timothy's murder. I told him I'd talked to Meredith afterward, but I left out Amelia's involvement, not wanting Cavanaugh to come down hard on her.

He wasn't happy about it, but he motioned for me

to continue without much more than a warning look.

I told him about the possibility of Timothy's stash, about Meredith's money troubles. I told him about the fight between Junior and his dad, and even mentioned my theory that Junior could have come back to kill Timothy without anyone seeing.

Detective Cavanaugh listened attentively, if not with a scowl of disapproval on his face. When I finished, he didn't look impressed by the glut of information.

"That's all?" he asked.

"It is." I felt small, but refused to back down. "Junior had more of a reason to kill Timothy than Ben. Even Meredith had a better motive, not to mention opportunity." I hated throwing Meredith under the bus, but it was Ben's freedom we were talking about.

"They might have," Detective Cavanaugh allowed. "But that's for me to decide, not you."

"It's not a crime to talk to people," I said. "Duke and I have known each other for years."

"And Ms. Hopewell?"

"We've had occasion to speak," I said, face growing hot.

"Mr. Fuller says you've been coming around, hounding him about his father's property," Cavanaugh said.

"I have not!" I looked past him to find Junior inside the kitchen, watching us. "I came here looking for Stewie, and that's all."

"He said you forced your way into the house yesterday."

My blush deepened. "I might have come in without knocking," I said. "But I had reason! I heard shouting and thought someone might be hurt."

"And were they?"

"Well, no," I admitted. "But he had Stewie cornered. The poor dog was barking his head off, and was scared out of his mind. I don't think Junior knows how to handle him, yet he insists on taking him, despite his father's wishes."

Cavanaugh's sigh sounded frustrated. "I can't have you running around town, causing trouble, Mrs. Denton," he said. He held up a hand, cutting me off before I could speak. "I understand that it's your son who currently has his feet to the fire. I also understand you are worried about the dog's well-being. But you have to let me do my job. I can't do that if every time I turn around, someone is calling me about you."

"Someone called you about me?"

His eyes narrowed.

"All right, I'm sorry." I lowered my gaze. He was right. If I kept getting in the way, it wouldn't help Ben's cause. Cavanaugh *was* a police detective. Finding murderers was his job.

"Can I at least see Stewie?" I asked. "I want to make sure he's okay. The stress has to be getting to him."

Cavanaugh motioned for Junior to join us. "Where's the dog?" he asked him.

"What dog?" Junior asked, acting as if he had no idea what I was talking about. Alexis came up to stand next to him, looking confused, as if even she was at a complete loss.

"Stewie," I said, keeping my voice as level as I could manage. The man was infuriating. "Timothy's Pomeranian."

Junior rolled his eyes. "He's fine."

"Fine where?" I asked. "Did you leave him alone?

Or is someone watching him? You do know he'll need to go out. And you can't leave him without fresh food and water." I wouldn't put it past Junior to leave him locked up and alone, in a small cage, only letting him out once or twice, and even then, only when necessary.

"I said, he's fine," Junior said, and then, to Detective Cavanaugh. "Could you please get her out of here? I'm tired of humoring the woman who obviously broke in and ransacked the place. She was likely trying to steal the dog out from under me."

I groaned audibly. "I didn't break in! And even if I had, why would I look for Stewie in the cupboards? You aren't making sense."

"Who knows what goes through the heads of people like you."

My fists clenched and I might have done something stupid, but then I remembered Clarence, sitting across the street, where he seemingly always was.

"I might have proof," I said, hoping I wasn't going to make a fool out of myself.

"Proof?" Detective Cavanaugh asked. He looked ready to leap at any opportunity to settle the matter. "Proof of what?"

"That I had nothing to do with any of this," I said. "The guy across the street, Clarence. He was outside when I pulled up. He might have seen who broke in."

"They came in through the back door," Cavanaugh pointed out.

"But whoever it was might have driven by," I said. "And even if he didn't see who broke in, he can tell you that he didn't see my van until I just pulled up a few minutes ago. You've seen it. It's kind of hard to miss."

Junior didn't look like he cared whether or not Clarence could prove my innocence, but didn't protest when Cavanaugh started for the door.

"Then we'll go talk to him," the detective said.

All four of us trooped across the street, to where Clarence was still sitting. The old man continued to rock, seemingly unconcerned as we approached.

"Good afternoon to you, Detective," he said. "I'd offer you some coffee, but I'm fresh out." He showed us his empty mug. "Didn't expect guests or I'd have made more."

"That's all right, Mr. Ellison," Cavanaugh said, taking the lead. "We'll only take a moment of your time."

Clarence merely nodded. "I figured you might come see me," he said. "Could hear the ruckus even from here. It's been wild around here lately. Not sure if I remember it ever being this crazy." He shook his head, but was smiling as he did so. "What is it I can do for you, Detective?" His gaze moved my way. "Mrs. Liz."

I didn't fail to note how he completely ignored Junior and Alexis. By Junior's scowl, I doubted he missed it either.

"Do you recall seeing anyone enter Mr. Denton's house today?" Cavanaugh asked. "Or seen someone poking around where they shouldn't be? A strange car driving slowly by, perhaps?"

"Today?" Clarence asked. "I don't recall seeing anyone today until you lot showed up."

"What about late last night?" Cavanaugh asked.

"I'm an old man, Detective. Bedtime comes early for me. If someone was there past dark, I was too busy counting sheep to notice."

"Did you hear anything?" I asked, earning me a

sharp look from Cavanaugh. But at least he listened for an answer.

"There might have been a few thumps earlier this morning," Clarence said, nodding slowly in remembrance. "I can't say for sure if it came from the house, but I do recall hearing something. Didn't pay it no mind, though. Did something happen?"

Cavanaugh ignored the question. "What about Mrs. Denton here," he asked. "Did you see her today?"

Clarence gave me a fond smile. "Mrs. Liz came and visited me yesterday," he said. "Saw her a little later, but she didn't do nothing wrong."

"Today?" Cavanaugh asked.

"Not seen hide nor hair of her, until now."

"Liar," Junior muttered under his breath.

We all ignored him.

"Thank you for your time, Mr. Ellison. If you think of anything else, you have my card."

"I do." He patted his shirt pocket, as if it was there. "I hope you figure this thing out, Detective. I miss the quiet."

We returned to Timothy's driveway a few minutes later.

"Satisfied?" I asked Junior, unable to stop myself.

He snorted, looked away.

"I'm not," Cavanaugh said. "You shouldn't be snooping around, talking to witnesses."

"I'm sorry," I said. "I wasn't snooping." Well, I suppose technically I was, but I didn't think of it that way. "He's the one who saw Ben that day. I wanted to hear exactly what it was he saw, straight from him."

"I understand why you did it," Cavanaugh said. "But you need to understand my position. If you were to threaten or attempt to coerce him . . ."

"I'd never do such a thing." I took a calming

breath, stifling the urge to argue, before going on. "I won't come back," I said. "Not unless Junior is ready to give up Stewie, who by rights, belongs to me."

"Hasn't the poor doggie suffered enough," Alexis asked, speaking for the first time since I'd been there.

Before I could retort, Cavanaugh held up both hands, silencing everyone.

"You," he said, looking to me. "Go home. If I need to follow up on anything you told me, I'll call you."

I ground my teeth as I nodded.

"And you two," Cavanaugh said, turning on Junior. "If the dog belongs with her, I expect you to get it to her in the next day or so. I don't need this petty argument fouling up my investigation."

Junior looked as if he wanted to argue, but surprisingly, simply nodded.

"I'm going to do my job here, talk to a few people, and by tomorrow, I want your differences worked out. I'm tired of the arguing. A man is dead. Your *father* is dead," he said, staring hard at Junior. "I expect everyone to act with a modicum of respect."

Everyone lowered their gazes in shame. Well, everyone but Cavanaugh, who was in the right, as much as I hated to admit it.

He huffed, turned to Junior. "Now, let's go inside and see if we can figure out if something is missing."

Dismissed, I returned to my van. I felt ashamed, and rightfully so. During all of this, I was too concerned about Ben, about making sure he got out of this okay, without ever really considering others who were affected by Timothy's death.

Junior wasn't a nice man, just like his dad. But that didn't mean he didn't have feelings. As far as I knew, he was hurting inside, which in turn, was causing him to lash out at everyone around him. Alexis might be the only thing keeping him from completely losing it.

As I started up the van, I caught movement at the door. I looked up to find Junior glaring at me, murder in his eye.

Quite suddenly, I no longer felt bad for him.

He slammed the door hard enough to rattle the frame, which I hoped earned him a firm reprimand from the detective, but I wasn't counting on it.

"Jerk," I muttered. And then, thinking of how I'd treated Amelia, I amended the comment to include myself.

I backed out of Timothy's driveway, and turned toward home. It was time to make things right with my daughter.

16

Loud electronic music was playing in Amelia's room when I got home. I approached the door, but reconsidered. She was mad, and rightfully so. While I wanted to talk to her about what had happened, it would probably be best if I gave her more time to calm down. I didn't want a fight. I was pretty sure she didn't either.

I backed away from the door and retreated back downstairs. Okay, so maybe I wasn't quite ready to talk yet either.

So, instead of having what would inevitably be a heated conversation, I decided to clean the room Toby and Leroy had recently occupied in preparation for Stewie's upcoming stay.

There wasn't a lot to do since the two older dogs hadn't been too messy. The room did smell like beagle, but a quick mop of the floor and wash of the bedding, and you'd never know they'd been there.

I took my time, relishing the smell of cleaner. The

floor, the blankets and pillows, all got deep cleaned. Even the food and water dishes got a thorough scrubbing. It took a good two hours for me to be satisfied, and by the time I was done, my back was barking and I had the beginnings of a headache. But at least the room smelled fresh, without a hint of dog.

Amelia was waiting for me at the dining room table when I left the room, carrying a bucket of dirty water. I took it to the bathroom, dumped it, and then stowed the bucket in the laundry room before joining her.

"Wheels needs some food," she said. The cat in question was sitting at her side, purring. "I put the last in her dish when I got home."

"All right. I'll get it in a little while," I said, sitting down across from her with a groan. I rubbed at my back, once more missing Ben to no end. He usually helped with the cleaning.

Amelia stared at me, chewing her lower lip. There was still defiance in her eye, but she didn't seem angry anymore. That was good. In the shape I was in, I wasn't looking forward to an argument.

"I filled the police in," I said, taking the lead. "Detective Cavanaugh listened, but I think he already knew about Meredith's money issues and Timothy Fuller's hidden cash. If he didn't, he does now, and I think he'll look into it."

"Good." Amelia dropped her eyes briefly before meeting mine again. "He seemed like he knew what he was doing when he questioned me."

A flare of anger shot through me, but I suppressed it. *He was only doing his job.* Still, every time I thought about him going to her school to talk to her, it made me want to give him a piece of my mind.

"Someone broke into Timothy's house too," I said. "It looked like they were looking for something. The place was a disaster."

"Do you think whoever it was, was looking for the hidden money?"

"It's likely," I said. "Junior was pretty upset. He blamed me, saying I was trying to ruin him. That man has it in for me, and I don't even know why."

Amelia's brow furrowed as she thought it over. "We were with Ms. Hopewell right before that," she said.

"We were. But the break-in might have happened earlier. I don't think anyone was at the house until shortly before I showed up, so no one really knows when it happened. It wouldn't surprise me if the thief broke in last night." Which meant, just about everyone could be a suspect.

We both fell silent. Amelia seemed to be chewing over what I'd told her, while I was sitting there, waiting for her to tell me how she got involved in Ben's case. I understood *why* she did it, just not the how.

"Amelia, what's going on?" I asked her when it didn't appear as if she was going to speak on her own. "Why were you talking to Meredith?"

"I wanted to prove Ben's innocence. Ms. Hopewell seemed like a legitimate suspect, so I figured I'd press her and see what she had to say for herself."

"So, you decided to go alone?" I couldn't help it; my voice rose, more in panic than anger. "Amelia, if she was Timothy's killer, that meant you were walking into a bad situation with no backup. No one knew where you were."

"You were there." Bitterly.

"That was pure luck," I said. "If I hadn't seen you, you would have been all alone. What if something had happened? What if you were right and when you started asking questions, she decided to silence you?"

"Mom, I can handle myself."

"I know you can, Amelia, but you shouldn't have to. Why go alone when you could have called me? Or had one of your friends go with you?"

She reached down and ran a hand down Wheels's back. The cat's purr got louder. She rose from her place at Amelia's feet and paced back and forth, soaking up the attention. The wheels seemed loud in the silence.

"I want you to be safe," I said, calmly, lovingly. "Someone is out there right now, someone who killed a man. Nothing says they'll stop at just Timothy Fuller. Any one of us could be next." Not a comforting thought, but I hoped it proved my point.

"I know," she said. "But I thought that since it was about money, I'd be okay. I bet whoever killed him, didn't mean to do it."

"I'm not sure you can accidentally stab someone," I said. *Especially in the back.* "How did you even know about the money anyway?"

"I hear things," Amelia said, not meeting my eye.

"You hear things? Amelia . . ."

"What? I did a little research, asked around. It wasn't too hard."

I gaped at her. *Research? Asked around?* "Should you be doing that?" I asked.

She shrugged, and then gave me a crooked smile. "At least we're making progress, right?"

I wanted to tell her that *we* shouldn't be doing anything at all, but held my tongue. While Amelia had confronted only one person, I'd gone and talked to nearly everyone involved with Timothy Fuller or his dog, Stewie. It's kind of hard to yell at someone who was doing the same thing I was.

"Who is C. Chudzinski?" I asked, abruptly changing the subject.

Amelia's smile faded. "How do you know his name?"

"I saw it," I said. "I went into your room to see if you were there and it was on the shelf by the door."

"You were snooping?"

"No." Well, yes, but I didn't want to tell her that. "I saw the card with his name on it, and I'm curious about who he is. I just want to make sure I shouldn't be worried about him."

Amelia rolled her eyes. "Mom, you don't need to worry about me."

"Yes, Amelia, I do."

She heaved a sigh, jaw firming like she was going to sit there in stoic silence until the walls fell down around her ears. I'd run into her stubbornness more than once, and was willing to wait her out.

She seemed to realize the same. After only a few seconds, her shoulders sagged, and she looked down at her hands.

"He's just someone I know," she said.

"A boyfriend?"

"Ew, no. He's like three times my age."

"So, he's the man I saw you with earlier?"

She nodded. "I've met with him a few times. We were talking." She looked up, met my eye with a hard stare. "*Just* talking."

"Okay, you were talking. What about?"

"About Ben. About the case. He knows a lot about stuff like that."

"Does he now?" The skepticism was thick in my voice. It wouldn't be the first time an older man claimed to know things, just so he could attract a younger woman.

"Yes, he does," Amelia said. "He's a private investigator."

That stopped me short. "He's a what?"

"A private investigator," Amelia repeated. "He was a guest speaker in one of my classes a few months ago. I enjoyed his talk so much, I stayed after to talk to him about it. We've kept in touch since."

The worry that his motives weren't pure was back, but it was overwhelmed by my confusion. "You hired a private investigator for Ben?"

"No," Amelia said, sounding frustrated. She lifted both hands, dropped them heavily onto the table, before picking at her fingernails. "He's sort of my mentor."

"Mentor?" The confusion kept growing and growing. "What are you talking about, Amelia?"

She bit her lower lip, glanced up at me, looked away, and then looked up again. She was more than nervous; I could see the fear in her eyes, like she thought I was going to explode when she finally told me what was going on.

"Amelia," I said, keeping my voice level. "I'm not going to be mad." Or at least, I hoped not. "Just tell me why you're talking to a private investigator."

She took a few moments more to collect her thoughts. She licked her lips, rose, and grabbed a water from the fridge, before returning to her seat.

"Chester is a nice guy," she said, speaking slowly, and carefully, as if she was thinking through each word before she said it. "He's been in the business for a long time. I guess he's helped the police solve a few big cases in his time, though these days, he mostly does small-time stuff, like checking on cheating husbands and things like that."

I could imagine. There really wasn't a lot of major crime happening in Grey Falls. I was surprised we even had a private investigator at all, to be honest.

"So, he gave that talk I mentioned, telling us about some of his cases, how he worked them, what went wrong. Stuff like that. It was in my criminal justice class."

"You take criminal justice?"

She smiled. "I did. It was a really neat presentation and it sounded exciting, so I asked if we could talk about it some more sometime. We'd occasionally get together after class, but yesterday, we met early because he had somewhere to be that evening."

Which was why she'd left so early. There was nothing nefarious in it.

"But, why?" I asked, still confused.

"I like it," she said, growing excited as she spoke. "To piece things together, to find the clues, the patterns. It drew me the moment he started speaking. I'd been taking classes like that for a while, but it wasn't until he gave his talk that I realized it was what I wanted to do."

It took me a moment to realize what she meant. "You want to be a private investigator?"

She lowered her gaze, appeared embarrassed, or perhaps, ashamed. "That or a police detective."

I sat there, dumbly, for a good couple of minutes as I thought it through. This seemed to have come out of nowhere, yet it sounded as if she'd been thinking about it for a long time. Not only that, but she was passionate about it. I could see it in her eyes, by the sound of her voice. This was what she wanted to do with her life.

How could I have not known?

Because she never talked about it, that's why.

"Why didn't you tell me before now?" I asked.

"Because I thought you and Dad might be mad at me."

"Mad at you? Why would we be mad at you?"

She refused to look up as she spoke. "You and Dad and Ben are all involved with animals. You have the rescue. Dad's a veterinarian. Ben's probably going to be a vet too. I felt like I was letting you down by not following in your footsteps. You always ask me if I want to help out. Dad asks if I want to come in and help sometimes. I was afraid that saying no would make you hate me."

"Oh, honey, you aren't letting us down. And we definitely don't hate you. Actually, I'm proud of you."

"You are?" she asked, skeptically.

"I am." I stood and rounded the table to wrap her in a hug. She squirmed briefly before giving in and accepting it. "You've found your calling," I said, releasing her. "There's nothing wrong with that."

"Even if it means I don't help out much with the animals?"

"Even then," I said. "I'm happy if you're happy."

"I am."

"Then there's nothing to be angry about."

She didn't look entirely convinced, and we still
had to break the news to Manny, but I was pretty sure
he would be just as thrilled about her finally finding
a direction for her life as I was.

Of course, there was one caveat.

"As happy as I am for you, Amelia, I don't think
you should be looking into Ben's case."

"Why not?" she asked, stubbornly crossing her
arms.

"Because you are related to him. The police won't
be able to use whatever you bring them." Well, I'm
sure they could, but it would be with a healthy dose
of skepticism.

"If it's true, then they'd have to."

"Maybe," I said. "But it's risky."

She pouted, and I knew that no matter what I said,
she was going to do whatever she could to help Ben.
A warm, fuzzy feeling filled me then because I knew
I'd raised both my children right.

"What do you know about the case?" I asked, par-
tially giving in. I had to admit, I was curious as to
what she'd uncovered. And while I didn't want her
going to Detective Cavanaugh with anything she discovered, I had no problem doing it for her.

Amelia sat up, entire demeanor brightening. "Not
much, yet," she said. "But I've been working on it.
Chester says that these things take time sometimes, and
that you just have to keep pressing. I've only got bits and
pieces right now, but I'm sure I'll be able to use them
to get to the truth."

"Okay, tell me what you have."

"You know about the Ms. Hopewell thing. She's
short on cash, and might lose her house. If the ru-

mors of Mr. Fuller's money are true, then she had every motive in the world to go after it."

"But to kill him?"

"If he refused to give it to her, she might have gotten angry. Or she thought she could find the money before the house was sold. She just needed the old man out of the way, and opportunity to search the place. If she was the one who broke in, she could have done it last night, and then faked everything we saw today."

"And then there's Junior," I said. "When he showed up to care for his dad, he could have messed up her plans."

"Exactly," Amelia said. "And Timothy Jr. isn't exactly rolling in dough either."

"He's broke?"

"Mostly." She gave me a satisfied smile. "Apparently, his wife, Alexis, came from a rich family, who disowned her for marrying a man they believed beneath her. She has expensive tastes, and expects him to support her. Junior doesn't have that kind of money coming in."

"So, he thinks he can get his sick, dying dad to give it to him."

"But when he tries . . ."

"The old man says no."

"And with Ms. Hopewell already trying to find the money, Daddy would only get in the way."

I thought about it. Both of them were likely suspects, and if both of them were hurting for cash, it could very easily motivate them both. Meredith feels she's owed, as does Junior. They clash. And they're both on a time limit. Once Timothy is sent to the

home, the house would go up for sale, and if it sold
before they found the money, it might be lost forever. If he died, then the house would be stuck in
limbo until everything was sorted out.

But in that scenario, Timothy's death benefited Junior the most. Once Timothy was gone, Meredith
wouldn't have a reason to go back to the house. Junior could go through it at his leisure.

Did he hasten his father's demise along, just to be
rid of Meredith? And was that why the murder took
place in the barn? If it happened in the house, then
the place would be locked up as a crime scene, not to
mention searched. He couldn't afford to let anyone
else find the money, not with the stipulation in Timothy's will that everything should go to Stewie.

"Then, who went through the house?" I asked,
thinking we might be on to something. "The place
was trashed and Junior seemed pretty upset about it."

"Both Ms. Hopewell and Tim Jr. had reason to,"
Amelia said. "Though, at this point, I think Tim Jr. is
the more likely suspect."

"Junior called the cops," I said. "Why would he do
that if he was the one who wrecked the place?"

"Maybe he was trying to scare someone else off?"

Yeah, but who?

Amelia didn't know much else, but swore to me
she was on it. When she went to her room, presum-
ably to make a call to Chester Chudzinski, I let her go
with a warning to be careful. I wasn't going to stop
her from doing what she loved, but I also didn't want
her getting hurt.

But she *had* given me something to think about. It
was sounding more and more like Timothy had died

because of his secret stash—if it even existed. And if it did, was it now currently in possession of the man or woman who killed him? Or was it still tucked away, hidden in a house that would soon pass on to someone else who didn't even know it existed?

17

I spent the next hour waiting for a call that never came. I wasn't sure what I expected. It wasn't like Detective Cavanaugh had promised to tell me if he learned anything about who had broken into Timothy Fuller's house, yet a part of me hoped he would.

Amelia left thirty minutes into my wait, promising she wasn't going to get herself into any trouble, and that all she was going to do was study with a friend. I had a feeling that wasn't the entire truth, but I let it slide. If she was to somehow come up with Timothy's killer, it would save Ben. I was okay with that.

Eventually, I couldn't take it anymore. I gathered my purse, made sure my phone was charged and tucked away, and then headed out the door to do a little shopping.

Pets on Main was a locally owned pet store where I shopped for both Wheels, and the rescues, exclusively. Their prices were sometimes higher than what I could get at one of the chains, but I preferred to support smaller, locally owned businesses. And some of the local products they carried couldn't be found anywhere else.

As per its name, the pet store was located on Main Street, which ironically enough, wasn't actually downtown, or a main road. It was situated on the north end of town, in a shopping district that was beginning to bloom as more and more businesses came into Grey Falls. It was where the mall, and many of the restaurants—locally owned and chains—were located.

I pulled into the lot, which was shared with a car dealership. Most of the spaces were taken up by cars with price stickers in them. Before long, there wouldn't be anywhere for Pets on Main customers to park. Eventually, I feared it would force the owner, Jamison Crowley, to close up, or move. If he left, I didn't know where I'd get Wheels her food.

Pets on Main was a small, squat building that looked more like an old grocery store than a pet store. In fact, I believe it was once an Aldi that had moved to the other side of town. Only the name out front, and the dog houses that lined the sidewalk, indicated that it was, indeed, a pet store.

I parked close to the doors and went inside. Jamison wasn't at the counter, but I could see him stocking one of the shelves farther to the back. He often worked alone. Unmarried, and uninterested in relationships, he'd made Pets on Main his life's work. When he wasn't in, his only employee, Zack Traylor, was.

He looked up as I entered, and waved. I returned the gesture, and then picked up a basket. Jamison was in his early sixties, but looked far older. He'd survived a house fire when he was little, but he hadn't

gotten out unscathed. Half of his body had been se-
verely burnt, giving him a perpetually wrinkled ap-
pearance. Some found him frightening, but there
was nothing scary about Jamison Crowley.

I went down the cat food aisle and filled up on
Wheels's favorites. She got canned cat food twice a
day, dry as a snack. I would have cut down on the
canned, but due to health issues resulting from her
deformity, she needed the extra moisture in her
food. It would probably eventually cause her weight
problems, but for now, it kept her flowing regularly,
and that was what was important.

A meow from the end of the aisle caught my attention. Jamison kept six cages at the back of his store
where he kept rescues or shelter animals. Today, three
of the cages held kittens. The other three were empty,
which I took as a good sign.

I took a moment to reach through the cages to pet
the kittens. They mewled and batted at my fingers
playfully, looking as cute as could be. They wouldn't
last long. White, with black around their eyes, they
looked like cute little bandits. I'd be surprised if they
weren't gone by the end of the week.

Telling the kitties goodbye—and forcing myself to
walk away lest I buy one of them myself—I started to
head for the checkout, when I changed my mind and
veered off toward the dog food aisle.

I still had some food left over from when I took
care of Toby and Leroy, but thought it might be a
good idea to get something special for Stewie after
he'd suffered such a harrowing couple of days. I was
positive I'd eventually gain possession of the Pomeranian, and I wanted to ease the transition as much as possible.

I need to find out what he usually eats, I thought. The

best way to ensure the smoothest transition would be to make sure he got the same food, was fed at about the same time. And with a dog Stewie's age, his system was likely sensitive to anything new, so changing it up on him could have negative consequences.

Still, I could splurge and get him something, perhaps one of the expensive brands, just enough to make him feel wanted. Once I got the chance, I'd have to ask Meredith what Timothy usually fed the Pomeranian and pick some up for him.

I turned the corner, mind elsewhere, so I didn't see someone coming down the aisle until our baskets collided.

"I'm sorry," I said, hurriedly grabbing at a display I very nearly knocked over. "I didn't see you."

"Liz?" Courtney's hand fluttered near her mouth, before settling back onto the handle of her basket. "Fancy meeting you here."

"Courtney." Of all the people to run into, it had to be her. "It's a pet store. I practically live here."

Her basket was filled with tiny little cans of dog food, the kind meant for smaller dogs. You know, like Pomeranians. She noticed me looking and waved it off.

"I'm stocking up for an influx of puppies," she said. "Cute little things. Momma was a bad doggie and got out one day, and well, here they are."

"I see." Someone hadn't gotten the memo about spaying and neutering your pets. Even inside dogs should be fixed, lest something like this happen. "Given up on Stewie?"

"You can have your old dog," she said, making a face like the idea of the elderly Pomeranian sickened her. "I'm not interested in that anymore."

I couldn't help myself. "That's not what Duke said."

She froze. "Duke? What does he have to do with anything?"

"I talked to him earlier today," I said. "It was quite interesting." I stared at her, waiting for her to react, but she merely stared at me, so I continued. "He said you told him to sneak Stewie away from Timothy Fuller while you and I talked."

"Really?" The shock in her voice was clearly faked. "I don't know what you're talking about." Her eyes darted around the room, as if seeking an escape.

I wouldn't let her get away that easily. "He said you let him out just down the street. He never got the chance, though, did he? Murder kind of puts a kink in plans like that." Of course, the way Duke told it, he was walking away when Timothy Fuller died, so he hadn't seen or heard it happen. Still, it sounded better the way I said it.

Courtney laughed, though it was a nervous sound. "You can't really blame me for trying, now can you?" she said, surprising me by not denying it. "I mean, you butted in on my pickup, so it wasn't like I did something you wouldn't have done."

I bit back a protest. Arguing with Courtney about it again would be as helpful as a pooper scooper without a handle.

Besides, I believed her when she said she was no longer interested in the older dog. Puppies were definitely more her speed.

But it did make me wonder; why was she so interested in Stewie in the first place? I'd never known her to be interested in an animal she couldn't make a profit off of. An old dog, one who might have health issues, was definitely not easy to move.

"I've heard a rumor," I said, fishing. "About Timothy Fuller and a possible secret stash of money. Do you know anything about that?"

Her eyes widened briefly, before she looked away. "Really? I hadn't heard."

Really, indeed.

It kind of made sense. Courtney was always all about the money. She liked animals, sure, but wouldn't do anything that would cost her too much cash. If she heard about Stewie, and Timothy's money, maybe she thought she could get her hands on the cash at the same time as the dog.

It would also explain why Duke was so nervous about going back to the house. Was he told to not just get Stewie, but to find the money as well? Had he tried? Could he have gone in after Junior left, looked for the hidden stash, but was caught by an already upset Timothy? I didn't see Duke as a murderer, but if he panicked, who knew what could happen?

"Are you feeling all right, Liz? You look funny."

"Hmm?" I came back to the here and now. "I was just thinking."

She raised her eyebrows at me as if she was shocked I even knew *how* to think. *Like she's one to talk.*

"Are you sure you knew nothing about the money?" I asked, pressing her because I knew she was lying. The question was, why lie? Why not admit it and move on? At this point, it wasn't like she could get her hands on it.

"I'm sure." She stepped past me, though her basket jammed me hard in the ribs as she passed. I had a feeling it was on purpose. "If you'll excuse me, I've got to get home to prepare for the little guys."

She hurried to the checkout counter. Jamison was already there, waiting on her. Courtney glanced back at me twice while he rang her up, seemingly concerned, before she finally paid. When she left, she practically ran out the door.

I watched her go, wondering. I couldn't see Courtney as a killer, nor could I see Duke killing anyone. Yet, strange things happened when money was involved.

Yet, nothing in Duke's demeanor when I'd talked to him earlier told me he was lying. In fact, he seemed pretty calm about everything, all things considered. If he'd killed Timothy, I figured he would have acted more nervous, or tried to deflect.

But that didn't mean he, or Courtney, hadn't returned later, searching for the money. Could one of them have broken into the house last night?

It was something to think about.

"Is there anything more you need?" Jamison asked, raising his voice as if he'd already asked me once before.

"Yeah, sorry." I hurried down the dog food aisle, grabbed a couple cans of the expensive stuff, and then carried my basket to the checkout.

"I saw you talking to Ms. Shaw," Jamison said, ringing me up. "Didn't know you two were friends."

"We aren't really," I said. "But we kind of run in the same circles, thanks to our rescues."

"I see." He squinted at the register. One eye was milky, the other pinched. I worried that one day, he'd lose his vision entirely. I hoped that day was a long day in coming because I couldn't imagine not seeing him here. "Something strange about her today," he said. "She acted funny."

"I noticed."

"She's not normally so flustered." He glanced at me with his one good eye. "I think your conversation had something to do with that."

I shrugged and smiled, acting as if I had no idea what he was talking about.

But it did make me wonder. I'd gotten to Courtney, and I really hadn't said too much. In fact, all I really did was tell her stuff she already knew. No accusations, no threats.

And yet she was worried. What about? The money? The murder?

Or was there something else going on with her, something she knew I wasn't going to like?

I paid, bid Jamison a fond goodbye, and then got into my van. A part of me hated myself for even suspecting Duke or Courtney of any wrongdoing, but I couldn't help it. Someone had killed Timothy Fuller. And, as Jamison had said, Courtney was acting strangely. There was definitely something going on with her.

I was about to pull out of the lot, when I noticed a couple in the lot across the street. I crept up to the stop sign and stopped, watching them.

The two were laughing, which was innocent enough. It was the *who* that was the problem.

Selena was dressed in one of her short skirts and a shirt that bared her belly button. Jason was across from her, holding keys in the air, playing what looked like a game of keep away.

Selena reached for the keys and he pulled them back. She lunged again, pressing herself against him as she did. He took advantage, pressing his lips to hers, free hand finding the middle of her back, even as her fingers closed over the keys.

I fully expected her to pull back, shocked by his advances. I definitely didn't expect her to lean into it, but that's exactly what she did. They kissed for a good couple of seconds, the familiarity between them speaking of years together, not minutes. When they finally did part, she had the keys in hand, and together, they got into her car, still laughing.

Motherly instincts shouted at me to confront her. Ben was in trouble because of her. If he hadn't been drawn to her bikini-clad body, then he would have come with me to Courtney's and would likely be sitting beside me even now.

As she started the engine and pulled away, I simply sat there and watched them drive off. I shouldn't have been surprised she was already seeing someone. And just because she was cozy with Jason, it didn't mean she wasn't interested in Ben too. Not everyone was content with seeing one person. Some people—like Ben—reveled in playing the field. There was nothing wrong with a woman who liked to do the same, even if it might hurt my son.

Yeah, keep telling yourself that.

A horn honked behind me. I waved to whoever was there, and then pulled forward. I wouldn't confront Selena about Ben now, but I had a feeling that before this was over, she would leave me no choice.

18

The house was unbearably quiet. I was sitting on the couch, Wheels snoozing at my feet, trying my hardest to be patient. I could hear every tick of the clock, every groan of a board settling. If I continued to sit there, it was going to drive me crazy.

I stood and started pacing, careful not to disturb Wheels. How did other parents manage when their kids were in trouble? The waiting, the worrying, the anger. It was almost too much to bear. Manny was able to work, but I was positive he was as stressed as I was. Maybe that's what I needed. Work would occupy my mind.

But my work consisted of taking care of animals in need of homes. I was supposed to be taking in a certain Pomeranian, one that was currently in possession of a man who shouldn't be allowed *near* a dog, let alone own one.

The animals were my life, as were my family. Ben should be here with me now, not sitting in a cell. We should be playing with Stewie, keeping the dog's spirits up, before finally taking him to his furever home. How did things go so wrong?

Selena Shriver, that's how.

Anger simmered just below the surface. If she hadn't led Ben on, then none of this would have happened.

So, what did I know of Selena?

It was obvious she liked to garner attention by wearing skimpy outfits. Clarence had said she spent a lot of time in a bikini, and that was exactly what had drawn Ben's eye. If she'd put on some more clothes, would he have been as interested? Was it intentional? Had she seen Ben, decided to flirt, and put on the bikini to draw him over? Or was it by pure luck she happened to be standing outside as we were about to leave?

I didn't know, and wouldn't know, not unless I asked Selena about her motives.

What else did I know about her? By all appearances, she was dating Jason Maxwell. She'd insisted they were just friends, but I'd never kissed a friend like that.

But if they were dating, why hadn't he corrected her when she told me there was nothing between them? Was I overreacting? Was there something else going on between them, some new dating fad I didn't understand? It wouldn't be the first time I showed my age when it came to dating.

The biggest problem I was facing was that I didn't have all the information. Who was Selena really? Why did she live alone in that house at such a young age? I could see her in an apartment, or perhaps living with some friends, but alone? You never saw that.

I grabbed my phone and dialed, thinking I might know someone who could tell me something about Selena.

It rang twice before a distracted answer of, "Hello?"

"Hi, Deidra," I said. "It's Liz. I'm sorry if I'm bothering you."

"Liz? Hey! No, I just wasn't expecting a call. Is everything okay? Nothing else happened to Ben, did it?"

"No, nothing like that," I said. "Ben's still in jail, but I'm hoping you might have some information that might help him."

"Me?" Deidra asked. "I'm not sure I can help, but I'll try. What do you need to know?"

I took a deep, relieved breath. I didn't know why, but a part of me was afraid she'd shoot me down on the spot.

Then again, she didn't know what I was about to ask either.

"I was wondering if I could ask you a question about a girl you might have had in class a few years back."

"Sure," she said, sounding both wary and intrigued. Deidra was a high school teacher who rarely liked to talk about her students outside of class. "Which student are we talking about?"

"Do you remember someone named Selena Shriver?" I asked. "This would have been a few years ago, maybe five or six." I wasn't even sure Selena went to Grey Falls High, but it couldn't hurt to ask.

"Selena Shriver . . ." I could almost see her tapping her lip with her finger as she thought about it. "Oh, yeah, I remember Selena," Deidra said. "I never had her in class, but I saw her around. Her mom is a pretty big deal at the school. The family has money, and they're not shy about throwing it at anyone who gives them what they want."

Which would explain why such a young woman had a house all to herself.

"What can you tell me about her?" I asked. "Selena, not her mom."

"Well, she was pretty popular back then. She hung around all the pretty, rich kids." Deidra chuckled. "You know how it is. It wasn't quite a mean girls clique, but it was darned close. They pretty much ruled the school, and since the Shrivers donated so much money, she could get away with practically anything she wanted. Gotta love the politics."

"Did Selena have a boyfriend?"

"Sure. I can't remember his name though. Girls like Selena always have guys chasing after them. It would be an interesting study. You see all these pretty girls getting all the attention in high school, but what about afterward? How many of them get chewed up once they're out in the real world and looks and popularity no longer matter as much?"

"I don't know. It would be interesting to find out," I said, mostly to humor her. Deidra loved to debate that sort of thing. "Does the name Jason Maxwell ring a bell?"

"I think so. If that's who she's seeing now, then that's likely the same guy she was seeing in high school."

"Why do you say that?"

"Jen—that's Selena's mom—always talked about how faithful her daughter was. I don't think she much liked Selena's boyfriend, but from what I gather, there were plans for a wedding. I'm not sure if they actually got married, or if it's on hold, but the way I heard it, it's inevitable."

"Really?" Then why had she invited Ben over? And why didn't she just come out and tell me she and Jason were dating? If the marriage was still on, then it made her actions seem that much more sinister and calculated.

"As far as I know, that's the case. I remember a lot of guys hanging around Selena, but only one that ever got close to her. It might be Jason, it might be someone else. You know how things change once high school ends. And it wasn't like I paid too much attention to the kids' social lives, you know? If it wasn't for Jen, I probably wouldn't even remember Selena dating anyone at all."

"I see." If Selena *had* been seeing Jason as far back as high school, and if she was indeed planning on marrying him, then something was definitely not right with her story. I'd brought Ben up, right in front of Jason, and he hadn't batted an eye. If he felt Ben was a threat, he gave no indication. In fact, it was like he didn't care one way or the other who Selena was spending her time with.

Did that mean the relationship had faded and they really were just friends? It happened from time to time, though it was pretty rare for people who were considering getting married to call it off and then continue to spend time with one another like nothing had happened between them. And then there was that kiss . . .

"What's this about, Liz?" Deidra asked. "I didn't even know you knew the Shrivers."

"I don't, really," I said. And then, not wanting to drag Deidra into it any more than I already had, "I bumped into her and Jason and was curious to know more about them."

"I see. Well, I'm glad I could help." I could tell she didn't buy my admittedly weak explanation. But thankfully, she didn't press.

"I'd better go," I said. "I'll talk to you later."

"Okay. You'd better fill me in when you do. This sounds as if it could be an interesting story."

"I'll do that," I said. "If anything comes of it, you'll be the first person I call."

"I'd better be."

I hung up and tapped my phone thoughtfully against my chin. Selena was Timothy Fuller's neighbor. She might have heard the rumor about the old man's hidden stash. If that was the case, could she have planned to steal it for herself?

I wasn't sure how she'd pull such a thing off with Ben right there, or why she'd even drag him into it in the first place. It also didn't explain why Clarence saw Ben going into Timothy's house, and then fleeing back to Selena's place a few minutes later. I was definitely missing something here.

And there was likely only one way I'd get the answers I needed.

I grabbed my keys and headed for the door. Selena might not want to talk, but darn it, I wasn't going to let her be the reason my son ended up in jail.

I jerked open the door and was forced to duck back when a fist came flying for my face.

Courtney yelped as she nearly went over on top of

me. She staggered, letting go of the storm door, and placing both hands—thankfully open—on my shoulders to steady herself.

"Oh, I'm so sorry, Liz," she said, pulling back and wiping her hands on her clothing. "I wasn't expecting you to open the door on me like that. You startled me."

"It's okay," I said, heart resuming a more natural pace. There's nothing like nearly getting punched in the mouth to get your blood pumping. What was Courtney trying to do? Knock the door down when she knocked? "What are you doing here, Courtney?"

She glanced back toward her van, which was parked right beside mine. I half expected to find Duke sitting in the passenger seat, but no one else was inside as far as I could see.

"I wanted to talk to you for a few minutes," she said, gaze moving past me, into the house. "Alone, if possible."

I really didn't want Courtney in my house, especially after seeing the perfection of her own place. I mean, my house wasn't a pigsty, but it wasn't all that clean either. With Ben's incarceration, and the fight with Junior over Stewie, I hadn't been keeping up with the sweeping. Neither had Manny or Amelia, for that matter.

"It's about the money," Courtney added.

"Fine," I said, stepping aside. "But make it quick. I have somewhere to be."

Courtney stepped past me and immediately started nosing around. She looked appalled by the fur on the floor, and especially by Wheels, who'd woken and was zooming around the dining room, chasing after a catnip mouse. When Courtney finally moved farther into the house, she moved gently, like she was afraid she might step in something.

"What do you want, Courtney?" I asked, letting my impatience show.

She reached into her purse and extracted lip balm, which she applied before speaking. "As I said, I wanted to talk to you about the money, and figured it best if we get it out of the way now."

"What money?" I asked, though I had a good idea what she was talking about.

"Timothy Fuller's money," she said. "We talked about it earlier today."

"You said you knew nothing about it." I crossed my arms over my chest, but managed to keep myself from tapping my foot or raising my voice in accusation.

"I know," she said, shoulders slumping as she shoved the balm back into her purse. "You caught me off guard and I wasn't quite sure how to handle the situation."

"You could have told the truth."

She laughed, as if I was joking. I wasn't.

"Courtney, a man died," I said, not so much as cracking a smile. "And Ben's in jail, falsely accused of murdering him. I have a feeling that Timothy's money might be the reason he was killed, so if you know something, then spit it out."

Her laughter died away, as did her smile. She looked ashamed, and a whole lot worried.

"I don't really know anything," she said. "I admit; I knew about the money, had known for some time. It was why I went after Chewy when I did."

I didn't bother correcting her. "How did you expect to get the cash?" I asked. "Did you think Timothy would give it to you out of the goodness of his heart?"

"Well, no." Her face reddened, and I realized that was exactly what she'd thought. "I didn't think there was any reason not to try. I mean, it wasn't like he was going to need it any longer, you know? What harm was there in asking?"

"He died. I'd say there was a whole lot of harm in it."

"I didn't kill him!" Courtney's eyes went wide, and she took a step toward me, like she might grab hold of me to plead her case. "After I left with you, I never went back to that house, I swear."

"But you sent Duke back."

"I did," she admitted. "He was supposed to get Chewy and take a look around, but he never made it inside the house. And I never did get a chance to ask Timothy about the money either. The entire thing was a disaster!"

"Did you send Duke back later?" I asked, remembering the state of the house the last time I'd seen it. "Someone broke into Timothy's house."

"Of course not," Courtney said, sounding appalled. "By then, I'd completely given up on it." She took another step toward me and lowered her voice. "But then, after I talked to you, I got to thinking."

I refrained from making a joke about how rarely she thought about anything. "About?" I asked.

"You knew about the money, and from what I've heard, you've been back to the house quite a few times now."

"I was trying to find out what really happened to

Timothy Fuller so I could help Ben," I said. "I wasn't looking for money."

"I'm sure you weren't." She winked. "Did you find it?"

"Find what?"

"The money." She glanced around the room as if she expected someone to be hiding behind the couch, listening to our conversation. "If you found it, we could split it."

I gave her an incredulous stare. "We can what?"

"Split it. Fifty-fifty. I won't tell anyone about it, and you can use your half to pay someone to help your son. It's a win-win for the both of us."

I stood there, mouth agape, not quite sure what to say. I wasn't the least bit surprised Courtney had known about the money, and I wasn't really all that shocked she'd be willing to take it, but to think I would have stolen it and would share it with her? She must be insane.

"Liz, I know you could use the cash." She made a face, eyes darting around the room in disgust. "So, I don't hold it against you for taking it. But since we were both there, and were both looking out for the best interest of Chewy . . ."

I held up a hand stopping her. "It's Stewie," I said. "With an *S*."

"Whatever."

"And I never took the money," I said. "I haven't looked for it, don't care to. If it belongs to anyone, it belongs to Junior." Even with as little as he deserved it.

"I promise not to tell."

"Courtney!" It was all I could do to keep from screaming at her. "I don't have it. Someone else ransacked the place, so if anyone has it, it's likely that person."

She pouted, before she stepped back and brushed at her shirt, which had attracted a few stray hairs from Wheels. "Well, then," she said. "I don't even know why I came over."

Neither do I, I thought, but kept it to myself. "I'm sorry, Courtney, but even if I did find the money, I wouldn't be keeping it. It's not mine."

"Uh-huh." She huffed. "Well, if it does somehow magically fall into your hands, let me know. I'm sure we could work something out."

I should have continued to argue, but what was the point? No matter what I said, Courtney would still think she deserved a share. I wasn't even sure the stash existed, yet it appeared everyone in town was interested in it. Was I the only person who hadn't known that Timothy might be secretly loaded?

"If I find it, I'll let you know," I told her, just to make her go away.

Courtney nodded once, glanced around my place one more time, and then made for the door. "You do that," she said, and then she was gone.

I stared after her, not quite sure I could believe what just happened. I knew Courtney was shallow, but geesh, this was really low, even for her.

I waited until she backed out of my driveway and was down the road before I left. I noted Joanne was standing outside, looking toward my house, a disapproving frown on her face. I think she was worried Courtney's pink van would become a fixture in my driveway. If I'd had it in me, I might have done something to make her think it was, just to see her sweat.

But I was in no mood for another argument, at least, not a pointless one.

I waved to Joanne, who sniffed and went back into her house. So much for playing nice.

I drove by, putting my neighbor—and Courtney—out of my mind. Ben was what was important. And to save him, it looked like I was going to have to pay Selena Shriver another visit.

19

Clarence was sitting outside when I pulled into Selena's driveway. It was becoming a habit, one I hoped I'd be able to break soon. I'd lost count of how many times I'd been to Selena's place over the last couple of days—or Timothy's house for that matter. Hopefully, the next time I was on this end of town, I'd be here to pick up Stewie, or spend a quiet few minutes with Clarence.

I waved to him as I got out of my van. He raised his ever-present coffee mug in salute, and then continued to watch. I wondered what he thought of my constant visits, and then decided that I probably didn't want to know, considering his near-crude comments about Selena the last time we'd talked.

Selena's car was in the driveway, but I was worried she wasn't home. She could have come back, and then left again with Jason, with him driving this time. As much as I wanted to confront her about how her relationship with Ben affected her relationship with her boyfriend, I wasn't going to wait around to do it.

I knocked, and was pleasantly surprised when the door opened and Selena peered out at me.

"Mrs. Denton," she said, taking an abrupt step back. "I wasn't expecting you."

"Can we talk?" I asked. Motherly anger was trying to bubble up, yet I suppressed it. She might have a perfectly good explanation as to why she was with Jason earlier. Nothing said she'd actually led Ben on, though from where I was standing, I wasn't sure what else you could call it.

"Uh, sure." Selena stepped aside, sounding, and looking, uncertain.

"Is Jason here?" I asked, going straight for the kitchen, and peering out back. No one in the pool, or around it.

"No. Why would he be?" Nervous.

I glanced around the kitchen, noted the lack of food dishes on the floor. There wasn't cat food anywhere in sight, nor did it smell like a cat lived here. Selena's house wasn't all that big, so it wasn't like she had many other places to hide a pet, or its things.

"You don't have a cat, do you?" I asked, facing her.

Her eyes darted around the room before they finally firmed on me. "No, I don't."

"But you told me you did."

"So?" she asked. "Telling white lies isn't a crime."

"No, it's not," I said, "but it *is* suspicious. Why would you tell me you have a cat, when clearly, you don't? Do you have something to hide?"

Selena didn't respond, just stood there, looking at me, face unreadable.

"You said Jason was just a friend," I said, not backing down. This girl lied to me, more than once, and I couldn't imagine any other reason why she would, outside of her being involved in Timothy's death in some way. It was the only thing that made sense.

"I did."

"You didn't say what kind of friend."

"What's that supposed to mean?" Some of her stoicism broke as worry creased her brow.

She knows I know.

"He's your boyfriend, isn't he?"

She opened her mouth, and I got the distinct impression she was going to deny it, before she shrugged and looked away. "What business is it of yours whether he is or not?"

"You pretended you two weren't together. Why would you do something like that? And why would he go along with it?"

Selena continued to hem and haw around without actually saying anything. She brushed some crumbs off the table, rearranged the salt and pepper shakers, before fiddling with a book on a nearby table.

I waited her out. Selena was a grown adult, albeit a young one. I had quite a few years on her, and I bet she still viewed me like most teenagers did anyone older than them. I doubted she respected me—she wouldn't have lied if she did—but she would assume I believed I had some sort of authority over her.

I crossed my arms and pointedly tapped my foot hard enough so she could hear it. She glanced up at me, entire demeanor tightening, as if my impatience was merely going to cause her to pull within herself even more.

So, she was going to play it like that, was she? Well,

I wasn't going to let her get off with stubborn silence. "I saw you with him," I said. "I was buying cat food and just so happened to see you two messing around in a nearby parking lot. That kiss looked like a lot more than what two friends would share."

Selena eased down into a chair. "Okay," was all she said.

"Okay, what?" I pressed.

"He's my boyfriend."

I crossed my arms and just stared. I knew the two of them were closer than they'd let on, but hearing it actually hurt. *Oh, Ben, how could you be so stupid?*

"I'm sorry," Selena said, clearly unsure what she should say. "It wasn't like we planned it or anything. Jason . . ." She scowled down at her hands. "I didn't mean for anyone to get hurt."

My chest tightened. Was that an admission of some kind? "Tell me."

Selena took a moment to gather her thoughts, and I let her. If she was involved in Timothy's death, I didn't want to scare her off, press her until she clammed up.

"I like him," she said, voice soft, almost shy. "Ben, I mean." Her gaze lifted, met mine. "I really do."

"But you're with Jason."

"I know." She slumped back. "We've been together for a long time, but honestly, I think it's over. He's been pulling away for months now, and while we still have fun sometimes, there's just not the same spark as there was before."

"But the kiss . . ."

She shrugged it off. "It happens from time to time. We *are* still together." The "for now" was implied.

I mentally sorted through what I knew and asked, "Someone told me the two of you might be getting married."

Selena actually laughed. "Maybe like two years ago," she said. "We talked about it then, but I'm not sure either of us were too serious about it. Then, after I heard he was running around with Carly . . ." Old anger seemed to bubble up, and then dissipate. "I just don't care anymore."

I still wasn't quite getting it. How did this have anything to do with Timothy Fuller?

"Why did you lie to me?" I asked. "When we first met, you told me it was a cat in the house. It was Jason, wasn't it?"

"It was," she admitted. "I didn't know what to do. Jason knew Ben had been here, but I didn't want him to know anything else. As far as he knows, Ben and I are just friends. I mean, I guess we are. Were. I don't even know what we are. Or what we could have been if, well . . ." She motioned in the direction of Timothy's property.

"So, you're interested in Ben?"

"Yeah." A shy smile crossed her lips. "He's nice." The smile faded. "I said what I did about him when Jason was here, just to throw him off. I didn't mean for it to sound like I was accusing Ben of something."

"What do you mean?"

"About Ben, about him leaving for a little while." She reddened, refused to look up. "When Jason got here and found out some guy was here, I had to say something, so I told him Ben was a friend from school. Then, when you showed up, I hoped that saying I dozed off, and that Ben left, he'd leave it alone."

It sounded awfully convoluted to me, but what did I know? I'd never been in a situation like this before: torn between two men, and having it happen right when a murder takes place next door. Selena was probably just as confused about the whole thing as I was.

"So, you lied to me because you didn't want Jason to know you were interested in Ben?" I asked, just to be sure.

"I know," she said. "It sounds stupid, but I panicked. Mr. Fuller was murdered, and I was having problems of my own, and I just didn't want to deal with it. I thought if I made everyone believe there was nothing between Ben and me, then it would all go away."

"Until you broke it off with Jason," I said.

She nodded. "I was thinking of doing it soon, I swear." Then, she sat forward, finally meeting my eye. "I didn't want Ben to get into trouble. I'm sure he had nothing to do with Mr. Fuller's death. I didn't mean to make it sound like he did, not really. I was just so scared."

"You could tell the police he was with you the entire time," I said. "Let them know he couldn't have killed Timothy."

"Well . . ." She looked like she was going to tell me something I wouldn't want to hear when she sucked in an excited breath, and abruptly stood. "The car!" She hurried to the back door and went outside. I followed after her, but if there was a car back there, I sure didn't see it.

"What car?" I asked, when all she did was stand there, looking out toward a back alley that ran along the rear of both properties. I touched her arm and asked again. "Selena, what car?"

"It wasn't when Ben was here," Selena said. "But afterward, that night."

"Okay?"

"I was sitting out here with Jason, just chilling, when I saw it. I didn't really think much of it since you can't really see anything."

Which was true. A couple of small trees sat at the edge of Selena's property, as they did next door. If a car were to drive by, it would be mostly obscured, right up until it vanished behind Timothy's barn.

"It was just getting dark," she went on. "And I might have had one or two too many to drink." She glanced at me. "It was a stressful day, so, you know, I might have overdone it."

I nodded and motioned for her to go on.

"Anyway, I was sitting here when I noticed the headlights."

"The car was coming this way?"

She shook her head. "I only noticed them when they snapped off. The car coasted down the alley, then went quiet. I didn't see anyone, or hear anything after that, but I found it odd."

"Someone broke into Timothy's house," I said. "It might have happened late at night." Could the car she had seen been driven by the person who'd broken in? I found it likely.

"I heard." She shuddered, hugged herself. "I'm not sure if anyone actually got out of the car, because, like I said, I'd been drinking, and Jason was here. We went inside a short time later, so if someone did break into the house then, I didn't see it happen."

My mind raced. Who would have wanted to sneak in, unseen? Junior had a key, and honestly, had every right in the world to be there. Jason was supposedly with Selena at the time, and Ben was in jail.

So, who did that leave? Duke and Courtney might have come looking for the money, but I somehow doubted they'd go so far as to break in to look for it. Courtney might be the type, but Duke wasn't. He would have talked her out of it.

There was always Meredith. She might have come back for the cash, figuring it best to do it at night since Junior seemed to hang around during the day. She didn't live too far away and after the abuse she'd suffered from Timothy, she felt she was owed. Other than that, I couldn't think of a single person who would snoop around in the middle of the night.

Amelia, maybe? She could very well have snuck out and come out here, just to have a look around. I wasn't sure what all her interest in being a detective had her doing. Could she have been waiting for the killer to return to the scene of the crime?

"Look, Mrs. Denton, I'm really sorry about Ben, and I really do hope he gets out of this okay," Selena said, drawing me out of my thoughts.

"I hope so too," I said. And then, because I couldn't let it go, "Have you seen anyone hanging around next door lately? Anyone who doesn't belong?"

"I wish I could help," she said. "But I've told you everything I know. I'm sorry."

The house next door practically grinned at me. There were secrets there. I could feel them, tucked away in dark corners, in hidden crevasses.

And all of those hidden secrets appeared to lead right back to Timothy Fuller and his money.

"Do you think it would be all right if I went to see

him?" Selena asked, drawing me out of my thoughts yet again.

"Who? Junior?"

"No, Ben." She scuffed one shoe on the patio. "I was thinking that if he did get out of this okay, that maybe we could catch a movie or something."

"You can try," I said. Though, honestly, I didn't really want her hanging around my son, not until she broke it off with her current boyfriend. Ben had already been through enough, he didn't need his heart broken on top of everything else.

I wondered if I should tell him about Selena's two-timing, or if I should make her do it, especially if he wanted to see her again. I knew it wasn't my place, but he was my son. I couldn't let him make a mistake when I knew I could do something to stop it.

He might be mad at me after, but as long as he didn't end up with his heart broken, I was okay with that.

I left Selena a few minutes later, thinking I might go see Ben. Perhaps there was something he remembered, something I could use to help him. I wasn't sure what that something might be, considering he'd likely told everything to the police already.

I was about to get into my van when a faint sound came from Timothy's house. I froze and held my breath to listen, not quite sure I'd heard it right. Nothing happened for a good ten seconds.

And then it came again.

A pair of high-pitched, angry yaps.

There was no car in the driveway, and I hadn't seen one out back when I'd been looking.

Had Junior brought Stewie back to the house, only to leave him unattended?

There was no way I could let that stand.

Leaving my van in Selena's driveway, I marched across the yard, ready to give Junior—or anyone else who would abandon a dog like that—a piece of my mind.

20

I'd just reached the front door to Timothy Fuller's house, when a crash sounded from inside. It was quickly followed by a heavy thump that shook the door in its frame. My heart rate ratcheted up as I pressed my ear against the door.

No one was speaking, and the barking had either been muffled, or had stopped. Remembering how Junior had cornered Stewie before, I wondered if that was what was happening now.

But if that was the case, where was Junior's car?

Someone had already broken into the house once already, so it wouldn't be a surprise if it happened again. But in broad daylight?

I glanced to the house across the street, but Clarence was no longer outside. A flutter of fear shot through me. What if something had happened to the old man? Maybe Timothy Fuller's death had nothing to do with money. Could there be an elderly man killer on the loose?

I suppressed the thought. There was no need to panic quite yet.

Maybe I should call Detective Cavanaugh, I thought, torn between running across the street to check on Clarence and investigating Timothy's house. The detective could deal with the situation far better than I could.

But what if he was too slow in getting here? If it was someone looking for Timothy's stash, they might find it at any moment.

Then sit back and watch the house. There was no reason to go inside and risk my life when I could wait for whoever was inside to leave. I had my phone; I could snap a few pictures to take to Cavanaugh later.

Another crash came from within. It was followed by the startled yip of a Pomeranian.

Nope, there was no way I was going to stay out here if someone was hurting Stewie.

I tried the door and found it to be locked. Cursing under my breath, I peered in through the windows, but the blinds were closed, obscuring my vision. Even if I could see through them clearly, the crashes sounded as if they were coming from farther into the house, likely from upstairs, if I was hearing right.

"The back," I muttered, as I hurried around the side of the house to the back door. Fearing it was going to be locked like the front, I tried it, and was relieved to find the door unlocked. I stepped inside as another series of barks and yips came from upstairs. It was followed by a thud I hoped wasn't someone throwing heavy objects at the dog.

I started toward the stairs—which were situated between the dining room and living room—but paused halfway through the kitchen. I took a quick look around, and then spotting the knife block, I grabbed the butcher's knife. Thusly armed, I headed for the stairs.

Since Timothy's house was an old farmhouse built sometime in the early 1900s, if not before, it creaked with every subtle shift of weight, making my ascent sound like a chorus of groans and squeaks. Thankfully, the intruder was making even more noise, and with Stewie now barking at a near constant clip, I probably could have run up the stairs unnoticed.

The stairwell was hot and suffocating, the stairs themselves thin and weathered. There was no railing, just two walls that felt far too close together, making the stairwell narrow and claustrophobic. My left shoulder rubbed against the faded wallpaper as I tried to peer up the stairs and discern where the noises were coming from.

The distinct sound of a drawer opening and closing clued me in. The intruder was in the far back room, which would be behind me as I reached the top of the stairs. I hurried up the last three steps, and spun, knife held out before me. I was trembling, mentally cursing myself for not calling Detective Cavanaugh before entering the house. I wasn't a fighter. If I was about to face off with Timothy Fuller's killer, I was going to be in some serious trouble.

A bathroom was off to my left. A small storage room to my right. Both rooms were a disaster, their contents tossed on the floor. Straight ahead was the slightly open door. A shadow passed before it, and then vanished. Stewie let loose with another set of yips.

I crept down the hall, wincing at every creaking step. A cascade of thumps masked my progress. It sounded like someone had dumped a full shelf of books onto the floor.

I sidled up to the door, back pressed against the wall so that if whoever was inside the room were to look, they wouldn't see me. Using my free hand, I reached out and gently pushed open the door, just enough so I could see inside.

Stewie was standing in the corner, facing a bed that probably hadn't been slept in for years. Drawers from the dresser were tossed in a pile, their contents spilled out in a heap. A board had been pulled from the wall, exposing the slats beneath. Beside that was a bookshelf, now void of books. They were currently scattered across the floor in a jumbled mess of bent pages and torn covers.

And kneeling, arm reaching beneath the bed, was Timothy Jr.

"What are you doing?" I demanded, stepping into the room. The knife was clutched with both hands now, just in case he came at me. I doubted I could bring myself to use it, but I hoped the threat of it would keep him at bay if the thought crossed his mind.

Junior jerked, smacking his head on the bottom of the bed. His hand immediately went up to rub at the spot, but instead, he cracked his knuckles on the wall, right above the gap he'd made. He cursed, crawled backward, and then got to his feet. The glare he gave me could have curdled milk.

"You," he spat. And then, to Stewie, who was yapping up a storm. "Shut up!"

"Don't talk to him like that."

"I'll do what I want." Junior rubbed at his head. "And what I want to do, is call the cops."

"I was thinking the same thing," I said, lowering the knife, but only a little. I still didn't trust the man, though he wasn't making any move toward me.

Stewie lunged toward the distracted Junior, who scuttled out of the way as if he were being attacked by a Doberman. Stewie didn't bite him. Instead, he let loose a series of threatening barks, bouncing on his little legs with each one.

Junior made a frustrated sound. He looked angry enough to kick, so, taking my chances, I dropped the knife and went over to pick up the enraged Pomeranian. Stewie snapped at me once in surprise, and then let me pick him up. As soon as the dog was in my arms, I took two quick strides away from Junior.

"Take him," he said, waving a dismissive hand at me. "The damned thing is useless."

"You were scaring him," I said, looking around the room. It was completely trashed. The closet was hanging open, the clothes having been pulled from it and thrown into a pile. Everything had been removed, every box or door opened. Nothing was left untouched.

"I was trying to find . . ." He glanced at me and glowered. "Never you mind what I was looking for."

"Your dad's money?" I asked, petting the dog to calm him. Stewie's eyes never left Junior. I could feel the tension running through him. Every muscle was tense, and he trembled ever so slightly.

Junior's eyes narrowed. "How do you know about that?"

"Everyone in town does," I said. "Is that why you came to Grey Falls? To look for your father's money? You should be ashamed of yourself."

"I deserve it," Junior said, sitting heavily on the bed as if exhausted. He kicked at a pile of Timothy's things. "I put up with that man all my life, and what do I have to show for it? An old house with a bunch

of junk I'll be lucky to sell for more than scraps?
What a waste."

Stewie calmed as soon as Junior sat, though the
tension was still there. I had a feeling if I were to set
him down, he'd bolt from the room and hide.

"What makes you think the money is here?" I
asked. "He might have hidden it somewhere else." I
remembered what Evelyn had said about walking in
on Timothy hiding the money all those years ago. It
seemed likely he'd be more careful about where he
hid it after getting caught once before.

"Where else would it be?" Junior said. "He rarely
left the house. And when he did, he had that nurse
of his with him, so it wasn't like he'd have an opportunity to hide it anywhere else."

Which was all true, though I did wonder how Junior knew that. Had he been keeping a close watch
on his dad, hoping the old man would slip and reveal
his hiding place? I wouldn't put it past him. "He
might not have hidden anything at all," I said. "He
could have spent it years ago."

Junior came up off the bed, startling both me and
Stewie. The dog instantly started barking, and I took
two quick steps back toward the door, kicking the
knife with my heel in the process. It slid out into the
hall, where it bounced off the wall, to come to rest
near the stairs.

"He hid it all right," he said. "And I'm going to
find it. Unless . . ." He strode toward me, eyes dan-
gerous slits. "Did you take it? You were the one who
broke in here, weren't you?"

"Of course, I didn't," I said, backing out of the
room. Stewie was struggling to be put down, but I refused to release him. Maybe if Junior came at me, I

would set him free. The Pomeranian might be small, but his teeth were sharp.

"The nurse, then," Junior said. He looked wildly around the room, like Meredith might be hiding somewhere inside it. He looked unhinged. "She had to have known about it." He strode forward, past me, toward the stairs. He stepped over the knife like he didn't even see it.

"Where are you going?" I asked, hurrying after him.

"I'm going to find her and make her tell me what she did with the money." Junior started down the stairs. "You can have the dog. It didn't know."

"Didn't know what?" I asked. He descended quickly, while I went down them slowly. Not only did I have a squirming dog in my arms, but I wasn't used to the steep decline. He'd already reached the bottom before I was two steps down. "Junior, wait!"

Surprisingly, he did. He spun around, ran his fingers through his hair. His eyes were wild, unfocused. I wondered if he'd been sleeping, or if the stress of everything was getting to him. "I thought the dog would recognize the spot," he said. "So, I brought him to sniff out the cash. All he did was bark and bark and bark. Useless!"

"Maybe he didn't know what you wanted," I said, though I wasn't sure why I was feeding into the delusion. Even if Stewie knew where Timothy had hidden his money, how was he to know that Junior brought him over to find it? Or even, what to do if he did know. Dogs were smart, but not *that* smart.

Junior merely smiled, baring his teeth in a wolf's grin. "Sure, he didn't. The mutt is just like the old man."

"Is that why you wanted him?" I asked, finally reaching the bottom of the stairs. "To find the money for you?"

"Not at first," Junior said. "But Alexis told me about a story she read where a dog helped find its missing owner. She thought Dad's dog could do something similar and help us find the money."

That's insane, I thought, but wisely kept it to myself. Maybe with training, Stewie could have helped. "The money will pop up," I said. "You don't need to use a dog for that." Or tear the house down, but I kept that to myself too.

"I won't," Junior said, sneering. "Take him. Give him to someone who cares." He spun away.

"Wait!" I said, but this time, he kept walking. "You can't go after Meredith."

He glanced back. "And why not?"

"Do you really think she'd tell you if she took the money?"

That caused him to come to an abrupt stop. I very nearly walked into him.

"She'd have to," he said, but he didn't sound convinced.

"If she took it, she's probably already hidden it somewhere. And *if* she *did* take it," I said, stressing the words, "she has to know that the police might think she killed your dad for it. She won't tell anyone, not even you."

Junior's jaw tightened. "So, what? I let her have it?"

"No," I said. "But you wait it out. If you go pounding on her door now, you might spook her. She could pack her things, grab the money, and leave town. If she does that, you'll never see her, or the money, again."

He huffed and clenched his fist as if he might punch the wall. Thankfully, he just stood there, scowling. "Maybe it was that son of yours," he said, but without conviction.

"Ben had nothing to do with your dad's death. He didn't steal the money either. He never had the chance."

Junior closed his eyes, seemed to center himself. When he looked at me again, he looked less crazed. "Fine. I'll leave her be for now. But don't think I won't be telling the cops about my suspicions."

"Go right ahead," I said. "If she did kill your dad, or stole the money, then she should be caught." And if it helped exonerate Ben of the crime, all the better.

I was also considering calling the cops to let them know what I saw here today. I wasn't above pointing Detective Cavanaugh Junior's way. With the way Stewie looked at him, I could tell the dog hated him with a passion.

I kept thinking back to what Ray had said about how Stewie was protective of Timothy. If he saw who killed his owner, didn't it make sense that he'd want to go after them? So far, Junior was the only person Stewie seemed to genuinely hate. Coincidence? Or did the Pomeranian's wrath point to the killer?

Junior walked over to the sink and grabbed a plastic cup from the counter next to it. He filled it halfway, and then downed the water in one swallow. He turned back to me, wiping his chin.

"Why are you still here?" he asked.

I edged toward the back door, dog in hand. "So, there's nothing else?" I asked, even though he hadn't asked me in. I was just glad he wasn't going to call the cops. Yet.

"No. Go." He waved a dismissive hand. "And take the mutt. He's only given me a migraine."

I didn't hesitate. Afraid Junior might change his mind about the dog, I hurried out the back door.

Junior followed me out, locking the door behind him. I hoped it meant he was done searching for the day, not that he planned on ignoring my advice and was going to go after Meredith.

I was almost to the edge of the house when curiosity got the better of me. I turned to find Junior walking past the barn, toward the alley, where I assumed he'd parked.

"Did you check the barn for the money?" I asked him.

He never broke stride, nor did he answer. I, for all intents and purposes, could have been invisible.

I returned to my van, which was still in Selena's driveway, wondering why he hadn't parked out front. Unless he'd walked from wherever he was staying, it appeared Junior had parked out back, car hidden by the barn where hardly anyone could see it. *Just like the person Selena had seen last night.*

I settled the Pomeranian into a carrier, gave him a few treats to calm him, and then jumped into the driver's seat. Junior was acting erratic, secretive. I wasn't sure that made him a killer, but it didn't do him any favors.

As I started the engine, a car pulled into the driveway beside me. Jason Maxwell got out, brow furrowed, as he watched me back out. I pretended not to see him, lest I lay into him for unwittingly hurting Ben.

I'll have to face the Selena situation eventually. But not right now.

"Let's get you checked out," I said, glancing back toward Stewie.

He gave a yap in what I took for assent, and then, we were on our way.

21

"Aww! Who's our little friend?" Trinity asked, coming around the counter, a big grin on her face.

"Stewie," I said. The Pomeranian was leashed, and looked nervous, which wasn't much of a surprise considering where we were. He knew what happened at a vet's office. "He was Timothy Fuller's dog."

Trinity's eyes went soft. "The man who died?" When I nodded, she dropped to her knees. "You poor thing." She rubbed behind Stewie's ears. The dog, of course, soaked it in.

"Is Manny free?" I asked, smiling. Sometimes, I was a bit cynical when it came to Trinity and her good looks, but she *was* good with the animals. Take away the snapping gum and phone addiction, and she might make a great veterinary assistant someday.

"He's finishing up with Ms. Keller's pooch," Trinity said, not taking her eyes off Stewie. The dog was butter in her hand. "He shouldn't be much longer."

"Thanks, Trinity."

I left Stewie in Trinity's capable hands and walked

past the exam room doors. It appeared Manny was the only one currently with an animal. Ray was likely in the back somewhere, running tests or cleaning up. I didn't think any animals were currently being housed overnight, but that could have changed.

Manny was in exam room two. I waved through the window when he glanced up from Cathy Keller's miniature poodle, Winnie. He returned the gesture, and shot me a smile, which caused Cathy to glance back. When she saw me, she practically beamed, before leaving both Winnie and Manny, to join me.

"Liz!" she said, giving me a quick hug. "It's so good to see you."

"Cathy. How's retirement treating you?"

Cathy patted at her curly white hair. "I should have done it much earlier, if that tells you anything." Cathy had been an elementary school teacher since I could remember. She was in her eighties, but moved and acted like a woman half that. I'm not sure if it was her diet, or hanging around all those little kids, but she seemed to have found the fountain of youth.

"I think we can all agree with the sentiment," I said.

She laughed. "How are Ben and Amelia? I haven't seen either of them in ages."

"Amelia's good," I said, deflating. "Ben is, well . . ." How do you explain to someone's old elementary school teacher that their favorite student was now in jail for a crime they didn't commit?

"I hope it's nothing serious," Cathy said, noting my hesitation. "Ben was such a good boy. Why, I remember that time when he glued his hand to his desk and panicked because he thought he'd be stuck there forever." She laughed, a full-bodied laugh, that shook her entire frame.

"He'll be okay," I said, not wanting to bring her down with tales of murder and money. I was actually surprised she didn't know, considering it was likely all over the news by now. "Just a little bit of trouble."

"Oh, dear. Is there anything I can do to help?"

Before I could answer, the door to exam room two opened.

"Mrs. Keller, Winnie's ready to go," Manny said, poking his head through the doorway.

"Oh! Thank you, dear." She turned back to me. "It was good seeing you, Liz. We should all get together sometime and catch up."

"I'd like that," I said, and I meant it.

She went back into the exam room, gathered up Winnie, and then with an animated wave goodbye, she left.

While Manny cleaned up after the poodle, I retrieved Stewie from Trinity. She was practically lying on the floor by now, playing with the old dog, who was eating up the attention. When she saw me coming, she groaned, and kissed the Pomeranian on his head.

"See you soon," she promised him, before returning to her spot behind the desk.

I took Stewie to exam room two. Manny had just finished wiping down the table with a disinfecting wipe. He glanced up when we entered.

"Who do we have here?" he asked. When he saw the Pomeranian, his eyes widened. "Is this who I think it is?"

"It is," I said, setting Stewie down carefully on the table. "Ray said Stewie has been here before, so you should have his records on file."

"Fantastic," Manny said, stroking the dog to earn

his trust, while looking into his eyes, likely checking for signs of disease. "So, you managed to get him after all."

"I did, though it wasn't easy." I gave him a quick rundown of what had happened, including why Junior had been so keen on keeping the dog around.

"That's crazy," Manny said. "He's not trained for that sort of thing."

"I know. I don't think Junior was thinking too clearly. He seemed off when I talked to him."

Manny, by now, had Stewie's nerves calmed enough, he could start checking his joints and teeth. The dog didn't like the manhandling, but accepted it well enough. There was no barking, no growling.

"I did notice something odd," I said, watching my husband work with admiration. I appreciated the care he took with the animals, but there was no way I could ever become a vet. For every animal he helped, there was always one who was too sick to be cured. It would break my heart every single time, and unlike Manny, I'm not sure I'd get over losing someone's pet.

"What's that?" Manny asked, gently squeezing Stewie's front legs. "Something odd with Stewie?"

"No. Well, yes." I waved a hand in uncertainty. Stewie watched it, eyes growing bright. He was likely hoping for treats. "It's about Junior, really."

"Okay?" Manny finished checking the basics, and resumed stroking the Pomeranian, who was being awfully good. Even the most well-behaved dog didn't like getting poked and prodded by a stranger.

"It was something Ray had said. He told me that Stewie had a tendency to defend his owner, Timothy. He'd bark and get a little aggressive, though I don't think he actually bit anyone. And while I know Pomeranians like to bark quite a lot, there is one person who seems to really get under his skin."

"Let me guess, Junior?"

I nodded. "Every time I saw them together, Stewie would bark at him and cower away like he was afraid of Junior. He's the only person with whom I ever saw him like that."

"Dogs can sense when people don't like them," Manny said. "If Junior is as bad as you say, then it's likely the reason why Stewie acts as he does toward him."

"Could there be more to it?" I asked.

Manny's brow furrowed. "Meaning?" Before I could answer, he held up a hand. "Hold that thought." He poked his head out the door. "Hey, Trinity, can you get me Stewie's records. They'd be filed under Fuller, Timothy. Thanks." He popped back in. "You were saying?"

"Do you think it's possible Stewie saw the murder and is barking at Junior because he was the one who did it?"

Manny appeared surprised by the question. "Do you think that's what happened?"

"I don't know," I admitted. "But as far as I can tell, Stewie only acts that way with Junior, which has to mean something, doesn't it? He's never barked at me, and he seemed fine around Timothy's nurse, Meredith."

"I suppose it's possible," Manny said. "But you can't use his barking as proof of a crime. In fact, I'm more apt to believe he simply doesn't like Junior, than he witnessed a murder and is reacting because of it."

That wasn't what I wanted to hear, but I wasn't really all that surprised. It was a long shot. "Junior is pretty obsessed with finding his dad's money," I said. "If anyone had motive to kill Timothy, it was him."

Manny gave me a sympathetic smile and walked over, took my head in both hands, and brought my forehead to his lips. "I know what you're trying to do," he said.

"What's that?"

"You want to help Ben. I understand that, and I love you for it."

I could feel the "but" coming. I stepped back and waited.

"But you need to let the police deal with it," he said. "I want to help too, but what if you do something that messes with the investigation? We have to be careful, Liz. Tell the police what you know. If money is involved, I'm sure they'll find it. Now that you have Stewie, there's no reason for you to talk to Junior again. I don't want something to happen to you."

"I know, but . . ."

"I understand," Manny said, though I hadn't actually said much of anything. "I want to rush to the police station and demand they release Ben. I want to check the scene myself, see if I can find something the police have missed." His fists clenched, some of his composure slipping. "But I know I can't. If I do, I'll mess it up somehow. I couldn't live with myself if I did that. So, I'm here."

"I feel the same way," I said. "It's just so hard to do nothing. And come to find out, the girl Ben was hanging out with at the time of the murder already has a boyfriend. I keep wondering if she was a part of it somehow. And then after what happened with Amelia, I'm afraid I'm losing complete control of everything."

Manny went completely still. "Something's happened to Amelia?"

Oh, crap. I hadn't meant to say anything about her. That's what I get for babbling on like a fool. "It's nothing," I said. Not very convincingly, I might add.

"No, Liz. What's going on with Amelia?"

Reluctantly, I told him about my visit with Duke, and how I saw Amelia with the older man afterward. I downplayed the whole thing about me following her, saying I'd been heading in the same direction, but told him about it nonetheless. I ended with what she'd told me about wanting to be a detective or private investigator when she finally graduated college.

Manny was silent for a couple of minutes afterward, digesting everything I'd said. I couldn't tell if he was upset, angry, or thrilled. He paced over to Stewie, who was watching us, head cocked to the side like he'd been trying to follow the conversation, before Manny spun, a wide smile on his face.

"This is fantastic news," he said.

"It is?"

"It sounds like Amelia has finally found her calling." He grinned. "I was starting to get worried there for a while."

"I told her we'd support her," I said, relieved. While I might have told Amelia we'd both be happy for her, there'd been a niggling of doubt in the back of my mind that Manny wouldn't approve of her career choice.

"You know, we should celebrate," he said. "Tonight." The door opened and Trinity entered. She handed Manny Stewie's file, giving us each a curious look, before heading back out front. "We should show her we support her, make a big deal out of it. She'll probably hate it at first, but I bet she'll appreciate it in the end."

"That actually sounds like a good idea," I said, thinking it through. With everything bad that's happened lately, it would be nice to focus on something positive for a change. Amelia wasn't big on us showering her with attention, but I thought she'd approve.

"Let me finish up with Stewie and we can make plans."

"Sound good."

"This is great," Manny said, turning to the Pomeranian. "Don't you think so, buddy?"

I left him with the dog, and went outside to make a call. Manny was right; I needed to let the police handle Ben's case. I'd tell Detective Cavanaugh everything I'd learned since we'd last talked, and then I'd step away. There was no reason for me to keep going back to Timothy's place, let alone Selena's house, now that I had Stewie in custody.

I dialed the detective's cell—I'd found his number in the van—and waited as it rang. Eventually, it went to voicemail, but I clicked off without leaving a message.

I started to dial the police station, but only made it halfway through the number before I canceled the call and shoved my phone into my pocket. If I truly thought about it, it was unlikely Detective Cavanaugh would want to hear from me again today, even if I had information for him. He had a pretty full plate already, and what I had to say might not have anything to do with Timothy's murder. I could always save it for tomorrow.

By now, Cavanaugh probably already knew about the money and everyone's interest in it. And what difference did it truly make that Selena already had a boyfriend when she was flirting with my son? It wasn't a crime—though in my mind, it should be.

Trinity was back behind the desk, attention focused on her phone, when I came back inside. When I peeked into the exam room, both Manny and Stewie were gone. I assumed the dog was getting weighed. Afterward, tests would be done, many of which, would likely leave the Pomeranian grumpy.

Instead of returning to the exam room, I sat down in the waiting area, on the dog admittance side. A woman sat across the way, a pair of black-and-white kittens in a carrier. She must have come in while I was on the phone, though I hadn't seen her walk by. She cooed at the mewling kitties as she awaited her turn to be seen.

Theresa Rush came from the back a few minutes later, rather than Ray, who I'd expected. Theresa was five years older than me, and while we got along all right, I don't think she really cared for me all that much. She saw me, gave a half-hearted wave, and then took the woman and her kittens to exam room one.

Fifteen minutes later, Manny came out, leading a surprisingly happy-looking Stewie on a leash.

"He's all done," he said. "He handled the exam like a pro."

"Did everything check out?" I asked, accepting the leash when Manny offered it.

"It did," Manny said. "He's far healthier than I expected. No cataracts or signs of disease, other than maybe a little arthritis in his legs. Mr. Fuller took good care of him." He rubbed behind Stewie's ears.

"The blood work won't be ready for a day or so, so I can't be sure, but I'm almost positive our friend here is going to get a relatively clean bill of health."

That was good to hear. Maybe everything in the world wasn't falling apart, despite how it seemed.

"Thanks, Manny," I said. "I'll start getting everything prepped for his adoption." I looked down at the dog, and a pang shot through me. I liked the little guy, even though I hadn't spent much time with him yet. This one was going to be hard to let go of.

Then again, weren't they all?

"You calling them tonight?"

"No, I think I'll wait until tomorrow," I said. I didn't want the Lincolns to get their hopes up if something came up in the tests overnight.

Or if Detective Cavanaugh called, wanting to see the dog. I still couldn't shake the feeling that Stewie knew more about who killed Timothy than he could tell us. I doubted Cavanaugh would have any more luck than the rest of us getting it out of him, but I wouldn't put it past him to try.

"I can keep him here overnight, if you want?" Manny asked, concern in his voice. "It'll be no trouble."

"That's all right," I said, forcing myself to smile. "Stewie and I can get the room set up together, right, Stewie?"

The Pomeranian yapped in agreement.

Manny laughed. "If you say so." He gave me a quick hug, and then stepped back as the door opened and a couple came in with a Labrador. "If you change your mind, just let me know. We've got room here."

"I won't," I assured him. "I'll see you tonight."

"Liz," Manny said as I started to walk away. "Remember what I said."

I flashed him a smile, and then left, a happy dog trailing behind me. When I opened the back of my van, he pranced in place, as if he actually wanted to be picked up and put into the carrier.

"Things are looking up for you," I said, picking up the dog and putting him into the back of the van. He ran into the carrier, and immediately curled up and lay down. Apparently, the exam had taken more out of him than he'd let on.

I closed the back of the van, content. Stewie was going to a loving home. And while his former owner was gone, I was pretty sure the Lincolns would make sure he remained happy. Things were definitely going his way.

I just hoped that some of his good fortune would eventually rub off on me.

22

Stewie yapped and then skipped sideways, tail wagging a mile a minute. In response, Wheels rolled to his left, circling the excited dog, causing Stewie to spin so fast, he very nearly fell down.

"They look like they're getting along," Manny said, leaning over to kiss me on the cheek before tossing his keys on the coffee table.

"They've been playing since we got home," I said, smiling. I was sitting on the couch, cup of coffee in hand as I watched the dog and cat play. When I first brought Stewie in, he didn't seem too sure about the cat with the wheels strapped to her backside. After only a few minutes of sniffing—and a playful swat or two—they'd seemingly become best friends.

Manny sat down beside me, letting loose a heavy sigh as he landed. He pulled off his shoes and then rubbed at his arches. "He's handling it pretty well, all things considered."

"He is. For as mean as Timothy Fuller was to everyone around him, he really did care about his dog.

And then when you consider the time Stewie spent with Junior, it's no wonder he's in a good mood now that he's not around him anymore."

"Mm-hmm," Manny said in agreement.

Wheels spun in a tight circle, causing Stewie to lose his mind and start hopping on stiff legs as he yapped excitedly. The cat came to a stop, staggered two steps, and then rolled toward the Pomeranian, who fell over backward, before leaping to his feet and running away. Wheels, of course, gave chase.

I watched them go, still smiling. Wheels was used to having other animals in the house since we were always temporarily fostering them, but I wondered if it might not be a good idea to get her a permanent play buddy. It didn't have to be a dog. Another cat would work. Even a rabbit or a ferret would, since Wheels had never been violent toward any other animal before, regardless of species. I'd brought in a guinea pig once, and the two of them had played like the best of friends.

I sipped my coffee and sighed in contentment. For the first time in what felt like a long time, I was relaxed. Just because Ben was in trouble, it didn't mean I had to wallow in misery.

Of course, merely thinking of Ben caused my smile to slowly fade. Here I was, sitting in the comforts of my own home, watching the animals play, while he sat in a cold cell, on a hard cot, fearing for his future. What kind of mother was I?

"Where's Amelia?" Manny asked, working at his other arch. Normally, I would have offered to give him a foot rub, but I was afraid to put down my coffee mug. As much as I'd like to think I was holding it together, I was one more disaster from completely losing it. I was grasping the mug like it was my sanity.

"In her room," I said. "She came home a little while ago. I think she's studying, but you'd have to check on her to be sure."

"Amelia!" Manny called, though we both knew it would be no use. He gave it a count of three, and then rose. "I'll be right back." He headed for her room, where he'd likely find her sprawled across her bed, earbuds crammed into her ears, with the music loud enough that everyone in the room could hear it. It was a wonder that she wasn't deaf by now.

I considered getting up and warming up some food for Manny, who'd worked late tonight. Apparently, he'd gotten an emergency call that turned out, thankfully, not to be as big of an issue as first assumed. Amelia and I had eaten quietly, conversation focused mainly on the Pomeranian, before she'd retired to her room. I assumed Manny had already grabbed a bite to eat since he hadn't said anything when he'd come in, but I couldn't be sure without asking him.

I waited until Manny returned before finally rising from my cozy spot on the couch. He made directly for the kitchen, and I followed him in, thinking I'd make the offer to heat something up, when I noted a bag sitting on the counter.

"What's that?" I asked.

"A cake," he said, pulling said dessert free. "For our little celebration tonight. I picked it up on the way home, figuring you wouldn't have had a chance to grab something. I guess I should have called and asked. You didn't bake anything, did you?"

I stared at him blankly for a long couple of seconds before it dawned on me. "For Amelia?"

He popped the top of the plastic container, revealing a chocolate cake. Nothing was written on it. "I wasn't sure what to grab," he said. "So, I went with chocolate. No celebration would be complete without cake, am I right?" He grinned.

"What are we celebrating?" Amelia asked, coming into the room. Her phone was shoved into her pocket, earbuds hanging loose around her neck. I could hear the buzz of music coming from them.

I went to the cabinet to retrieve plates, figuring I'd let Manny take the lead on this one.

"You!" he said, wrapping her in a hug, which she stood stiffly for. "I heard you've finally found your calling. I couldn't be happier for you."

"Really, Dad?" Amelia said, face growing red as she pulled away. "You don't need to do this."

"Oh, yes I do."

Amelia looked to me for help, but I merely shrugged.

"Fine," she said, though I could tell she was pleased. "I want your icing." The last was directed at me.

"It's all yours."

Manny cut each of us a piece of chocolate cake. I scraped off the icing on my piece and slid it over onto Amelia's plate. I liked cake, but I wasn't a big fan of ultra-sugary icing. I could stand it in small quantities, but I'd usually split it between my children just to avoid the inevitable tummy ache. Now, without Ben, however . . .

No, Liz. Enjoy this.

We carried our plates to the table, and I went back for some milk. Nothing went better with chocolate cake than a cold glass of milk. The same went for cookies, and pretty much any dessert, if you asked me. I poured three glasses, and Amelia came in to carry hers and Manny's back to the table. Once that was done, we sat down, and immediately dug in.

"No," Manny said when Stewie realized we were

eating and rushed over to his side. "You can't have chocolate."

Stewie yapped in response, and then tore after Wheels, who zipped by, swatting at the dog's backside as she sped past.

Amelia laughed, which made the ache in my heart ease. I kept telling myself I'd focus on the good things in my life, yet every time I turned around, I was thinking of Ben and everything that had gone wrong over the last couple of days.

"So, what have you learned about being a detective?" Manny asked, shoving a piece of cake into his mouth.

Amelia shot me a worried look before answering. "Not much," she said, easing around the issue. Like me, I wasn't sure how Manny would take it if she admitted to looking into her brother's case on her own. "I really only just got started."

"Have a good teacher?"

"A couple of them." She chewed, focusing a little too hard on her cake.

"She has a mentor," I said. "Apparently, he's been showing her the ropes."

"Really?" Manny said. "He put you on any cases?"

He'd meant it as a joke, but Amelia didn't take it that way. She immediately stiffened, a panicked look coming over her face.

Manny looked from her to me, eyebrows slowly climbing.

"I, um . . ." Amelia cleared her throat, and then looked to me for help.

Decision time. On one hand, Manny had every right to know his daughter was looking into his son's case. He'd worry about her, but that's what parents were supposed to do.

Then again, adding that worry to everything else might push him over the edge. I'd never known Manny to freak out too badly about anything, yet we'd never experienced anything quite like this before.

In the end, I opted for the truth. "She looked into someone involved in Ben's case," I said. "It's just your basic background check, so she isn't putting herself in any danger."

Okay, so maybe I chickened out and didn't tell him the whole truth. Everything had turned out fine, and I doubted Amelia would be knocking on any other murder suspect's door any time soon, so there was no need to worry him.

Manny's brow furrowed in concern for a moment, before he smiled. "Well, if you learn anything, be sure to tell that detective. What's his name?"

"Detective Cavanaugh," I provided.

"That's the one," he said, pointing his fork at me. "Maybe if you come up with something useful, he'll decide to take you on as an intern or something. Are there detective assistants?"

"Not really," Amelia said, still blushing furiously.

"Well, there should be," Manny said. "I'm sure he's under a ton of stress, and could use someone to help him out with the small stuff."

Thankfully, conversation turned to more pleasant things then—mainly Stewie and Wheels. The dog looked ten years younger as he ran around the house, chasing after the cat. I think the sound of Wheels's wheels on the hard wood had a lot to do with that. Every time the cat zipped by, Stewie's ears would turn, and then he'd bounce after her, yapping away.

I knew it had to be getting on Joanne's nerves, but right then, I didn't care. If she came knocking, I'd put her in her place, and then walk away. Let her call the police. There wasn't anything they could do.

We finished our cake slices nearly at the same moment. Amelia begged off seconds, claiming she had to study. Manny considered another, but opted to head for the shower with a warning that he was likely going to bed early tonight. He was yawning even as he left me alone with the animals.

I was tired too, but wasn't so sure I'd be able to sleep. I put away the cake, cleaned up the dishes, and then decided it might be a good idea to at least try to catch a few hours of shut-eye.

"Come on, Stewie," I said, leading the dog toward the room where he'd be staying the night. He ran inside, sniffed at the food and water, and then turned to me and whined. Wheels was behind me, watching, a forlorn look on her face. She knew what the room meant; it would be the end of her playtime.

"I can't watch the two of you while I'm in bed," I said, but even as the words came out of my mouth, I knew I wasn't going to press the issue. "Fine," I said, stepping aside. "Have at it."

Stewie rushed toward Wheels, who spun in a wide circle. Her left wheel caught the wall, nearly tipping her over, but she managed to right herself and speed off before the Pomeranian could catch her. She skidded around the corner, and they were off toward the kitchen.

I let them play until the shower shut off and I heard Manny getting ready for bed. I forced the two of them to stop playing for a few minutes so I could take Stewie out for his nighttime potty break. He made quick work of it and whined to get back inside. As soon as Wheels saw him, she took off.

"Please, try not to destroy the house tonight," I

said, as I checked to make sure all the doors were locked. Once that was done, I headed to the bedroom. Manny was lying in bed, eyes already closed, and was snoring lightly. Amelia's light snapped off as I got dressed in my PJs, telling me she was heading to bed as well.

I climbed beneath the covers, and despite the certainty I'd be getting no sleep, I found myself dozing off almost immediately.

It felt like a single minute had passed when my eyes shot open. I sat bolt upright in bed, head swimming with sleep. I had no idea what had awoken me, but whatever it was, it had Manny up too. He looked to me, eyes wide, and then quickly stood and went to the window to peer outside.

"What was that?" I asked as Amelia's door opened. She poked her head out, hair a mess atop her head. I vaguely recalled hearing something, but couldn't place what it was that had woken me.

"I don't know," Manny said, keeping his voice low.

Somewhere downstairs, Stewie started barking and growling. I was on my feet in an instant, heart pounding in my ears.

"Stay in your room," Manny hissed, pointing at Amelia, who looked like she might argue at first, but thought better of it as she ducked back into her room and closed the door.

I started to follow Manny out of the bedroom, but he shook his head, pointing toward the bed like he expected me to stay there. I, of course, ignored him. There was no way I was going to stay behind when the animals could be in danger.

Please, let it be something the animals broke. But I knew it was unlikely, not with the ruckus the dog was making. Stewie didn't sound like he was barking at a broken vase. Something—or someone—was out there. I didn't know if it was in the house, or outside it, but something was indeed prowling around.

Manny peeked around the corner at the bottom of the stairs, and then started to back up, only to bump into me. He gave a little yelp, and then glared when he saw me.

"I told you to stay in the bedroom," he whispered.

"Is someone out there?" I asked, refusing to get into it. I was already there, so there was no point in arguing.

He nodded. "I saw a shadow move outside. I'm going to call the police." He retreated back upstairs, and into the bedroom, where his cell phone was charging.

The smart thing to do would be to follow him and wait until the police arrived, but Stewie was really barking and growling now. I'd also heard the faint tinkle of glass, as if someone had knocked a few shards free from a window. It was followed by an increase in the yaps, and I knew someone was trying to get inside.

Instead of heading for the bedroom, I found myself moving toward the dining room and the sound of the barks. I would *not* allow anything to happen to Stewie—not on my watch. I slid into the dining room, to the hutch there. I remained at a crouch as I opened the drawer and removed a large pair of scissors I kept there. Duly armed, I made for Stewie, who was at the back door.

I saw nothing at first. Wheels was nowhere in sight, and I hoped that meant she was hiding somewhere safe. Stewie was lunging at the back door, and I thought I heard someone hiss in a pained breath. *Good dog,* I thought. I hoped he'd drawn blood.

Scissors clutched in hand, I eased forward, eyes wide in the dark. I couldn't see much of anything, at least, not at first. A hand appeared, reaching in through a busted window beside the back door. Fumbling fingers reached for the latch, but before they found purchase, Stewie leapt up, teeth gnashing. The hand withdrew quickly.

Heart in my throat, I considered my options. Someone was trying to break into my house, but Stewie was holding them at bay for now. How much longer before they risked a bite to get inside? So far, it didn't appear as if the would-be thief had noticed me. The only lights on inside were two night-lights. One was upstairs in the hall by the bedrooms, the other in the hall near where the fostered animals would stay. No lights were on outside, and the moon was mostly covered by clouds, making it practically pitch-black out there.

I could very likely get to the door without the would-be intruder knowing, and then stab them in the hand when they next reached through. But, Stewie might react to my presence, giving me away.

And what if they have a gun?

There was no question who would have the advantage then.

But I couldn't stand there and do nothing.

I started forward, not sure what I was going to do, only knowing that I wasn't going to let whoever was outside in. I was almost to the door, scissors poised and ready, when the dining room light flicked on, blinding me.

"Liz?" Manny asked, but I paid him no mind. A

yelp, followed by the sound of scuffling feet, told me the intruder was beating a hasty retreat.

I rushed for the door and tried to jerk it open, but was stymied by the lock. Cursing under my breath, I flipped the lock, opened the door, and hurried outside, making sure to close the door behind me so Stewie wouldn't follow me out.

Eyes scanning the dark backyard, I didn't see anyone at first, and then I noticed movement to my left. It was a person, but they were wearing a hoodie, with the hood up, and loose-fitting pants, so I couldn't tell if it was a man or a woman. They weren't much bigger than me, which I took as a good sign. If it came down to a struggle, I hoped I could hold my own.

"Hey!" I shouted, scissors still clutched in my hands. "Stop!"

Needless to say, they didn't listen.

I gave chase, but after only three or four steps, I stopped. I was in my bare feet, in my pajamas, with only scissors for a weapon. Not only was it unlikely I'd catch the intruder in my current state, but I had no idea how well prepared they were for a fight. A knife would work just as well as a gun at stopping me.

"Liz!" Manny shouted behind me. He sounded panicked.

"I'm okay," I said, turning back to him. The intruder was long gone. An engine fired up down the street somewhere, and wheels screeched as the intruder raced away.

Manny gathered me into his arms. "Don't do that to me!" he said, hugging me tight.

"I'm all right." I turned back to the house so he wouldn't see the worry in my eye. I might not be hurt, but I was trembling. *Someone tried to break into my house!* "Let's get inside." I said, voice surprisingly strong. "They're gone."

Manny peered into the darkness, and then nodded.

Together, we headed inside to wait for the police to arrive.

23

I nearly jumped from the couch at the knock on the door. My heart, which had just resumed its normal pace, started thumping again. I felt sick, violated, and the intruder hadn't even gotten into the house. The more time I had to think about it, the worse I felt.

"I'll get it," Manny said, rising. "It's probably the police." He headed for the door.

"We're okay, Mom," Amelia reassured me. "Nothing got stolen. It's just a broken window."

"I know." I tried on a smile, but it faded quickly. A broken window was one thing; a broken sense of security was another.

Stewie was sleeping at my feet. The old dog had either not heard the door, or chose to ignore it. I'd spent the last ten minutes petting him, telling him how good of a dog he was for warning us that someone was trying to break in. If he hadn't been there, running free, there's no telling what would have happened. Were we dealing with a thief? Or was it the killer, come to silence those of us looking into Timothy's death?

Wheels was beside Amelia, squirming to be let down. Amelia kept her hold on her, not wanting to risk losing the cat. For all her reassurances, I could tell she was shaken, and was scared not just for us, but for the animals as well.

Manny returned, Detective Cavanaugh in his wake. The detective looked tired, as if he'd been sleeping when he'd gotten the call. Why they hadn't sent a regular cop, I didn't know. It probably had something to do with Timothy's murder, and our family's connection to it.

"Mrs. Denton," Cavanaugh said, stopping just inside the living room. He nodded once to me, and then Amelia, before his eyes started roaming, cataloging the layout of the house.

Manny sat down on the couch next to me, and put his arm protectively around my shoulders. I didn't sag into him, but appreciated the gesture nonetheless.

"Detective," I said. "Thanks for coming."

He grunted, and then his gaze fell on the snoozing dog. There was the briefest tightening of his jaw, but he didn't comment. "Is everyone all right?"

"We're fine," I said, though I felt anything but. "A window is busted, but otherwise, we're all okay. It was probably just a burglar."

Cavanaugh didn't look convinced. He strode across the room, to peer into the dining room, at the back door, and the window beside it. I'd swept the glass into a pile, but left it beneath the window in case he wanted to check it for evidence. He stared at it for a few minutes, and then turned back to us.

"Walk me through what happened."

"There isn't much to tell," Manny said.

"Humor me."

I took the lead and gave him a quick rundown of everything I knew. As Manny said, there wasn't much I could tell him, so it only took a couple of minutes.

"We were asleep when it happened," I said. "He broke the window, and when Manny turned on the light, he ran."

"Are you sure it was a he?"

"No," I admitted. "But something about the way he moved makes me think it was. It's nothing I can put my finger on."

"Is that all you can tell me?" Cavanaugh asked, looking down at his notepad. There hadn't been much for him to write down.

"That's it," I said. "We woke up to the sound of Stewie barking, and then I chased off the would-be thief. After that, it's been quiet."

"I see." This time, when Cavanaugh went to the dining room, he went all the way to the back door and looked outside. He tried the door, found it to be locked, and then unlocked it. Without so much as another word, he opened the door and stepped outside.

"Stay here," I told Manny and Amelia, rising.

"Are you sure you should go out there?" Manny asked.

"I'll be fine," I said. "The burglar's gone, and the detective is here. I want to make sure there's nothing else he needs from me."

Manny nodded, but didn't look comfortable with letting me go. I squeezed his forearm, shot Amelia a comforting smile, and then followed the detective outside.

Cavanaugh had a small penlight on and was using

it to scan the ground around the broken window. A couple shards of glass twinkled in the light, but, as far as I could tell, there was little else.

"Which way did he go?" he asked, turning the light on me.

I pointed. "He went that way. I heard a car start up shortly after I lost sight of him. I'm guessing he parked down the street and took off from there."

Cavanaugh stared off in the direction I pointed, as if he could see into the past. I had to admit, he had detective eyes. It wouldn't surprise me if he *could* deduce something just from looking at where the culprit had been.

"Any idea how long it took before you heard the car? A minute? A few seconds?"

"I'm not sure," I said. "I think it was only a few seconds, but in all the excitement, it could have been longer."

"And you didn't recognize the person?"

"Like I said, I never got a good look at him." I followed Cavanaugh's gaze, but there was nothing to see. "It could have been a random break-in," I said.

"Do you really believe that?"

"Well, no. But I don't want to think about the alternative."

"You say the dog woke you?"

"He did. He was barking up a storm and growling. It scared me. I'm not sure, but I think it was the glass breaking that woke me. I was dreaming one second, and wide awake the next, with no real idea why, until I heard Stewie."

Cavanaugh turned off the penlight, but didn't make for the door. "There's been no recent reports of break-ins around here," he said.

"We could have been the first. Or maybe it was a one-off job, kids causing trouble or something."

"The dog wasn't caged?" Cavanaugh asked, sounding as if it surprised him.

"No, he wasn't. He got along with Wheels just fine, so I figured it wouldn't hurt anything to leave him out to play."

"Wheels?" Cavanaugh asked, sounding skeptical.

"You saw her," I said. "It fits."

"I see." He cleared his throat, frowned. "It seems that dog has been at the center of quite a lot of trouble lately, hasn't he?"

"It's not his fault."

"No, I'm sure it's not." He stretched and rubbed at the back of his neck, before stifling a yawn. "But someone finds him interesting."

"You think someone came here to steal Stewie?"

He spread his hands. "I'm not sure what to think. The dog was present when Mr. Fuller was murdered. Now that he's here, your house gets broken into."

"Almost," I said, though the distinction was minor.

"You've had no issues before with break-ins. There's no recent activity in this area. No warning signs. Whoever was here, I'd put money on it that it had something to do with that dog."

My chest tightened. "Could it have been something else?" If someone was indeed after Stewie, I wasn't sure what I was going to do. I couldn't protect him, not indefinitely. And I definitely couldn't pass him on to the Lincolns if there was a chance someone might come after him there.

"Could it?" Cavanaugh asked. "Have you seen anyone strange around here lately? Any cars or people walking slowly by?"

"No."

"Any random calls? People calling at late hours, hanging up when you answer?"

"None that I recall."

"Have you interacted with anyone involved in the murder? Talked to them about the case, about Timothy Fuller or his dog?"

"You know I have."

"What about other times, when I wasn't present? Have you run into them outside their homes? Gone to see them without my knowledge?"

I tensed, thinking of Amelia's and my visit to Meredith. And then there were my trips to see Selena. And that's not to mention Duke and Courtney, or all the times I ran into Junior at the house. It seemed like every time I turned around, I was coming into contact with people involved in the case.

"I've bumped into some people," I said. "But nothing that would have led to this." I motioned toward the hole in my window.

Cavanaugh frowned, eyes narrowing as he regarded me. "You haven't been snooping, have you?"

"What? Me? No."

It must have sounded as exaggerated as it felt coming out of my mouth because Cavanaugh's frown only deepened.

"Seriously," I said. "I might have talked to Selena Shriver about her relationship with Ben and this other guy, Jason, but otherwise, I'm trying to stay out of it."

"And how did you get the dog?" he asked. "Last I heard, he was still in Mr. Fuller's possession."

"I went to talk to Selena," I said, choosing my

words carefully. "About Ben. When I was about to leave, I heard Stewie barking inside Timothy's house. I went over to make sure everything was okay, and that he wasn't left there alone. Junior was ransacking the place and was frustrated because he thought Stewie might lead him to Timothy's hidden stash of money. He realized it wasn't going to happen, so he told me to take the dog."

"Just like that?"

I shrugged. "He doesn't like animals, I don't think. He wanted Stewie because he thought he knew where the money was hidden. He no longer needs him."

"Because he found the money?"

"No, because he doesn't believe the dog can help. He thinks someone else took the money."

"Like who?"

Cavanaugh seemed suddenly interested. He removed his notebook from his pocket and clicked his pen.

"He accused me," I said, not wanting to lie to the detective. If he talked to Junior, I was sure my name would be the first out of his mouth. "And then he accused Meredith Hopewell, Timothy's nurse, of taking it. He was thinking of confronting her about it, but I talked him out of it."

"Does he have any reason to believe either of you would have taken the money?"

"Me? No," I said. "I think he blamed me because I was convenient."

"And the nurse?"

"She was with Timothy all the time," I said. "If anyone would know where the money was hidden, it would be her."

Cavanaugh looked thoughtful as he wrote something down. He tapped his pen on the pad of paper twice, and then pocketed both.

"Is there anything else you can tell me?" he asked. "Anything you've conveniently left out until now?"

I squirmed under his stare. "Not that I can think of," I said, though I could tell him all about Selena and Jason; not that I thought it had much to do with Timothy's murder. Just because she led my son on, didn't make it a crime.

"You sure about that?"

"Yeah," I said. And then, because I really wanted to know, "Do you have any idea who could have done this?"

He shook his head. "I can't say for sure, but I would recommend you keep to yourself for a few days. I don't want you looking for whoever did it, and I definitely don't want you asking questions."

I wanted to protest, but held my tongue. The more I thought about it, the more I was starting to wonder if Junior might be responsible for the attempted break-in. He'd parked in the alley, behind the barn, at his dad's place, when it would have been closer to park in the driveway. Whenever he was doing something underhanded, did he always park out of sight? Was it a pattern?

But why? He'd given Stewie to me, so it seemed strange he would want the dog back. Unless, of course, he changed his mind and wanted to give the Pomeranian's money sniffer another go.

Or if he thought I had the money here.

If that was the case, then what would stop him from trying again? It was obvious he was after the money, and if he truly thought I'd taken it, could he have figured the dog might lead him to it here? Was that why he let me take Stewie?

And then another thought seeped into my brain, one I liked even less.

What if it was Duke?

Junior didn't know where I lived. I guess he could have followed me, or happened across my van, which was sitting in the driveway, but I found it unlikely. Courtney was interested in the money, had said so herself. Maybe she, like Junior, thought Stewie could lead her to the cash. Or perhaps she figured she'd have a look around, see if I had it lying around my house.

Cavanaugh was watching me intently as I thought it through. While it would serve Courtney right if I were to tell him my suspicions, I didn't want to start pointing fingers. All I had were unfounded suspicions, and sending Cavanaugh on what could be a wild goose chase would help no one, Ben included.

I forced a smile, and gave him my best innocent look. "Is there anything else I can do for you, Detective?"

"I think I'm done here," he said, eyeing me. "Not unless you have something else you can tell me?"

"Not a thing."

He didn't look convinced, but, thankfully, he didn't press.

I led him back inside, to where Manny and Amelia were still sitting. Amelia's eyes were droopy, and Wheels had gotten down. She was sitting on the floor, next to Stewie, who was still snoozing away.

"Mr. Denton," Cavanaugh said, shaking Manny's hand. "I'll be in touch if I figure out who did this, but

I wouldn't count on it. These things happen, and often, the thief never returns."

"Thank you," Manny said. He walked Cavanaugh to the door. They spoke briefly, voices low, before the detective shook his hand once more, and then left.

"Crazy night," Manny said, returning.

"Yeah."

"The detective told me he's keeping Ben for another twenty-four hours," Manny said, but before I could get angry, he added, "He did sound as if it was more a precaution than anything. I'm starting to believe he's on our side."

"He'd better be," I muttered.

Manny stretched, eyes traveling toward the dining room. "We should do something about the window." He punctuated the comment with a yawn.

"Go ahead and get to bed," I told him. "You've got to work in the morning. I can clean up the glass and tape up some cardboard until we can get it fixed."

"You sure?" He yawned again.

"I'm sure."

He kissed me on the cheek. "It'll be fine," he said, though it sounded like he was trying to convince himself, more than me.

"It will," I said. "Go to bed. I've got this."

He nodded, and then headed for the bedroom.

Amelia rose with a yawn of her own, causing Stewie to rouse from the floor, tail wagging. She patted him on the head, and then turned away, feet dragging, as she headed for her bedroom.

"Amelia, hold on a sec."

She turned back to me, eyes heavy. "Yeah?"

"Did you talk to anyone other than Ms. Hopewell?" I asked. If she'd asked questions of the wrong person, then perhaps she'd stirred something up, something that would lead to someone trying to break into my house.

Amelia scratched her head, seemed confused by the question for a moment before, "Not about Ben," she said. "All I did was drive by the scene once and take some pictures. There wasn't anyone there. I did it mostly for the practice."

"So, no one saw you?"

She smacked her lips, trying to work out the sleep. "I don't think so," she said, before changing her mind. "Actually, there was some old guy across the street. He waved at me. And I guess someone might have looked out a window and saw me, but it would have been next door. I'm positive no one was at the Fuller house when I was there."

I wanted to press, ask her how close she got to the house, if she'd gone around back, or if she'd stayed in her car, but I could tell she was barely hanging on. The excitement from our late-night visitor had worn off, and she was dead on her feet.

"Thanks, Amelia. Go get some sleep."

"Goodnight, Mom." She turned and slouched down the hall. Stewie followed after her, leaving me alone with Wheels.

I watched them go, thinking. Just because she didn't see anyone at the house, didn't mean they weren't there. If Junior saw her snooping, or if whoever really killed Timothy had, then perhaps they'd stopped by for revenge.

But why? It wasn't like she'd found or saw anything.

Had she?

No, I was beginning to wonder if it was my own

poking around that had triggered the break-in. Junior was angry with me, as was Courtney. I was almost positive it was one of them.

But there wasn't anything I could do about it tonight. Stifling my own yawn, I turned to the closet and removed the broom and dustpan, and got to work cleaning up the mess.

24

Manny was gone by the time I woke up. I vaguely recalled him giving me a goodbye kiss on the cheek, but I was so out of it, I wasn't sure if it had actually happened, or if it was a dream. I'd lain awake most of the night, waiting for the window breaker to return, though he never did show again. I finally dozed off just before sunrise.

To say I was tired would be an understatement. But I didn't let it stop me. I scarfed down breakfast, and then grabbed the phone, ready to get to work.

"Hi, Sue," I said when my call was answered. "Good news! I have Stewie, the Pomeranian, for you, if you're still interested?"

Sue gasped in happy surprise. "Oh, Liz, thank you! I am. When can we get him?"

"He still has to pass all his tests, but I'm pretty sure it won't be any more than a day or two. If you want to see him before then, I can arrange a get-together whenever you'd like."

"No, that's all right, I can wait. I'm not sure I

could resist taking him home with me if I were to see him." She laughed.

"I'll call you as soon as all the test results are in."

"Thank you, Liz. We're both so excited to meet him. I think it'll do us both a lot of good."

"Oh, I'm sure he will. Tell Barry I said hi."

"Will do."

We clicked off.

I was thrilled to start my day off on such a high note. Sue and Barry Lincoln would make good pet parents for Stewie, even if he was older than they were—in dog years, that was. Hearing the joy in someone's voice when they learn they'll be taking in a new pet is part of the reason why I did what I did.

Speaking of Stewie, I found him lying next to a dozing Wheels, and took him out into the backyard to let him take care of his business. As he sniffed around the yard, I considered what I needed to do today. Calling someone to fix the window was high on the list, as was making sure I'd gotten all the glass when I'd swept last night. I didn't need Wheels stepping on a missed shard and injuring one of her front paws. The same went for Stewie.

Once the dog was done and ready to go back inside, I took him back to Wheels, and then checked around the window. The glass was gone, both inside and outside. I did put on a pair of gloves and wiggled a few loose shards from the windowsill before boarding it back up. I didn't want one of them falling out while I wasn't around to clean it up.

Satisfied, I made a quick call to a contractor I knew, arranged for them to stop by later, and then grabbed my keys and purse. I wasn't about to sit around and wait for them to show; not when there was something else I was desperate to do.

I started for the door.

"Where are you going?"

I nearly jumped straight out of my shoes. I spun to find Amelia standing in the hallway, hand on her hip in a way that was a spitting image of me—and before me, my own mother.

"Don't you have class today?" I asked, masking my embarrassment by asking a question.

"I took the day off," she said. "Are you heading out?"

"For just an hour or so," I said. "I thought I might check in on Ben and make sure he's doing okay."

Amelia's eyes widened briefly before she held up a finger. "Hold on one sec." She spun and vanished back down the hall.

She returned only a few seconds later, her backpack thrown over one shoulder.

"I'm coming with you," she said, her tone saying she wouldn't take no for an answer.

Honestly, I'd be glad for the company.

"Let me call Lenore," I said, taking out my phone and hitting her number. While I'd been content to let Stewie have the run of the house a few minutes ago, now that Amelia was coming with me, I was hoping we'd be out longer than the hour I'd planned for. "Maybe we can get lunch afterward," I told her as my phone rang.

Amelia nodded and waited while I asked Lenore if she could doggie sit. The older woman was more than happy to, and promised to be right over.

"How did you sleep last night?" I asked Amelia when I hung up.

"All right, I guess." From the bags under her eyes, I could tell that was a lie.

I didn't call her on it, however. All things consid-

ered, losing a little sleep was far better than the alternative. Thinking of Stewie's warning barks, I grabbed
him a treat and gave it to him, once more thanking
him for being so vigilant.

"We should get a dog," Amelia said, likely thinking
along the same lines as me. "A permanent one. If he
hadn't barked last night . . ."

"I know." I rubbed him behind his ears, and told
him how good of a dog he was. He soaked up the attention.

I took a few minutes to set out some things for
Lenore so she wouldn't have to look for treats for the
animals, or a snack for herself. I was just finishing up
when she arrived.

"Where is he?" she asked the moment the door
was open.

Introductions only took a few minutes, with Lenore
immediately cooing over the Pomeranian. I don't
think she heard half of what I'd said, she was so taken
with him. Stewie was just as happy as she was, if not
more so. He yapped twice, spun in a circle, and then
promptly rolled onto his back, if not a little stiffly.
Lenore gave him the belly rub he was asking for.

Amelia and I left them to it, and got into the van.
A moment later, and we were on the way.

We remained silent during the drive, each of us lost
in our own thoughts. Worry kept working through me,
and an urge to call the house to make sure Lenore was
okay hit me every mile or two. Nothing said the intruder hadn't been watching the house, waiting for
an opportunity to strike again. Now that we were
gone, and all that was there was a little old woman,
he could easily make his move.

Stop it, Liz, I silently reprimanded myself. *She'll be
fine.* Paranoia didn't suit me.

I pulled into the police station lot, a bundle of nerves. It had only been a couple of days since Ben had been taken in, yet it already felt like a lifetime. I wasn't sure I could take it much longer, and I wasn't even the one who was locked up. I didn't even want to think about how he must be feeling.

Amelia and I headed inside, immediately bumping into an exhausted-looking Detective Cavanaugh, who appeared as if he was about to leave. His eyes tightened and his mouth pressed into a fine line when he saw me.

"Did something else happen?" he asked.

"No," I said. "But thank you for coming out last night. I've never had anything like that happen before. I was afraid he was going to come back."

"He didn't," Cavanaugh said, leaning against the wall like it was the only thing keeping him upright. "I had a car drive by every few hours. As far as I can tell, whoever tried to break in is long gone. I doubt they will try again."

"I hope so."

Cavanaugh rubbed at his chin, eyes going from me, to Amelia. "Is there something I can do for you ladies?" he asked. By his tone, I think he already knew what we wanted.

"We'd like to see Ben," I said. "Just to talk and make sure he's doing okay."

Cavanaugh remained silent as he regarded the two of us. I could tell he was thinking about it, but wasn't sure whether or not he should relent. As it stood now, Ben was a murder suspect, and I was sure there were rules against letting people come and go as they pleased.

"Please, Detective," Amelia said. "I haven't seen

my brother since before you arrested him." She gave him puppy dog eyes, which had *me* nearly in tears.

Cavanaugh heaved a heavy sigh and pushed away from the wall. "All right, I suppose at this point, it can't hurt. But don't expect this to keep happening." He looked as if he wanted to say more, but instead, all he said was, "Wait here," before he turned and walked away, rubbing at the back of his neck as he went.

I was hoping his willingness to let us see Ben meant most of the pressure was off him, and that Detective Cavanaugh had a new top suspect, not that he was giving us one last visit before locking him up for good.

The police station was buzzing with a low level of activity. A few cops paused to look at us, but no one approached. I didn't see Officer Mohr anywhere, or even Officer Perry. I missed the familiar faces, especially since I was standing there with all those eyes watching us. It made me feel like a criminal.

Thankfully, Detective Cavanaugh returned a few short minutes later. "This way," he said, motioning for Amelia and me to follow.

He took us down the same hallway as the last time I'd visited, but instead of taking us to the same room as before, he opened another door. The room was larger than the last one, but not by much. It held a table and a few chairs that were pushed around it haphazardly, as if a group of people had recently sat there and all got up and walked out at once. A whiteboard was pushed against the wall. A few stray black marks were all that was visible on it.

A meeting room? I wondered, and then shook off the thought when Ben rose from one of the chairs, holding his arms wide. I rushed in for an all too brief hug. I stepped aside and Amelia took my place, surprising everyone by wrapping her brother in a hug.

"I'm so glad you're here," Ben said, sitting back down. He wiped at his eyes, a sad smile on his face. Amelia took the chair next to him, while I took one across the table. Cavanaugh closed the door, but remained inside, as expected.

"How are you holding up?" I asked.

"Better," Ben said. "It's hard, but they're treating me all right. Mr. Ives has been in to see me a few times already. He thinks I've got a good chance of walking away from this."

I glanced at Cavanaugh and was surprised to see compassion in his eye. He might think Ben capable of murder, but he still thought of him as human, with a family. It was sometimes easy to forget that when something like this happens.

"Have they charged you yet?" Amelia asked.

Ben looked to the detective, who didn't respond in any way. "I don't think so."

"They can't hold you for much longer if they don't, I think," she said, sounding uncertain. "There's only a certain amount of time you can be held without being charged before they are forced to let you go."

"I've discussed this with the detective," I said to her. And then, to Ben, "He said last night it might only be a day more."

"Unless he charges you," Amelia said, crushing my hopes that Ben might be home by tomorrow. "If that happens . . ." Her jaw tightened as she looked down at her hands.

"I'm okay, sis," Ben said. "I mean it. It was hard at first, but I'm getting used to it."

Amelia snorted. "Liking prison life, are you?" she asked. "And to think, all this for a girl."

"Hey," he said. "She's pretty hot."

Amelia rolled her eyes.

It made my heart ache seeing them like this. It was good to see they both still had their senses of humor, but darn it, they should be joking with one another at home, not here, not with Ben's life on the line.

And to make matters worse, I had to break him of any notion that he had a chance with Selena.

"She has a boyfriend," I said, feeling like a horrible person for telling him.

Ben's smile faded, before he shrugged. "I guess I'm not surprised. A girl that good-looking can't be single."

"I take offense to that, you know," Amelia said.

"Yeah, yeah. Gag." Ben stuck his tongue out at his sister, and then turned to me. "I should have known better. But when we were together, she never said anything about having a boyfriend, so it never crossed my mind to ask."

"You were probably too busy ogling her," Amelia said.

Especially with her in that bikini, I thought, but didn't say it. "It's okay, Ben," I said. And then, because I felt guilty for making his bad day worse, "She did say she and her boyfriend are having troubles. There's a chance they may break up soon."

Ben grinned. "That's good to hear. I wouldn't mind stopping by her place and swimming with her a few more times. She does look good in a bikini."

"Swimming?" Amelia asked. "You went swimming?"

"Yeah. We talked for a little bit, and then got into the pool. We raced a few times, and kinda wrestled around a little." His face reddened. "Afterward, we crashed in the deck chairs and let the sun dry us off. I think we both dozed off, it was so relaxing."

"You didn't have your trunks," I said, lamely. Never in my life could I imagine showing up at a stranger's house and getting into a pool with them. Ben definitely took after his dad in that regard.

"She had a spare pair," Ben said.

"And you didn't think that was weird?" Amelia asked.

Ben shrugged. "I wasn't thinking as clearly as I should have by then. She let me get changed in her bedroom, and then we went swimming. That was all I was focused on at the time. If you would have seen her . . ." He waggled his eyebrows, which drew a groan from Amelia.

"Wait," I said. "You got changed?"

"Well, duh. I wasn't going to get my clothes wet."

Amelia's eyes met my own. She was thinking the same thing as I was.

"Where did you leave your shirt?" I asked.

"In the bedroom," Ben said. "Why?"

"Did you put it on while you were sunbathing?" Amelia asked.

"No, what would be the point?" Ben said. "I didn't get dressed again until I heard the commotion going on next door."

Which meant, his shirt was lying in Selena's bedroom, unattended for a good twenty minutes, if not longer.

Enough time for someone to sneak in, put it on, kill Timothy, and then sneak back and drop it off?

I thought it likely. But who? And why go to all that trouble?

"Ben, you idiot!" Amelia was saying. "Why didn't you tell someone this before?"

"I did!" he said, and then, quieter, eyes going to

Cavanaugh, who looked extremely interested in the conversation, "Well, I think I did."

I rose, turning to the detective. "Do you know what this means?" I asked, voice pitched excitedly.

"It might mean nothing," he said, speaking carefully.

"Someone could have come in and stolen the shirt," I said, just in case he hadn't figured that out on his own. "When Clarence saw someone sneak into Timothy's house, wearing Ben's shirt, it wasn't Ben!"

"Maybe," Cavanaugh said. "But who would have done something like that?"

"Jason," I said. "Selena's boyfriend." I snapped my fingers, trying to remember his last name. "Jason Maxwell. He must have taken it. He could have been there the entire time, hiding in another room while Ben and Selena were swimming." I remembered hearing him inside Selena's house the day of the murder, when she'd said it was a cat. "He could have planned the whole thing!"

"Mrs. Denton," Cavanaugh said, but I wasn't going to listen to him tell me my theory wasn't worth considering. I knew it had holes, but it made far more sense to me than Ben killing a man he barely knew.

"Come on, Amelia." I glanced back at Ben. "I'll be back soon. Hang in there." I marched past Cavanaugh, and out the door.

Amelia followed after me, calling, "Mom, wait!" but I didn't stop until we were in the parking lot, standing outside the van. "What are you doing?" she asked.

"He doesn't believe him," I said. "The detective thinks Ben's lying." Or he thinks I'm reaching, which I honestly might be, but at least there was something to go on now.

"We can convince him otherwise," Amelia said. "I've been learning a lot about law and procedure lately. I'm sure we can figure out how to make him understand and act."

"I know you have, honey." I opened the van door. "But I have a feeling we need more than a theory to convince Detective Cavanaugh."

"What?" Amelia scrambled over to the passenger's side and got in as I started up the van. "Where are we going?"

I smiled at her and backed out of the parking lot. Detective Cavanaugh was standing outside the station, arms crossed, watching me with concern. He had to know I was up to something, yet he wasn't making a move to stop me.

A good sign? Or was he hoping I'd hang myself out to dry and prove myself to be Timothy's killer?

"You'll see," I told Amelia, dismissing Cavanaugh out of my mind, and pulling onto the street. "Just follow my lead. I have a plan."

25

"I don't get it." Amelia held up the blond wig and reading glasses. "What do you want me to do with these?"

I started up the van and pulled out of the parking lot. I'd made her wait in the van when I went in to grab her disguise, knowing she would protest if she knew what I wanted from her. A bag of clothes sat in the seat behind her.

"Put them on," I said.

"Okay, I figured that out. But why?"

I glanced at her before turning onto the road leading toward Timothy's house. "Put them on."

She gave me one of her best put-upon sighs, but did as she was told. She pulled the wig on, tucking her hair beneath it so it wouldn't show, and then slipped the glasses onto her nose. She squinted at me through the lenses.

"They suit you," I said, suppressing a laugh.

"Uh-huh. I can hardly see anything."

"They're low prescription. Just let them slide down your nose a bit and you'll be fine."

"I feel stupid."

"You look good."

She huffed and sat back in her seat, arms crossed. "Are you going to tell me what we're doing or not?"

"I am. Eventually."

Amelia groaned, but stopped asking. Instead, she pulled down the visor so she could look into the mirror. She spent the rest of the ride fiddling with her glasses and wig.

I was okay with that. I wasn't exactly sure how we were going to do this. The plan I'd come up with was more like a vague impression of what I wanted to do, with no real details. The only thing I was sure of, was I didn't want Selena to recognize Amelia, now or later.

I was running on the assumption Selena or her boyfriend had something to do with Timothy Fuller's death. They were neighbors, and while, sometimes, spats between people who lived so close together could turn deadly, it didn't feel like that was what happened.

But killing for money? I could see it.

I had no real proof that Selena knew about Timothy's hidden stash. But then again, everyone else seemed to know about it, so why not her? Jason and Selena could have been in the pool together when they saw us show up for Stewie. Then, as we were leaving, they came up with a plan. Selena draws Ben over, gets him to take off his shirt, and Jason steals it to trick Timothy or Meredith into letting him into the house. He gets in, looks for the money, and then what?

He gets caught, of course.

Timothy sees him snooping, and Jason takes him out to the barn to kill him, likely so Meredith wouldn't hear. Maybe it was an accident, maybe he was prepared to do it, but either way, he panics, and runs back to Selena's house, takes off the shirt, and hides until Ben leaves.

Admittedly, there were holes in the story, and it was a tad convoluted for an impromptu plan, but at least it was something to go on.

I pulled into Selena's driveway and parked, but didn't get out right away. I shut off the engine and let it rest.

"There's some clothes in the back for you," I said. "Get changed quickly."

Amelia looked as if she wanted to protest, but instead, unbuckled and crawled into the back of the van. She audibly groaned when she saw what I'd bought for her.

"Really, Mom?"

"Please, just put them on. I'll explain in a minute."

"What are we even doing here?" Amelia asked, thankfully doing as I asked.

"Give me a second."

No one was home next door, so I couldn't use Junior directly in my little scheme. Clarence was sitting on his porch, watching my van, cup in hand, but he was of no use to me. Otherwise, no one was around. If Jason was here, he'd ridden with Selena. Other than my van, her car was the only one in the driveway.

I kind of hoped Selena was out with Jason, and wouldn't be back for an hour or so. I'd have more time to think and come up with an even better plan that way. I was already seeing holes in my plan, like, why would someone not related to me be riding in my van?

But to wait would mean Ben would spend even *more* time in jail. I couldn't have that, not when I was pretty sure Selena had something to do with Timothy's murder, even if it was indirectly. I knew she would never admit it, and if Jason indeed was the one who'd stolen the shirt and killed Timothy, then he would be just as tight-lipped. Convincing either to admit to anything would be next to impossible.

Thankfully, talking wasn't what I needed out of them.

It was actions.

"Mom?" Amelia asked, voice pitched nervously as she eased into the seat next to me.

"Sorry," I said. "I was thinking." I glanced at her, mouth falling open in shock.

"Shut up," she said. "I feel stupid."

She didn't look it. Her normal clothing, which usually consisted of T-shirts and jeans, had been replaced by a smart pantsuit. With the wig and glasses, I hardly recognized her.

"You look great," I said. "I mean that."

"I think we need to focus," she said. "Someone was looking out the window at us." She motioned toward Selena's house. Whoever had been there, was gone now. "If you're going to fill me in, you'd better hurry."

"All right," I said. "I think I know what I want you to do."

"You think?"

"I'm making it up as I go," I said. "Cut me some slack."

Amelia tipped her head back to stare at the ceiling. "You're going to get me killed, aren't you?"

"No," I said. "We're just here to deliver some information."

"What kind of information?"

"The kind that will produce results." Or, at least, I hoped they would.

"Mom, what are you talking about?" Her gaze moved to the house. "Doesn't the girl Ben was with live here?"

"She does."

"So, why are we here? And why am I wearing this stupid outfit?" She touched the wig, acting as if it might be crawling with bugs.

It's now or never. "We're going to play a little pretend," I said. I took a few minutes to tell her what I was thinking. Amelia looked troubled at first, and then excited. By the time I was done, she looked raring to go. I, on the other hand, was beginning to question the sanity of my plan.

"What are you waiting for?" Amelia asked, reaching for the door. "Let's do this thing."

"Are you sure you're okay with it?" I asked.

She merely rolled her eyes and got out of the van for an answer.

I followed her out, and then led the way to the door. This was *my* plan, so I was hoping to do most of the talking. Amelia was merely a prop, one I hoped would garner only mild interest, and little in the way of scrutiny.

I knocked on Selena's door. Amelia stood behind me, looking nothing like the daughter I had raised. She stood tall, confident, looking for all the world like a businesswoman.

Now, that's not to say Amelia wasn't a confident woman. She was. She just tended to hide it behind

the youthful arrogance of someone who was still trying to find themselves.

The door opened, revealing Selena Shriver, hand
on her hip. She was wearing another tiny dress, and
looked as if she was ready for a hot date. I wondered
if she actually sat around the house looking like that,
or if I'd caught her just before she went out for the
day.

"Hi, Selena," I said, flashing her a smile.

Her eyes flickered past me, to Amelia, and back
again. "Why are you here again?" she asked.

"Just to talk," I said. "There've been some developments, and I was hoping you might be able to help us
with a little trouble we've run into."

Her gaze flickered back to Amelia. "Who's this?"

"This?" I glanced back at my daughter, hoping Selena wouldn't be able to see the family resemblance.
"This is Tina Templeton. She works for the company
that provided the medical equipment Timothy
used."

Selena's hand moved from her hip so she could
cross her arms. "All right?" She sounded as confused
as I'd expected her to be.

"Hello," Amelia said, flashing a smile.

Selena's mouth worked, but she seemed unable to
come up with something to say, until she managed,
"What do you want with me?"

"Well," I said. "Tina came to me after she tried to
contact Junior and failed. She heard I was taking in
Timothy's dog, Stewie, and thought I might be able
to help." I paused, hoping Selena didn't realize how
ridiculous that sounded. "She's been trying to get
into the house so she can pick up the equipment to
return to the hospital."

"What does this have to do with me?" Selena asked.

"It's more than just the medical equipment I need," Amelia said before I could answer. "There's something else inside that might help the police solve the murder, if only I can get to it."

Selena's eyes widened briefly, but she covered it well by stepping aside. "Maybe you two should come inside," she said.

I glanced back at Amelia, winked, and then thanked Selena as we entered her house. She led us into the living room, and offered us a seat. Neither Amelia nor I sat.

There were no other sounds in the house, so it appeared Jason wasn't there. I was disappointed in that, because I'd hoped he'd be here to hear what we had to say. I had to hope Selena passed on the message.

"So, what was it you were saying about something helping solve the murder?" Selena asked.

"We'd gotten reports of abuse coming from the Fuller household," Amelia said, taking the lead. "So, when we delivered one of the machines last fall, we had a camera installed in the hopes of getting to the truth. Unfortunately, the recorded information is inside the house where we can't get to it."

"I still don't understand what it has to do with me?" Selena said.

"It's Junior," I said. "He won't talk to Tina. He says that whatever is in the house, belongs to him now. He plans on selling the equipment to make a quick buck." I leaned forward, lowering my voice. "He doesn't seem to care that there might be evidence there that could find his father's murderer."

"But he was killed in the barn, wasn't he?" Selena asked. "How would a camera in the house help?"

A flare of panic shot through me as I tried to come up with something to say.

Amelia stepped in, saving me from ruining my entire plan. "The device is placed so that it can see into the living room, and the kitchen, which looks out over the backyard."

"They knew that Timothy liked to go out there to get away from everything," I put in. "So, whoever killed him will be viewable."

"Why not go to the police?" Selena asked. She was asking far too many observant questions for my liking.

Thankfully, Amelia seemed to have all the answers.

"The camera isn't exactly legal," she said. "It was installed without Timothy's, or his nurse's, knowledge. If I can get inside the house, I can retrieve it, and place it somewhere unconnected to our machines."

"And then, all someone has to do is tell the police where to find it," I said. "They'll assume Timothy set it up himself to keep an eye on the house."

Selena blinked slowly. She seemed genuinely confused, for which I didn't blame her. Our little story had sounded better when we'd discussed it in the van. Now, I was beginning to wonder if it was just a little too far-fetched for anyone to believe.

"We need your help," I said. "We need to get into the house."

"And you want me to do what?" Selena asked, eyes still bouncing between us.

"Junior has spoken highly of you," I said. "He said you've been a good neighbor to his dad." I leaned in and put my hand next to my mouth as I stage whispered, "Though I think he's more interested in your looks than your personality."

Selena actually blushed. I had a feeling that would work.

"We were wondering if you might be willing to talk to Junior for us. Ask him if he would let her into the house so she could collect the machinery. If it doesn't work out and he turns you away, then there's no harm. If it does, you'll be doing her a big favor."

"All I need to do is talk to him?" Selena asked.

"That's it."

Selena looked thoughtful a moment, before shrugging. "I suppose there's no harm in asking for you. If I see him, I'll talk to him."

"Thank you," Amelia said.

"I can't promise anything," Selena added. "I don't really know him all that well, so he might turn me away without listening to me."

"That's all right," I said. "All we can do is ask. We appreciate you trying."

Selena bustled us to the door, seemingly eager to be rid of us. *She's likely going to call Jason the moment we're out the door.* And if he showed, then it was only a matter of time before they made their move. I had no doubts that if he'd killed Timothy, he'd be looking for the camera by night's end.

Thanking Selena once more, Amelia and I got into the van. We pulled out of the driveway, and drove past Clarence's house, who to my delight, was gone. I didn't want him to see us when we doubled back, nor did I want too many eyes seeing Amelia and me together.

"Do you think it will work?" Amelia asked, practically bouncing in her seat. The wig and glasses were still on.

"I hope so." I made a U-turn and then found a place to park where I could still see both Selena's house and Timothy's house, but wouldn't be easily seen by Clarence if he were to return to his porch.

"What if it wasn't her? Or her boyfriend?" Amelia asked.

"Then we try someone else." Junior was next on my list, followed by Meredith.

A car drove by, and then was gone. I couldn't tell if it was anyone I knew, or just someone passing by.

"What now?" Amelia asked, pushing her wig-hair out of her face. She grimaced, clearly not liking the feel of it.

"Now? We wait."

"For how long?"

I checked the clock. It wasn't even noon.

"For as long as it takes."

"And then?" Amelia didn't sound like she wanted to sit in the van for the next couple of hours.

Admittedly, neither did I.

But I wasn't going to walk away now, not after we'd gotten the ball rolling. If they made a move for the nonexistent camera, I planned on being there to catch them in the act.

"We'll decide that when we see what happens," I said, hoping that whatever did happen, would put the nail in the coffin of someone other than Ben.

26

Something rustled in the tree overhead, causing me to tense briefly before I resumed my watch. When I'd first concocted my little plan to catch Jason and Selena in the act, I hadn't realized how boring the wait would be.

Night had fallen some time ago, and nothing but animals had moved. No cars arrived at Selena's, let alone Timothy's house, and there were no furtive movements from next door.

I was crouched outside, a dry hamburger from a fast-food place downtown in hand. Amelia had left four times now, once for the food, another to swap the van for her car, which was less conspicuous, and the other two times to check on Stewie and Lenore, who was perfectly happy dog-sitting for the day. I didn't blame her for wanting to leave. The wait was awful and I was beginning to wonder if I'd been wrong about Selena and Jason's role in Timothy's murder.

I took a bite from my burger and chewed with a grimace. Would it be so hard to put fresh condiments on the greasy meat? It was becoming clear the food was as bad an idea as my plan.

I considered calling Detective Cavanaugh to tell him what I'd done, but shelved the idea. He would probably laugh at me for doing something so stupid. I figured I could give it a couple more hours, and then I would have to give up for the night. There was no way I was going to stay out here until morning, especially since Manny would be home soon and would start calling, wondering where I was.

I shifted so I could lean against one of the trees bordering the property across the alley from Timothy's house. I couldn't see Amelia's car from where I was, but I was sure Amelia was still sitting there somewhere, watching. If nothing else, our little stunt would give her practice if she truly did decide to pursue a career in law enforcement. Detectives spent quite a lot of time sitting around, waiting for something to happen.

What was worse, I couldn't check my phone or make a call without giving myself away. The phones these days gave off way too much light, and if Selena or Jason were to peer outside at just the right moment, they would surely see me.

Shifting positions again, I rubbed at a cramp forming in my left calf. I could always go back to the car and wait there for a little while. I figured that if something *did* happen, we'd see a flashlight inside Timothy's house, or would hear something as they started searching the place.

But what if we didn't hear or see anything? Sitting back here might very well be the only way I'd catch them. Could I really risk missing it?

No, I decided. I could suffer a little while longer. It was for Ben, after all.

My doubts were heavy as I took another bite of the near-moldy burger. My stomach revolted, so I threw the rest away in the neighbor's trash.

I was about to give in for the night when I saw someone creeping around the side of the house. My breath caught as I watched the shape move slowly, circling around the property. I hadn't seen anyone leave Selena's house, but that meant little since I couldn't see her front door from where I crouched. Amelia had her eyes on the front, but since she was forced to park down the road a ways so no one would see her, she might have missed someone leaving.

The shape paused at the back door. I wondered if it was the same person who'd tried to break into my house last night. I couldn't make anything out about them, no facial features, and no real good estimate on height or weight. The intruder was crouched in a way that meant it could be anyone—Jason or Selena included.

Wishing I had a way to contact Amelia other than risking a phone call or text, I eased forward in an attempt to get a better look. The person was attempting to jimmy the back door lock, head constantly on a swivel. I still couldn't make out their features—whether it was Selena or Jason or someone else—but I was afraid to get too close.

Finally, the lock clicked, and they were in, vanishing into the house like a ghost.

No light clicked on. The door closed, hardly making a sound. I waited as my heart thundered in my ears, but from outside, I could see and hear nothing.

Call Cavanaugh or wait? I wondered, itching to do *something*, while fearing for my life at the same time. Nothing said this intruder was the same one that killed Timothy, but if it was, I would be putting myself at great risk doing anything more than calling the detective and telling him what I'd seen.

And what would Cavanaugh do once he found out what I'd done? I doubted he'd thank me. And if the intruder got away, what would we have then? My word against everyone else's. No one said it was Selena or Jason. It could very well be Junior, coming back to poke around for his father's money.

But why be so secretive about it?

I decided to risk it and shot Amelia a quick text, telling her someone was in the house and to call Detective Cavanaugh anonymously. At least then, we'd have plausible deniability if this blew up in our faces.

Now what? I wondered. I could sit back and wait, eyes on the house, hoping Cavanaugh got there in time.

But what if they checked every last spot where a camera could be hidden, only to find it nowhere in sight? If it was Selena or Jason, they'd immediately think I'd led them on. And if it was one of them who'd tried to break into my house last night, they could try again.

And if they left while I was sitting here, debating on what to do? This whole thing would be for naught, and Ben would still be stuck behind bars.

I refused to let that happen.

Creeping slowly forward, I made for the back door, hoping the intruder hadn't locked it behind them. All was quiet outside, though now, I could hear something coming from inside, a harsh sound, like plastic being pulled apart with force. I didn't have much time.

Testing the door, I sucked in a relieved breath when I found it was still unlocked. Oh so slowly, I opened it, teeth clenched out of fear I'd make a sound. I opened the door just enough for me to slip in, and then, very carefully, I closed it behind me.

The intruder wasn't in view, which I was thankful for. Since someone had ransacked the place before, tearing apart the equipment, it was all over the room, so there really was no telling which machine might hold my made-up camera.

Only the faintest of moonlight illuminated the kitchen. I crept to the counter to where I'd found the knives before, but was disappointed to find them gone. In fact, the entire counter had been cleaned off, and likely boxed away, leaving me with nothing I could grab as a weapon.

My eyes traveled to the drawers and cupboards, and I wondered if there was something I could use in there, when a muttered curse came from the other room. There was a thump, followed by another curse. It sounded like it was coming from the other side of the wall, mere feet from where I crouched. I practically stopped breathing as I slowly moved toward the doorway.

Just leave, Liz! The voice in the back of my mind sounded a lot like Manny's as it urged me to get out. *You don't have a weapon. The person in there could be a cold-blooded killer. Do you really want to confront him or her bare-handed?*

Well, no, I didn't, but I also didn't want Ben to spend the rest of his life in jail.

I took another slow, careful step . . .

Right on top of a dog toy.

The squeak seemed deafening in the otherwise quiet house. My breath caught in my throat and every muscle in my body seized. As the echo died away, the only sound I could hear was my own pounding heart, which was currently residing somewhere near my larynx.

Afraid to remove my foot from the toy, I remained as I was, hoping that somehow, the intruder hadn't heard the loud squeak. I couldn't hear them moving on the other side of the wall. There were no more curses, no sound of plastic being pried free from metal.

Seconds passed where nothing happened. I started to get dizzy from holding my breath, so I let it out slowly between my teeth. I sucked in a trembling breath, filling my lungs with air that burned.

"I hear you."

The voice sent icicles racing down my spine. It was said singsong, almost whispered. I couldn't place the voice, but I was pretty sure that whoever said it was male.

With nothing else I could do, I straightened, taking my weight off the dog toy. It exhaled yet another reverse squeak as air rushed inside it.

"Come out with your hands up," I said, feeling ridiculous. Even if he did what I said, I didn't have a weapon. It would take him all of two seconds to figure that out, and then what?

A grunt of a laugh came from the other side of the wall. I guess I didn't have to worry about that.

"The police are on their way," I said, hating how scared I sounded. "You've been caught red-handed."

"I have, have I?" The speaker stepped into view, face swathed in shadow. Now that I was up close, I noted he was taller than expected. This was definitely not Jason Maxwell, though the voice was vaguely familiar, if not gruff. I could tell he was masking it on purpose.

Clutching my phone like I might a knife, I readied myself. "Stay where you are."

This time, I was met with a chuckle. "Ah. Liz Denton," he said, shaking his head. "I knew you would figure it out. Didn't I tell you that when you came to visit me?"

The entire room seemed to wobble as I finally recognized the voice.

"Clarence?" I asked, not quite sure I believed what my ears were telling me.

But it all made sense now. Clarence was the witness who'd claimed to have seen Ben entering Timothy's house. If *he* was the one who killed the old man, then, of course, he would make up a story and try to pin it on someone else.

"Timothy wasn't as smart as you, no sir." He sucked in a breath through his teeth. "That man was stubborn as could be, yet never truly thought about the consequences of his actions."

"You killed him?" I asked at a whisper, though I already knew the answer.

"It couldn't be helped. He wouldn't let things slide, nor would he listen to reason. It really wasn't all that surprising, not if you knew the man." Clarence sighed, held out his hand. "Give me the weapon, Mrs. Denton. Please."

I took a step back, hiding the phone behind my back. It was then I noticed the pry bar in Clarence's other, gloved, hand.

"Now, I don't want to have to use this on you," he said, hefting it. "But I will if you make me."

"But . . ." A thousand thoughts zinged through my head. How could such a nice old man kill anyone? How had he known where to look for the camera? Would he kill me too?

And, most importantly, where in the heck was Detective Cavanaugh?

Clarence took a step forward. Moonlight from the window swept across his face. He looked so serene, so calm, it felt like I was dreaming. When he held out his hand again, a faint smile crossed his face, like he was simply asking me to dance.

"The weapon, please."

"What are you going to do to me?" I asked, refusing to show him my phone. *Please, let Amelia have seen my text.* The moment he realized I wasn't armed, was the moment he would make his move.

"Now, that's up to you," Clarence said, advancing a step. "If you hand it over, maybe we can work something out. We both know Timothy wasn't a nice man. He deserved what he got. Those of us forced to deal with him need to be compensated for the stress he put us through, don't you think?"

"I think murder isn't the answer."

Clarence shrugged, hand insistent. "Sometimes, it's all we've got."

The door was closed behind me. Ahead, the front door would be locked, and there was nothing upstairs that could save me. Clarence had just admitted to murdering Timothy Fuller. There was no way he was going to let me get out of this alive.

Not unless I took matters into my own hands.

"Catch!" I shouted, tossing my phone underhand at him like it was a live hand grenade.

Clarence's eyes widened as he tried to catch it, dropping the pry bar in his surprise. I came charging in, right after the phone, shoulder lowered like a linebacker, and hit him directly in the gut with all the force I could manage.

For an old man, he was surprisingly solid. He

grunted and staggered back a step, but didn't go down.

My phone clattered to the ground, and he stepped on it as he righted himself and shoved me backward. I went down, landing hard on my backside, and nearly cracking my head against the edge of the table. Clarence winced, and rubbed at his wrist, like the shove had hurt him just as much as it had me.

"Now, why would you go and do something like that?" He began to advance, eyes gone hard. Murderous.

Not wanting to be caught on my back, I scuttled backward, working my way to my feet. I was only a few inches from the door, and I risked turning to grab for it.

Clarence was faster.

His hand slammed hard on the door just as I started to pull it open. With his free hand, he grabbed for my wrist, but I was able to twist free before he could get a solid hold. I screamed for help, and then ran for the living room, and the pry bar, which had bounced just inside the room.

Of course, I managed to step on the dog toy again, and completely lost my balance. I staggered forward, catching myself on the wall, hitting the light switch as I did.

After squinting into the dark for so long, it was like someone had turned on the sun. Clarence cursed, coming to a sudden stop as he was blinded. Blinking away tears, I dropped down and felt around for the pry bar, black spots flashing in front of my eyes. My fingers hit metal just as Clarence kicked it away.

"I don't think so," he said, breathing hard.

I rose and held up both hands as I backed into the living room. The already dismantled medical machines were in small pieces, wires pulled free. He hadn't come snooping for Timothy's money, but had come after the camera.

How had he known?

If I thought I had time, I would have asked him.

But Clarence's good humor was gone. He advanced on me, face hard, uncaring. This wasn't the same man I'd sat with on his porch. I could see the killer in his eye when he said, "I'm sorry to have to do this."

"Me too." I lunged at him, shoving him in the chest. Startled, he staggered back, slamming into the wall so hard, his head snapped back and left a dent in the drywall. I spun, and rushed for the front door. If I could get it open, then perhaps Amelia would see what was happening and could call for help.

I fumbled for the lock, finally catching hold, just as Clarence roared from behind me like some sort of wild animal. I jerked the door open, and was about to rush out it when a shout rang out.

"Mom! Duck!"

I did just that as Amelia reared back and launched something over my head.

It shattered behind me, all too close for comfort. It was followed by the sound of something—or someone—hitting the floor hard. I looked back to find Clarence lying on the ground, blood dripping from his head. He groaned, but didn't attempt to rise.

Then, the blessed sound of sirens blared in the distance. A few minutes later, and a pair of police cruisers came to a screeching halt in the driveway.

As the police—including Detective Cavanaugh—piled out of their cars, I pulled Amelia into a tight hug. We watched as the cops rushed into the house, taking Clarence into custody.

"I feel bad," Amelia said, holding on to me for all she was worth.

"For what?" I asked. "He deserved it."

"*He* might have. But the dog sure didn't."

"The dog?" I glanced back to where Clarence had fallen, and for the first time noted the remains of the ceramic Pomeranian that had once sat outside Timothy Fuller's door. I turned back to Amelia and smiled. "You know, I think he'll be okay with it. Stewie got his revenge."

Detective Cavanaugh approached. "Anyone care to tell me just what happened here?" he asked. "Especially why there's pieces of a dog all over the place?"

Instead of answering, both Amelia and I burst into laughter.

27

Stewie yapped happily as Sue and Barry Lincoln gathered him into their arms. I was sad to see him go, but happy for him at the same time. He was going to live a good, happy life from now on.

They carried the dog to the car, deciding against a carrier. Barry drove, while Sue took the passenger seat, Stewie on her lap. He gave me one last yap before they drove away.

I wiped a tear from my eye as I put an arm across Ben's shoulder. He accepted it with only a little squirm. He was in his early twenties, yet sometimes, he still acted like a teenager, afraid to show his own mother affection.

"Think he'll be okay?" he asked, voice breaking slightly. He might have only spent a few hours with Stewie, yet I could tell he'd grown close to the Pomeranian. I think they shared a connection, thanks to Timothy's murder. It wouldn't surprise me if Ben ended up visiting the little dog every now and again.

"He'll be fine," I said, giving his shoulder a squeeze. "Just like the rest of us."

"Okay, Mom," he said, pulling away. "We're getting a little too sappy here."

I laughed. "Yeah, yeah. I think I deserve it, don't you?"

He rolled his eyes, looking a lot like his sister right then. "I'm the one who was stuck in a jail cell."

"All the more reason for me to give you hugs." I reached for him, but he scuttled back.

"Go find Amelia," I said with a laugh. "Your dad wants to have a cookout to celebrate. I think he's out back waiting for you."

Ben gave me a thumbs up, and then headed inside, seemingly none the worse for wear after his arrest. I was glad to see his good nature hadn't been dampened by these last few harrowing days.

I was about to follow him inside when a car pulled into the driveway and parked next to my van. Detective Cavanaugh got out, eyes darting around like he was arriving at a crime scene, before finally settling his gaze on me.

"Mrs. Denton," he said, bowing his head slightly in acknowledgment.

"Detective. What can I do for you?"

"I didn't get a chance to talk to you before," he said, referring, of course, to the night of Clarence's arrest. He *had* interrogated me, of course, but he'd been so busy dealing with Clarence, he didn't ask about much more than the basics. "I thought I'd come down here now and have my say."

I didn't like the sound of that. "If you feel it's necessary." I crossed my arms over my chest, defensively.

"You do know that you put yourself, and your daughter, at great risk, right?"

"I do," I said. "But it got the bad guy, didn't it?"

"It did," he admitted.

"And you weren't even looking at him, were you?"

"Not expressly." His face was starting to redden, so I eased off.

"It's all good then. The murderer is behind bars and everyone is safe and sound." Other than Timothy Fuller, of course. He might not have been a nice man, but that didn't mean he deserved to die.

Detective Cavanaugh sighed, ran a hand over his brow. "Good enough, I suppose. Just know, I won't stand for this sort of behavior in the future. If something like this ever happens again, I don't want you sticking your nose where it doesn't belong."

"I won't, just as long as you aren't arresting my children for a crime they didn't commit."

His eyes flashed. In anger, or in embarrassment, I'm not sure. "Mrs. Denton, please. Take my warning to heart. I can't have civilians interfering in my investigations. The next time it happens, I won't be so lenient."

"I'm sorry," I said, relenting. "I don't plan on making a habit of this, trust me."

"Good." He shuffled his feet, cleared his throat.

"Did you get him to confess?" I asked. "Clarence, I mean." Just because he told me he killed Timothy, didn't mean he'd spill the beans to the cops. If I had to testify against him, I would. I wouldn't like it, but darn it, I would do it. A part of me understood why he did it. In some ways, I supposed I could empathize. But to murder a man? For money? I couldn't imagine.

"He did," Cavanaugh said. "I think a part of him regrets what he did, but another thinks Mr. Fuller de-

served it." He shook his head as if unable to compre-
hend how anyone could think that way.

"How did he know to look in the house that
night?" I asked, more to myself than the detective. "I
told Selena Shriver, thinking she'd tell her boyfriend,
Jason, but never in a million years did I think she was
working with Clarence."

"She wasn't," Cavanaugh said, tugging at his collar. "In fact, she had no idea Clarence had any interest in the money, or what happened to Timothy
Fuller."

"Then how did he know?"

"He called her." A faint smile appeared. "Said he
was curious as to why you kept coming around. She
told him about the camera, where you said it was hidden, and said she was confused as to why you thought
she could help. Clarence took the information and
ran with it."

"Wow," I said. If he hadn't called, I would have
wasted my night, and he likely never would have been
caught. "I can't believe he could do such a thing. He
seemed like such a nice man."

"Really, I think he is," Cavanaugh said. "Mr. Fuller
apparently brought the worst out in people, especially
when they are stressed. It appears as if Clarence's retirement wasn't paying the bills, and he figured Mr.
Fuller owed him, so he headed over to see what he
could coax out of the old codger."

"Yeah, he told me." A cynical part of me wondered
if that meant when the time came, I could go next
door and demand restitution for all the hard times
Joanne had given me.

"I don't think he went over there to kill him," Cavanaugh said. "Timothy Fuller was already in a foul
mood when he arrived. I guess he'd just fought with

his son, and when Clarence came around demanding money, the old man snapped. One thing leads to another, and someone ends up dead."

"Kind of hard to feel bad for a man who stabs someone in the back, though." I hugged myself as I shuddered.

"True." Cavanaugh rubbed at the back of his neck. "Apparently, Clarence lost it when old man Fuller went to call for his nurse, who was still in the house dealing with the laundry at the time. It was probably a spur of the moment thing, but that still makes it murder."

"And then he uses Ben as a convenient scapegoat," I said.

"He did," Cavanaugh said. "Claims he saw him napping with Ms. Shriver, and when the police came knocking, Ben was the first person who came to mind."

We stood there in silence for a few moments, neither of us looking at the another. I wondered why he'd come all the way here just to tell me this when I could have learned most of it from the paper. Before I could ask, another question struck me.

"What about the blood on Ben's shirt?" I asked. "Any idea how it got there?"

Cavanaugh's face reddened, and this time, I was pretty sure it was anger. "No one wore it but your son," he said. "It appears one of the officers on site wasn't as careful as he should have been when he checked Mr. Fuller for a pulse. My best guess is he must have gotten blood on his hand, and when he took your son into custody, it wiped off on his shirt."

"That's a pretty big mistake," I said. If Clarence hadn't confessed, the shirt very well might have been the key piece of evidence that could have put Ben away for good.

"Tell me about it," Cavanaugh muttered.

I decided to change the subject.

"Did Clarence admit to trying to break into my house?" I asked.

"No. He claims he knows nothing about it. I'm liable to believe him too. He's copped to everything else."

"So, then . . . ?"

Cavanaugh shrugged. "If we catch someone in the act, I'll let you know. I'm guessing this was a one-time deal and you won't be bothered again."

It made me wonder, though. It seemed like an awfully big coincidence for someone to have tried to break into my house on the day I'd brought Stewie home. I had a feeling there was more to it than just a random break-in, but for now, it looked like I had to let it go.

"What about Timothy's money?" I asked. "Has anyone found it?"

"Not that I'm aware. If I were to guess, I'd bet there is none to be found."

Which would make Timothy's murder even more tragic. To die for something that didn't even exist? How is that fair?

Of course, fairness rarely plays a part with murder.

"Care to join us, Detective?" I asked, motioning toward the house. "We're having a cookout and I made lemonade." I wasn't sure why I asked, but it felt like the polite thing to do.

"No, thank you. I'd better go," Cavanaugh said. "You have a good day, Mrs. Denton. And please, leave the detective work to the professionals."

"I will," I said, thinking that soon, Amelia might very well be working alongside him as one of said professionals. I wondered how Cavanaugh would take that.

He waved to me as he got into his car. I returned the gesture, realizing that I didn't dislike the big detective, even if he'd arrested Ben. He'd only been doing his job. Can't fault a man for that.

And that's not to mention the fact he didn't hold my little stunt against me. Well, at least not legally. I'm sure he could have slapped me with a charge of some kind if he'd wanted to.

Cavanaugh backed out of the driveway just as the door opened and Manny stepped outside. He put his arm around me as the detective drove off.

"Who was that?" Manny asked.

"No one." I turned, putting both the detective, and the horrors of the last week, out of my mind. "Let's go out back and join the kids." Especially Ben. He was due for a few more hugs.

"You sure?" Manny asked, leaning in close and smiling. "Joanne is watching. We could always give her something else to complain about."

I laughed, shoving him playfully away. "I'm sure. Besides, I'm absolutely dying for a hot dog."

"There's plenty," Manny said.

"I know." I led the way back toward the house. "But I've learned not to take anything for granted. Best get to them before they're gone."

Grab These Cozy Mysteries
from
Kensington Books

Available Wherever Books Are Sold!

All available as e-books, too!

Visit our website at **www.kensingtonbooks.com**